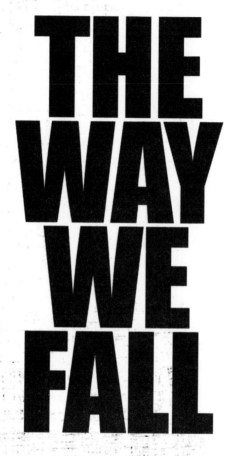

THE WAY WE FALL

MEGAN CREWE

HYPERION
NEW YORK

Text copyright © 2012 by Megan Crewe

Printed in the United States of America

First Edition
10 9 8 7 6 5 4 3 2 1
G475-5664-5-11319

Library of Congress Cataloging-in-Publication Data

Crewe, Megan.
  The way we fall/Megan Crewe.—1st ed.
    p. cm.
  Summary: Sixteen-year-old old Kaelyn challenges her fears, finds a second
chance at love, and fights to keep her family and friends safe as a deadly new
virus devastates her island community.
  ISBN 978-1-4231-4616-2 (Reinforced bdg.)
  [1. Survival—Fiction. 2. Virus diseases—Fiction. 3. Islands—Fiction.
4. Science fiction.] I. Title.
  PZ7.C86818Way 2012
  [Fic]—dc22   2011006504

Text is set in 12-point Adobe Garamond Pro.
Reinforced binding

Visit www.hyperionteens.com

For anyone who's ever fallen,
regardless how far

SEPT 2

Leo,

It's about six hours since you left the island. The way things have been, I know you wouldn't have expected me to come to see you off, but I keep thinking about how you waved and waved from the dock five years ago, when I was leaving for Toronto.

While the ferry was carrying you to the mainland, I was on West Beach with Mackenzie and Rachel. Mackenzie had decided we should have one last summer swim before school starts tomorrow, but the breeze was so chilly, none of us ended up wanting to go in the water. So we just walked on the sand, talking and speculating about how junior year will go.

The summer vacationers have all left, so no one was on the beach except for us and a few families having a barbecue by the rocks. I could see the white shape of the ferry getting smaller as it crossed the strait, and the knot in my stomach got tighter and tighter.

Mackenzie started gushing about her "awesome" summer in L.A. and the hot nightspots she'd gotten into, and Rachel and I mostly just nodded in the right places, like usual. Not that I mind. At one point Mackenzie turned to me and said, "Because the big city clubs are the best, aren't they, Kaelyn?" and all I could say was "Um, I guess," because I never actually went clubbing in Toronto.

2

If she knew I spent most of my time there at the zoo or the vet clinic near our house, not shopping and partying, I'm pretty sure she wouldn't have glommed on to me the second I moved back last spring. But I haven't gone out of my way to correct her. It's nice having people to hang out with like this, even if it's sort of under false pretenses. I was so focused on getting by on my own in the city, I didn't realize how much I missed being with friends.

And it was only today I realized how much I've missed you.

By the time the ferry was out of view, the spray from the waves was making us shiver. We went up to the grassy stretch by the road, and Mackenzie almost stepped on a dead bird. She yelped and hopped around, shaking her foot like germs might have leaped up onto it. Rachel couldn't stop laughing.

The bird was a black-backed gull, and it looked healthy—other than being dead, of course. Its feathers were shiny and I couldn't see any injuries. Really weird, the way it was lying there, like it'd just dropped out of the sky. I wanted to get a stick and move the body around to take a closer look, except Mackenzie would have completely freaked out.

You wouldn't have minded, Leo. If I'd been walking on the beach with you, the way we used to, you'd have watched while I checked out the gull, and asked, "Can you tell why it died?" And you would really have wanted to know.

Standing there, looking at the gull while Mackenzie wiggled her foot and Rachel laughed, it hit me harder than ever before. How stupid I've been to let one little argument screw things up so much. You were my best friend for as long as I can remember, and it's been almost two years since I last talked to you.

After a bit, Rachel stopped laughing and said she had to get going. Her mom's been bugging her to be home more since her dad broke his leg working the trawlers last week. We agreed to meet in the caf tomorrow to compare schedules, and then we headed back into town.

I didn't go straight home. After Mackenzie and Rachel took off, I wandered past the fisheries and up the path that leads through the pine trees to the cliff where the cormorants nest. It's so peaceful up there. Standing by the rocky edge, looking at the ocean with the cool wind gusting over me and the gulls coasting overhead, I can imagine what it's like to fly.

At least, I usually can. Right then I felt as if I had a weight strapped around my waist, holding me down, made up of all the things I should have said to you before you left.

The most important thing is the hardest to admit. You were right. When we moved, I was overwhelmed the moment the taxi drove us away from the airport into the city. The second I walked up to that huge middle school, swarming with kids who'd spent their whole lives around skyscrapers and subways, I was sure I didn't fit in. So I went off and watched the chimps play in the zoo and fed the kittens in the vet clinic instead of trying to make friends. I probably could have if I'd put in the effort—Drew was at the same school, just a grade higher, and by the end of the first month he was so busy exploring the streets with his classmates, we hardly saw him at home. But sticking to myself was easier. And by the time I got to the even bigger high school, the thought of doing anything else was scary.

You listened to me moan about the city and the kids at school so many times before you finally pointed out that half of the problem was me. I shouldn't have gotten so angry. But at the time, I felt like

4

you were turning on me. I couldn't see how right you were until we moved back here.

I figured I'd just fall in with the same people I'd known growing up, but everyone looked at me like I was a stranger. And I was still scared. I didn't know what to do or what to say, even to you. I'm so out of practice. It's ridiculous.

But that's going to change. Starting tomorrow, I'm going to be someone who talks to people in class even if they haven't talked to me first, and who hangs out in town instead of on cliff tops watching birds. I'm going to keep on being that person until I'm not scared anymore. And I'm going to use this notebook as a journal, to keep me on track and to practice saying everything I need to say to you, so the first time you come back to see your parents, for Thanksgiving or Christmas, I'll be able to apologize to your face and see if we can still be friends.

I promise.

SEPT 4

You must be settled in at your new school by now, Leo. Taking dance classes with the best teachers and hanging out with other supertalented people. I bet you're loving every minute.

I've been working on the brand-new Kaelyn. I said hi to at least ten different people at school yesterday while we were waiting to get our schedules. Everyone still seems kind of standoffish, like they suspect the me they knew five years ago might have gotten replaced by a pod person while I was in Toronto. I haven't managed anything other than "Hi" so far. But hey, it's a start.

Then today, after school, I put my ferrets (Mowat and Fossey) on their leashes and took them to Thompson Park instead of the backyard. I'm not sure anyone on the island has ever seen a pet ferret before, and the thought of people staring at me always made me nervous. But after a few minutes a couple kids came over and started asking all these questions, like "What do they eat?" and "Do they know how to swim?" and it was fun. Mowat and Fossey loved the attention, of course.

Mom came up to my room after I got back. "We're going to have dinner a bit late," she said. "There's an unusual case at the hospital they wanted your father to look at."

"Unusual how?" I said.

"He didn't know," she said. "He called me before he left the

6

research center. But he said he should be home by seven at the latest."

She hovered in the doorway while I pulled my textbooks out of my backpack. I was starting to wonder what was up when she finally asked, "How are you doing, Kaelyn?"

"I'm good," I said.

"I know you've had a hard time, moving to Toronto and then being uprooted all over again," she said. "If you ever need to talk, you know I'd be happy to listen, don't you? That's what I'm here for."

Her eyes misted up, probably because she was thinking about Nana—about Nana having the stroke and passing on when Mom wasn't here.

But what could she do if I told her about the fight with you, and how lonely I got in Toronto, and how out of place I feel here now? Not much. So I said, "I know, Mom. Really, everything's okay."

"All right," she said. She looked like she wanted to say something more, but finally she just left.

I hope Dad gets home soon. It's almost seven, and I'm starving.

SEPT 5

What a weird day.

Mrs. Harnett is already assigning group presentations in history, but at least she let us pick our partners. I'm working with Rachel since Mackenzie's not in our class. Which I didn't mind because Mackenzie would probably spend the whole time talking about movie stars she's seen and painting her nails while I did the work. Rachel actually cares about her grades.

We decided we might as well start working at Rachel's house since it's closer. I found Drew in the computer lab after school, showing some other seniors how he can hack into the teachers-only folders on the network, and asked him to tell Mom where I'd gone. Rachel said hi and started smiling all shy. Drew, of course, acted completely oblivious. If his personal life was mine to share, I'd tell Rachel there's no point in flirting with him, but it's not.

I started wondering, though, if maybe I hadn't given Rachel a chance. I mean, I've been hanging out with her because she's always with Mackenzie, but when Mackenzie was in L.A. all August, I never called Rachel up. Not that she called me either. But from what I've seen, I've got more in common with her than I do with Mackenzie. I should try to be more friendly. The new me definitely would.

"How's your dad doing?" I asked as we were walking over to her place.

"Okay, I guess," she said. "We'd better pick our topic for the project."

"Let's do something interesting," I said. We've covered Canadian Maritime history in pretty much every grade, and the last thing I want to do is regurgitate the same old facts and watch the class fall asleep.

"We should do the Acadians," Rachel said, and I made a face.

"Everyone's going to pick them," I said. "I heard people talking about it."

"Yeah," Rachel said, "because there's more information on them than anything else. I want to get a good mark."

"Maybe Mrs. Harnett would like something more original," I pointed out. "We could research the Mi'kmaq, or the Scottish immigration, or the fishing industry—I'm sure we could find out lots about any of those."

I wasn't trying to be argumentative—I want a good mark too. But Rachel gave me a frigid look and said, "Nobody cares about fish. If you don't want to do the project with me, you can ask for another partner."

Where the hell did that come from? I've gone over the conversation in my head a dozen times, and I still don't think I said anything that should have made her upset.

I wish people were as easy to understand as animals. You give a dog a treat, it's happy. You yank its tail, it's angry. Obvious cause and effect.

Maybe I'm the only one who has trouble. Maybe you would have seen right away where I went wrong, Leo. I still cringe remembering our big argument, how I said you couldn't know what it's like being an outsider—I mean, you were adopted *and* the only Asian kid on the island, and the stares and comments must have hurt even if you didn't let on—but you have to admit you're good with people, the way I'm good with animals. I doubt you've ever been at a total loss to figure out why someone did what they did.

But you weren't there, and I was, so I just said, "Okay, if you really want to, we'll do the Acadians." I spent the rest of the walk to Rachel's house wondering what to say next.

Then, after we'd been in her room scanning the history websites for about half an hour, her dad came clomping up on his crutches. He was coughing, too, and he sneezed a couple times as he got to the door. He must have caught a cold after his accident.

He stood in the doorway just smiling and scratching his elbow. Then he hobbled inside and wrapped one arm around Rachel. "My little girl," he said. "I missed you. And you brought a friend home!"

Rachel's cheeks went pink. She nudged him away. "Yeah, Dad, it's great to see you too," she said.

He coughed again, and turned his big smile on me. "It's Kayla, right?" he said. "Grace's kid?"

"Kaelyn," I said.

"Right," he said, leaning closer. His face was flushed, and I couldn't help wondering if he'd been drinking, but he didn't smell like alcohol. "I sure was glad when your family moved back," he went on. "That father of yours never should have dragged the bunch of you away. But what does he know? Always sad to see a mainlander snatch up one of ours, especially a woman as pretty as your mom. You know, even though she's a darkie, I might have chased her if I'd had half a chance. Why—"

"Dad, come on," Rachel said, sounding flustered. I sat there, my mouth half open, feeling like I was choking. What was wrong with him? Was he even listening to himself?

He scratched the back of his neck and then patted my shoulder. I flinched away, but he didn't seem to notice any more than he'd noticed Rachel's protest.

"There's been a lot of talk about what happened in the big city to bring you home again," he said, still grinning. "Your father strayed a little, maybe? Would be just like a mainlander. Or maybe *you* ran into some trouble?"

"My mom missed the island," I said, which was a really simplified explanation, but at that point I didn't feel like giving him a longer one. I stood up, adding, "I should get going. We'll work on the project some more tomorrow, okay, Rachel?"

I hardly waited for her nod. "Hold on, now," her father said, following me into the hall. "Got to be more to the story! All the temptations in the city—I hope you and your brother kept clear of the drugs and the gangs. . . . Why don't you invite her over for dinner, Rachel?" he called back over his shoulder. "Your mother's dying to hear the details!"

"Stop it, Dad!" Rachel said. She scooted past him and caught up with me at the bottom of the stairs. Her dad started coughing again, which was maybe the only reason he didn't keep talking.

"He's just sick," she said, looking down at her hands. "I don't know what he was going on about."

"Yeah," I said. "No big deal. But I really should go."

What he said was a big deal, though. The whole way home I couldn't get it out of my head. I know a lot of gossip travels around the island, about everything. I know lots of people resent mainlanders who've moved here, like Dad. And I know there are people who look differently at Mom and Drew and me, and everyone else who's not as pale as them. But no one's ever talked like that to my face so blatantly, and *friendly*.

My skin is crawling just thinking about it.

He must have been drunk. And he's sick too. And maybe going stir-crazy cooped up in the house when he's used to being on the docks or the water all day.

All I know for sure is, next time we work on the project, Rachel's coming over to my house.

SEPT 8

I think you could call today one step forward for the new Kaelyn and one step back for parental relations.

Dad already seemed stressed this morning, pacing in the kitchen while he waited for the kettle to whistle, but I didn't wonder about it much then. Meredith came over a little after breakfast, like she usually does on Sundays. She spent the morning making friendship bracelets with Mom, and the afternoon with me.

I don't mind having her around—she's a lot less bratty than most seven-year-olds I've seen. And she's been even quieter since Aunt Lillian left last year.

Can you imagine taking off on your husband and daughter without any explanation? Doesn't make sense to me. But then, I never got to know Aunt Lillian very well. Uncle Emmett did most of the talking.

I can't make up for Meredith's mom being gone, but I feel like a superhero if I can get her to laugh, showing her goofy videos I've found on the internet or letting her watch the ferrets chase each other.

We were sitting in my room with Fossey and Mowat bouncing around like they do, when Fossey knocked over my coyote notebook. Meredith picked it up and flipped through the pages.

"Cool!" she said, seeing my sketches. "Are you writing about dogs?"

"There's a family of coyotes living in the forested area north of the harbor," I said. "I've been watching them and writing down what they do."

"Are they dangerous?" she asked.

"Not really," I said. "I have to be extra careful if I want to see them, they're so scared of *me*."

She looked up with her eyes wide. "Could I see them too?" she said. "Can you take me?"

I've always gone by myself, but I thought maybe I should share the things that are important to me with other people more. Meredith was so excited, like we'd be on a real expedition. How could I say no?

Everything went perfectly. We walked out to the forest, and I showed Meredith the spot on the hill between two fir trees where I like to watch, because the breeze usually blows my scent away from the den instead of toward it. The sun was beaming, the grass smelling warm and green as if fall's still far away. We lay down on our stomachs, and after a few whispered questions Meredith stayed so quiet I could have forgotten she was there.

For a little while I was worried we wouldn't see anything. Then the parents and the pups, which are almost fully grown now, trotted back to the den from their day of hunting or scavenging. The pups started play-fighting. I saw more than I do most days when I'm on my own. I kind of kicked myself for not bringing the notebook along, but we weren't really there for me.

On the way home, I told Meredith about the first time I saw a coyote. You'd remember, Leo. The day Mom took you and me and

Drew out to pick blueberries, when we were five and he was six. At one point I looked up and saw a coyote standing a few feet away, watching me. I still remember those dark yellow eyes.

It's a good memory now, but back then I was terrified. I thought the coyote was going to eat me. I turned to yell for Mom, and the coyote flinched, spun around, and dashed away.

"But why would the coyote be scared?" Meredith asked.

"Because people hurt them a lot more than they hurt us," I said. "We assume we know everything about animals, like that certain ones are mean; but if you pay attention, you realize they're just looking out for themselves like we do."

Meredith couldn't stop talking about the coyotes after we got home, like seeing them had been the most amazing thing ever. I had no idea Dad was upset until after Uncle Emmett picked her up. He called me into the living room, with that stern expression Drew and I call his scientist face.

"I don't think you should take Meredith to the coyote den again," he said.

"What?" I said. After seeing how happy she was, I couldn't believe I'd heard him right.

"She's nine years younger than you," he said. "She doesn't understand how important it is to be careful around wild animals. You know there've been reports of coyotes attacking kids in other places."

"Only with kids a lot younger than Meredith," I said. "I was showing her how to be careful. She's—"

He cut me off. "We're not discussing this any further," he said, as if it'd been much of a discussion in the first place. "There are lots of other things the two of you can do."

And then he walked off into his study.

You know my dad—he's always been supportive of me studying animals. And I started going out to observe the coyotes on my own when I was only a little older than Meredith. I don't see why he'd be so worried now.

Maybe he's not really upset about the coyotes, just stressed out by whatever was bothering him before. I'll have to talk to him again later, when he's in a better mood.

SEPT 9

Rachel's dad was raced to the hospital last night.

I found out when I got to school this morning. A bunch of people were already talking about him—in hushed voices, but loud enough that I heard Shauna, who sits behind me in homeroom, say the words "psycho" and "ambulance" after Rachel's name.

Normally I'd have waited for Mackenzie to show up and gotten her to fill me in. Even when we were kids, Shauna would wrinkle her nose when I brought in tadpoles to show the class, and snickered if I turned up at school with bits of grass on my clothes, which wasn't unusual. But I figured the new Kaelyn wouldn't let a little nastiness years ago stop me from finding out what'd happened, so I swiveled in my chair and asked, "What's going on?"

Shauna did a double take, as if she couldn't believe I'd actually spoken to her. Her eyebrows rose into perfect arches. "You mean you don't know?" she said. I guess she assumed since I hang out with Rachel, I should be in the loop already.

I opened my mouth, but nothing came out, and a couple of Shauna's friends giggled. But it didn't really matter, because right then Mackenzie slid into her seat beside me. I turned toward her, hoping my face hadn't flushed dark enough to show.

"Pretty freaky, isn't it?" Mackenzie said.

"What?" I said. "I haven't heard yet."

"Rachel's dad," she said, and lowered her voice. "He went totally crazy last night. Woke up the whole street at two in the morning, banging on the backyard fence and shouting."

"Shouting about what?" I asked. I remembered how he'd acted last week, and suddenly I felt shivery inside. So he hadn't been drunk after all. There was something really wrong with him.

"No one knows!" Mackenzie said. "He kept going on about how he had to stop 'them,' but nobody was there! At least that's what I've heard. Someone called the police, and they brought a doctor to sedate him. Apparently he got sick with the flu after he broke his leg. My mom studied to be a nurse, you know—she said if your temperature goes high enough, you can get delusional, so maybe that's what happened. I mean, why else would he act so freaky?"

I could have told her the things he'd said last Thursday. But chances are Mackenzie wouldn't keep her mouth shut, and Rachel and her mom must be stressed out enough without me adding to the gossip.

"How's Rachel handling it?" I said. "I haven't seen her today."

"Me neither," Mackenzie said. "Looks like she stayed home, or maybe she's at the hospital. I can't blame her. I'd take any excuse I could to skip."

I hope Rachel's all right. I kept wondering about her and her dad all day, but I didn't want to call in case I interrupted her at a bad time. When I got home, it occurred to me that Dad might have heard something. Even though he's at the new ocean research center now, he still hangs out with some of the people he used to work with at the hospital.

After dinner he was sitting in the living room with one of his

Sudoku books. When I came over, he looked up and said, "Kae. How are you feeling?"

He's been saying that instead of "How are you?" since our summer visit here last year, when I got a bad fever and had to spend two days in the hospital. I could understand for the first week or so, but now it's kind of annoying. Like he figures I might still not be over one little bout of food poisoning.

"All good," I said. "I wanted to ask you something."

"Sure," he said.

But before I could go on, Drew dashed in and grabbed the TV remote. He had that determined look he always gets when he's about to push the issue. Dad obviously noticed too, because his shoulders stiffened up.

"Great episode of *Queer as Folk* on rerun tonight," Drew said as he turned on the TV. "Can't wait!"

Dad glared down at his book. "Maybe your sister would like to watch something else," he said, as if I wanted to be pulled into their passive-aggressive wrangling.

"Then she should have called dibs," Drew said. "Hey, you know how I helped build that petition website for same-sex marriage rights in North America? We've got more than a thousand names already. Pretty cool, eh?"

"Ah," Dad said, shifting his Sudoku book and raising his pencil, "the seven goes here."

The show's opening came on, and Drew flopped onto the couch. "Amazing how they managed to fit so many hot guys into one show," he said, turning up the volume.

Dad broke sooner than he usually does. He got up and stalked out of the room. Drew rolled his eyes.

You'd think, given how smart Dad is about science and medicine, he wouldn't be quite so stupid about Drew being gay. But he acts like the idea of having a son who's attracted to guys is so inconceivable he can't even acknowledge it. I doubt he'd have agreed to look for a job on the island so quickly when Mom suggested moving back if he hadn't walked in on Drew making out with his best guy "friend" a few months before. And Drew, of course, is determined to shove it in his face until . . . until he forces Dad into a total meltdown? I don't know what he expects to happen.

I realize Drew's completely in the right, but sometimes I want to scream at both of them.

Even if Dad had gotten over his bad mood from yesterday, I had a feeling his "conversation" with Drew made it come back. It didn't seem like a good time to bug him with a bunch of questions. At least Rachel's dad is being looked after now. I'll probably hear all about his recovery in school tomorrow.

SEPT 10

Rachel wasn't in school again. No word about her dad.

Mackenzie didn't seem to think her being absent was a big deal, but I couldn't imagine Rachel skipping school two days in a row unless her dad was pretty much dying—and *someone* would have been talking about it if his condition was that bad. This is the same girl who argued that she didn't need to go home after puking her guts out during last year's English exam, after all.

Rachel's never said anything, but I suspect there isn't enough money for her to go to college unless she gets a good scholarship. Her dad just has the fishing, which isn't going well for anyone these days, and her mom doesn't work at all. It's got to be tough.

So after school I called her to see how she was doing.

"Kaelyn!" she said when she picked up. "I'm so happy you called. I missed you!"

I hadn't been expecting such an enthusiastic response. "How's it going?" I asked.

"Oh, I've got this stupid cold and Mom said I have to stay home and rest," she said, and sneezed. "God, it's so boring. You want to come over? She probably wouldn't like that, but she's out grocery shopping, and what she doesn't know can't hurt, right?"

"Sure," I said. Maybe she was acting weird, but I'd wanted to be better friends with her. Seemed like a good time to try.

When I rang the doorbell, Rachel opened the door and flung her arms around me. She only let go to cough into her elbow and then scratch her collarbone. Her nose was red. Just like her dad when I'd been over before—sneezing and coughing and scratching.

I started feeling nervous then. But Rachel seemed so excited to see me, and a real friend wouldn't just take off. All she had was a cold. Her dad had gotten it really badly, but it wasn't like they'd put her in the hospital too.

So when she tugged my wrist, I followed her into the family room.

On the TV, a VJ was interviewing some hip-hop singer. Rachel pulled me onto the couch and slung her arm over my shoulder.

"Talk," she said. "I want to know everything I've missed. I've been stuck in this boring house too long."

There wasn't much to talk about. I didn't think she'd want to hear that everyone at school was gossiping about her dad. I told her they'd announced swim team would be starting soon, since I've decided I'll try out and maybe she'd want to come too, and then I remembered the story Mackenzie told at lunch—one of her usual "this famous person my parents know" deals, but really funny this time. As I started getting into it, Rachel grimaced.

"She's such a snot, isn't she?" she said.

I stopped and stared at her.

"I mean Mackenzie," she said, and rolled her eyes. "As if she's so special because she was born in L.A. She's always got her nose up in the air. God, I want to rip it off her face sometimes, don't you?"

Sometimes I do. But Rachel? She's always looked like she was hanging off of Mackenzie's every word.

When I didn't answer right away, Rachel kept going: "And she's so bossy too—it drives me up the wall! You know, I was kind of pissed for a while because she's my best friend, and you were, like, trying to steal her for yourself. But you're really so much nicer than she is. I'm so glad I've got you now! We can stick together, right?"

The weight of her arm across my shoulder had gotten uncomfortably heavy. "Yeah," I said. "Sure." Except the last thing I wanted to do right then was stick around. It wasn't just the sneezing and the coughing—she was *talking* like her dad did last week too. Like she was spewing out every unpleasant and embarrassing thought in her head.

I shifted away, and she started scratching at her collarbone again, hard enough that the neck of her shirt slid to the side. She must have been working at that spot for hours. The skin was pink—not a flushed pink from pressure, but a dark, raw pink, like the blood was about to break through. Looking at it made my stomach turn.

Rachel only stopped scratching when she had to sneeze. She dropped her arm for a second, and I leaped up. But a music video came on at the same time. Rachel squealed.

"I love this song!" she said, jumping off the couch and grabbing my hands. "It's so amazing!"

I bobbed along as she danced, wondering how I was going to get out of there. She raised her hands in the air and shimmied. "What d'you think?" she shouted even though the music wasn't that loud. "I've been practicing in my room. Sometimes a striptease too! You know, for when I get a boyfriend. I'm going to rock his world."

She spun around, laughing. The squeak of the front door opening right then was the most wonderful sound I'd ever heard.

"Rachel?" her mom called. "Sweetie, I told you to—"

She stopped short when she saw us. Rachel kept dancing,

thrashing her hair from side to side. I'm not sure what upset her mom more: the fact that I was there, or the fact that her daughter was acting like a maniac. But she was definitely upset.

"Kaelyn," she said, with a little tremor in her voice, "I don't think this is the best time for Rachel to have guests."

"I'm really sorry," I said, and I meant it. "I didn't know she was going to get so . . . worked up."

Rachel skipped after me to the door. "Mom's such a spoilsport," she said in a loud whisper. "She thinks the other parents on the island let their kids run wild. But wild is freakin' fun!"

She was scratching that spot again as she waved good-bye. I looked back when I was halfway down the block, and she was still standing there, waving and scratching.

I'm not just nervous now. I'm scared. I can't make myself believe Rachel was drunk, or any of the other excuses I could have used for her dad. She was just *not* herself.

What the hell is happening?

SEPT 11

Leo,

It's one in the morning, and I can't sleep. I wish I could call you. No matter what happened or how upset I was, you always found something to say that made me feel better. When we were still friends.

But I haven't got your number in New York, and even if I did, I doubt you'd appreciate me breaking two years of silence by waking you up in the middle of the night. It's my own fault for not talking to you sooner. So I'm crouched here on my bed with my reading lamp on, writing in this journal, because I can't think of anything else to do.

I couldn't stop worrying about Rachel after I got home this afternoon. Trying to figure out what weird sickness would make people act so strangely. But bacteria and viruses are Dad's area, not mine.

So when he and I were doing the dishes, I started telling him about what happened. The whole story ended up spilling out, about Rachel's dad last week too. I didn't look at him, just at the dish I was drying, because I thought maybe I was agonizing over nothing. But getting it out of my head was such a relief. I was starting to feel like maybe everything was okay when I raised my eyes and saw Dad's expression. His face had gone pale, and his hands were lying still in the dishwater.

"Her father touched you?" he said, sounding like he was trying very hard not to raise his voice.

"Just on the shoulder," I said. "Nothing inappropriate."

"And Rachel, today," he went on. "She was hugging you—have you been wearing the same clothes all day?"

My cheeks warmed because I'd felt like an idiot even while I was doing this.

"No," I said. "I changed when I got home, and took a shower. I couldn't help thinking—if what she's got is contagious—I don't want to catch it."

Dad's stance relaxed, which made me tense all over again.

"You think it is?" I asked. "Contagious?"

"It's always smart to be careful, Kae," he said. "You should run whatever clothes are in your hamper through the laundry tonight. And Rachel was at school last week, wasn't she? After you saw her father?"

I nodded, and he said, "You should stay home, then. Until the weekend at least."

"What?" I said. Part of the reason I'd been worried about getting sick was missing class. Maybe I don't need a scholarship, but I still have to get good grades to be accepted into any of the top university science programs. And staying home would mess with my new-Kaelyn project too. "Swim team tryouts are this week," I said. "Mrs. Reese said she's only going to let people join if they show they're committed right away."

"I'll ask someone at the hospital to write you a doctor's note," he said. "We have to be safe, Kae."

"Safe from what? We don't even know what's happening!" I said.

I heard Mom come into the kitchen behind me. She touched my back and said, "Gordon, you should just tell her."

"Tell me what?" I said, twisting to look at her and then turning back to Dad. His eyes were on her instead of me.

Mom doesn't like arguing—she says she finds it more effective to "gently but firmly nudge." But if something's really important to her, she's not afraid to put her foot down. Dad wanted Drew to lose his internet and phone privileges after the making-out incident, but Mom said he was being ridiculous, and that was the end of it.

"She's only sixteen," Dad said, as if that made me a toddler.

"Yes," Mom said. "And like any normal sixteen-year-old, she's only going to listen if you give her a reason to."

Dad took his hands out of the sink and dried them, then ran his fingers through his hair.

"What is it?" I said. If he'd told me what he knew before, maybe I wouldn't have gone to Rachel's in the first place. Did he really think keeping secrets would protect me?

"Rachel's father is very sick," he said. "We're not sure what's wrong with him."

" 'We'?" I repeated. "Did you go see him?"

He smiled tightly. "I'm the only microbiologist on the island," he said. "The hospital staff realized they couldn't identify the condition they were attempting to treat, so it made sense for them to involve me. We were hoping the cause might be something environmental. Two other fishery workers were admitted to the hospital last week, and another this morning, with similar symptoms: coughing, sneezing, persistent itching, and a fever, followed by a severe decrease in social inhibitions. And finally, panic brought on by mental confusion."

"They're hallucinating," I said, remembering Mackenzie's theory. "Because of the fever?"

"We're not sure," he said.

So basically some freaky disease is completely messing with people's brains, and no one has any idea what it is or where it came from. What's the point of having doctors if they can't figure out things like this?

Mom slid her arm around me and rubbed my shoulder. "Will that happen to Rachel too?" I managed to ask.

She had all the other symptoms when I saw her. Will she be going crazy in her backyard tomorrow? How are they going to help her?

"I don't know," Dad said. "I'll have to talk to her mother tomorrow morning about bringing her into the hospital so we can keep her under observation. But what concerns me the most is that, from what you've told me, we appear to be dealing with an infectious agent. It seems most likely Rachel picked up the condition from her father."

I remembered what Dad had said earlier, and my heart started beating faster. "You think she might have given it to me," I said. "That's why you don't want me to go to school."

"There's a small chance," he said. "Very small, because you were careful and the contagion doesn't appear to be spreading easily. Rachel's the only case I know of where the condition was clearly passed from one individual to another. But we can't be absolutely sure. And she may have infected other kids at school. I'm going to ask Drew to stay home as well."

"But she hasn't been at school since she got sick," I said.

"You can't be sure of that," he said. "We don't know how long the incubation period might be. She could have been carrying the bacteria or virus last week before the symptoms started showing."

I considered everything as calmly as I could. If anyone had caught this mystery disease from Rachel on Friday, the last time she was at school, they'd have come down with it by now, wouldn't they? I haven't seen anyone in class coughing or sneezing. And Dad thought I was probably safe. Rachel was *living* with her dad, after all. That's a lot more close contact than I'd had with her.

At the same time, I was imagining sitting at home for the next three days—on my own. I've been doing okay, but I still get nervous about speaking up in class, and to be honest, I'm a little terrified of showing up at swim tryouts on Thursday. Giving in to Dad would be an easy way out. Which was exactly why I shouldn't.

"What if I'd like to keep going to school?" I asked. "I mean, there's cautious and then there's paranoid, right? Only five people are sick. For all we know, they could get better tomorrow."

Dad exchanged a look with Mom over my shoulder. His mouth tensed, but he nodded.

"All right," he said. "But if you notice anyone in your classes with any of the symptoms I've mentioned—or if you feel at all unwell..."

I held up my hands. "I'll stay at home and I won't argue," I said. "I promise."

But even though I know if there was really an emergency, Dad would never have agreed, once I got up to my room, I couldn't make myself turn off the light. I keep wondering, what if those people don't get better? What if I did catch it, whatever it is?

I hope you're sleeping well out there in New York, Leo. Then at least one of us is.

SEPT 11 (LATER)

Rachel must be in the hospital by now, so the doctors can look after her. I hope she's okay.

No one's saying anything about the mystery sickness at school. Just the same old complaints about teachers and homework, and gossip about who's dating who. I can't be the only one who knows what's going on. The doctors and nurses know, and they talk at home, and some of them have kids here.

It's like we're trying to fill up every second of silence with meaningless talk so we don't have to say anything real or scary.

Every time someone clears their throat, I flinch. I saw Quentin scratching his arm during English, and I froze up until I noticed he had a mosquito bite there. And then in the cafeteria line, the smoke from the grill made me sneeze, and I felt like everyone around me instinctively shifted away.

I haven't seen anyone who looks like they have an actual cold, though. And just in case, I've been washing my hands between classes and trying not to stand too close to anyone. It's weird. I spent all last week trying to be Kaelyn the Super Friendly, and now I'm worried I'm endangering people if I breathe in their general direction.

I've been thinking maybe I shouldn't hang out with Meredith, just for this weekend. And then I wonder if any of those dockworkers who got sick has kids in the elementary school with her. Is anyone keeping an eye on them, making sure they're not infected? Maybe she should stay home until the doctors are sure.

I'm still going to swim tryouts tomorrow, and I haven't totally gone back to my loner ways. Tessa showed up late for biology this afternoon, and I noticed her standing in the doorway looking at the spot where she normally sits, in the back near Shauna. Shauna had called her friends over so they could whisper about boys and parties and whatever else they talk about, and Tessa's usual place was taken. The only seat left was next to mine, there at the front.

"Hey," I said, pointing to the desk. "You can sit here if you want."

I don't know Tessa very well, of course, since she moved here while we were living in Toronto. But anyone could see she doesn't care much about impressing people. She never dyes her hair to be "auburn" instead of carrot red, or puts concealer over her freckles, like Mackenzie does. And she's never talked much with Shauna, just smiles quietly when Shauna tries to drag her into a conversation. Really, she seems like she'd rather not be bothered with the rest of us. Well, most of us—obviously she bothered with you, Leo.

So I have no idea why, today, she looked at me, and at the empty desk, and then said, "That's okay." She walked right by me to Shauna's group and said something I couldn't hear. Melissa, who normally sits next to me, gave up Tessa's seat and came back.

My face got kind of hot, and I spent the rest of class staring at my textbook. I guess even though your girlfriend doesn't care about Shauna at all, she'd still rather be around her than me.

Maybe she's heard about the people getting sick, and she knows I was with Rachel a lot. It isn't important. But just writing down what happened, I feel uncomfortable, as if *I* did something wrong.

SEPT 12

Whenever I go into history, I can't stop looking at Rachel's empty desk. The longer I sit there, the more edgy I feel. Especially since everyone else seems to have forgotten about her. Mackenzie didn't even mention her today.

Mrs. Harnett remembers her, at least. At the end of class, she pulled me aside. "I understand Rachel may not be back at school for some time," she said. "You could finish the presentation project on your own if you'd like, or you could join another pair and we'll have one group of three."

She was talking about the situation so calmly, and all of a sudden my eyes prickled, like I was about to cry. I don't know why. It's just one project—of course Rachel can make up the grade later.

"I'll keep going by myself," I said. "Until she's better." I wanted to believe she might even get back before the due date.

But then when Dad finally got home last night, I asked him how Rachel was doing, how everyone's doing, and he frowned. It turns out the doctors have been checking the families of the other patients, and a bunch more people have symptoms.

"But you're working on it, right?" I said. "They'll get better?"

He hesitated, and I said, "Dad, I need to know! You can't keep not telling me things."

"It's hard to say at this point, Kae," he said. "We've been able to alleviate the symptoms in the short term, but we're still not sure how to eliminate them completely. And signs are pointing to the contagion being a virus, not a bacterial infection."

"Well, that's good, right?" I said. "That you're figuring out what it is?"

"In some ways," he said. "A virus is harder to tackle—our options for treatment are more limited. But you should know we're doing everything we can."

Which doesn't make me feel any better. I almost wish I hadn't asked.

SEPT 14

Yesterday, life started to feel almost normal again. Dad still worked late, but school was business as usual. Shauna was trying to convince Tessa to host a party at her house, because apparently her parents have gone off on some trip. I made it through both Thursday and Friday swim tryouts, and Mrs. Reese gave me a thumbs-up as I was leaving, so I think I'm on the team. And Mackenzie and I went across to the mainland to see the new Christopher Nolan movie in the big theater last night.

The guy at the concession stand was kind of cute. I chatted with him after the movie was over, until Mackenzie got impatient and said we had to go.

I couldn't stop grinning the whole way home. Not because I'm so crazy about him. I hardly know him. But it would be nice, you know, to crush on someone. Someone who might crush on me too.

But then this morning—five in the morning on a Saturday —Dad got a call and rushed off. He tried to be quiet, but we all woke up anyway. Once we realized he was gone, none of us could get back to sleep. So Drew and I sat at the table, still half asleep, and Mom fried hash browns.

She only does that for special occasions, or when she wants to make us feel better about something, because she says it's a lot of work for food she doesn't like to eat herself. She made hash browns the day she and Dad announced we were moving. So I could tell she's expecting bad news.

"Maybe they called him because someone got better in the middle of the night," I said, as if by saying it I could make myself believe it.

"We can hope," Mom said.

Even if they're the perfect combination of crispy and tender, hash browns are hard to swallow when it's two hours before you normally wake up and your stomach is full of knots. I only managed a few mouthfuls. Drew got through his whole plate, but he sat there chewing the last bite for a full minute before he swallowed. Mom didn't eat any. She just shrugged and scooped the rest into a Tupperware container for later.

We stayed at the table until the sun came up, eyeing the phone. Then Drew said, "Come on. It's Saturday morning. Let's see what's on TV."

Mom passed, saying she was going to try to get a little more sleep. Every second week she does a Saturday shift on top of her usual work at the gas station café, but I don't think she'll go in today.

The two of us went to the living room, and Drew flipped through the channels. Nothing was on except kiddie shows. Finally he settled on a Looney Tunes episode, and we watched Bugs Bunny taunt Elmer Fudd for a while.

Sometimes I can find that stuff amusing, but today the jokes just seemed stupid. I kept looking at the clock. If Dad takes a long time to call, is that a good sign because he isn't rushing to save us from some catastrophe? Or does that mean whatever happened is so terrible it's taking him forever to deal with it?

The little bit of hash browns I'd eaten must have been digested ages ago, but my stomach wouldn't stop churning. Drew was lounging on the couch, legs sprawled on the ottoman, like there wasn't anything more important in the world than a talking rabbit. After a while it got to me.

"Aren't you worried?" I said.

"Of course," he said, still focused on the TV.

"You're not acting like it," I said.

He reached for the remote and nudged the volume down. Then he turned to me.

"I think a couple girls in my classes are sick," he said quietly —I guess so Mom wouldn't hear, if she was still awake. Because if she had heard, she'd probably have reacted even worse than I did.

"What?" I said. I had to force myself to lower my voice. "Are you sure?" I asked. "What happened?"

"Nothing *happened*," he said. "Just, yesterday this one girl in my physics class was sniffling, and in the middle of law, Amy had to leave for a few minutes because she was coughing so hard. They probably just have regular colds. One always starts going around this time of year."

"Did you tell Dad?" I said.

He rolled his eyes. "Of course not," he said. "He'd have put us under lockdown. How's that going to help anything?"

"It'd stop us from being exposed," I said. "You really want to get sick too? And he could have made sure those girls got looked at in the hospital, just in case."

"If we're going to get sick," Drew said, "staying at home isn't going to help. We'll probably get it from Dad. He's the one spending twelve hours a day with the people we know for sure are sick. A guy I know on the soccer team—his aunt's a nurse. He told me she's being forced to stay at the hospital because she was helping treat the patients and now she's got symptoms."

He had a point. I knew that. But for some reason, that made me even angrier. It's easy for him to say Dad's just overreacting. He didn't see Rachel or her father—he has no idea how serious this disease is, how it can turn you into a whole different person. How scary it is that more and more people are catching it when the doctors still haven't found a cure.

"You could have at least told *me*," I said.

"Because you'd have done something differently?" he asked. "Is that how you'd want to handle this—by hiding at home?"

"I don't know!" I yelled. "At least I could have decided!"

I caught myself before I said anything else, and we sat silently and listened. Thankfully, there was no sign we'd disturbed Mom.

"I'm sorry," Drew said, after a moment. "I should have told you. I just hate the way Dad deals with problems by throwing up a wall, without even knowing what he's trying to 'protect' us from. And..."

When he didn't keep going, I prodded: "And?"

"And I've been even more pissed off at Dad than usual, for other reasons," he said, frowning. "A couple weeks ago, Aaron said there wasn't any point in us staying together, because Dad's not any closer to being okay with me having a boyfriend, and I guess Aaron doesn't like the 'drama,' even long distance. Even though *I'm* the one who actually has to deal with Dad."

"Oh," I said. I didn't know what else to say. We've never really talked about relationships, since I've never had much of one, and Drew's always kept the details of his private. "I'm sorry. That really sucks."

"Yeah," Drew said. "It does."

He stood up and walked out, and I didn't feel like watching TV alone. I was so tired, but when I lay down in my room and tried to sleep, my mind kept racing. I started writing to get everything out of my head.

Only now I'm thinking even more. Too much.

I heard Mom go into the bathroom a couple minutes ago, so she's probably up now. Maybe I'll ask her if

Dad finally called. Mom's still on the phone with him, so I haven't heard everything yet. But none of the news sounds good. Rachel's dad just died.

SEPT 15

We went over to Uncle Emmett's today so Dad could talk to him about the mystery sickness. I was going to take Meredith out for a bit, but Uncle Emmett insisted she should be informed too, so we all sat in the living room. I kept my arm around Meredith. She started chewing her thumbnail as Dad explained what's going on. Like she doesn't already have more to worry about than any seven-year-old should, now that her mom's gone AWOL, without hearing about worse-case scenarios and people dying. How much is she going to understand, other than the scary parts?

When Uncle Emmett had heard everything, he shook his head.

"Lot of good that fancy research center's done for the island," he said. "So glad you were studying seaweed while this disease was creeping up on us."

"Emmett," Mom said sharply, and he scowled at her.

I could have kicked him, but Dad didn't look offended. I guess he's used to Uncle Emmett making digs at him by now. "You might be surprised," he said. "The equipment's being put to good use, believe me."

Uncle Emmett stood up and said, "Well, I'll get started packing."

"What?" Mom said. "Where are you going?"

"Does it matter?" he asked, his voice rising. Meredith shifted, and I squeezed her closer. "You think I should wait around until this virus gets me or Meredith?" he went on. "If the situation is as serious as Gordon says it could be, there's no way in hell I'm staying here."

"It's not just about you and Meredith," Dad said. "It's about the whole world. For all you know, either of you could already be carrying the virus. You leave the island and you spread it further. We've contacted the Public Health Agency. They're talking about setting up a contained area on the mainland so people can safely leave. You'd have to stay under their supervision for the decided timeline, but when they're sure you're uninfected, you'd be able to go wherever you want. You just need to wait a few days while they get organized."

"A few *days*?" Uncle Emmett shouted. "Why don't they have a place for us already? I don't give a damn about the rest of the world—I have a right to protect my family!"

He kept going, but Mom shot me a look like a silent order, one I was happy to follow. I grabbed Meredith's hand and took her up to her bedroom, where most of her dad's words were muffled. Her hair was looking kind of raggedy, so I grabbed the brush off the dresser and sat down with her on the window seat.

Aunt Lillian used to do Meredith up with all these tiny braids. I was always jealous because I knew they'd never work in my hair, since even though mine's as dark as Mom's, it's fine like Dad's. I tried to copy her technique on Meredith, but my little braids looked puffy and straggly, not sleek like they're supposed to. So instead I made two big braids, like pigtails. Meredith got up to look in the mirror, and smiled at me, even though they were lopsided. Then the corners of her mouth drooped.

"Is what Uncle Gordon said true?" she asked. "Maybe I'm sick?"

My throat felt suddenly tight. "Probably not," I said. "Not many people are. And even if you do get sick, they haven't had much time to figure out how to cure it. Soon they'll be able to make everyone better. So don't worry, okay?"

I pulled her onto my lap, and she relaxed against me as we stared out the window together. Their house is right by the shore. A pod of harbor porpoises was bobbing through the water in the strait. Way off, the mainland lights were glittering as if everything was right in the world.

We stayed like that until Drew poked his head in to tell us we should come down to watch a movie.

"Mom got Uncle Emmett to promise he'd wait until the Public Health Agency gets organized," he said under his breath as we headed downstairs behind Meredith.

I know that's a good thing, but part of me understands exactly how Uncle Emmett feels. Part of me wishes he'd break his promise and get Meredith out of here, just in case.

SEPT 17

I asked Dad how many people are in the hospital now, before he rushed out the door this morning. "More than we'd like," was all he'd say.

They still haven't isolated the virus. And another patient died. I don't know how Rachel's doing. When I started to suggest maybe I could go visit her yesterday, Dad got this look like a blast of freezing air had hit him, and told me at this point she wouldn't get anything out of it.

Please let him find that cure I promised Meredith. For Rachel, and everyone else.

He called Gran and Grandpa in Ottawa yesterday to tell them to keep an eye out, just in case. And he's forbidden me and Drew to go to school, of course—really, from leaving the house at all. But after spending most of the weekend and all yesterday cooped up at home, by this afternoon I was ready to climb the walls. I kept thinking about what Drew had said, about hiding from our problems instead of facing them. The new me wouldn't be afraid to go out and see what's happening.

I told myself as long as I didn't get close to anyone, I was just as safe as if I stayed home. But my stomach started twisting up as I walked toward the school. I stopped under the oak tree outside one of the science-room windows. Mr. Grant was writing on the chalkboard in his wobbly scrawl. Everyone was flipping to a page in their textbook. It looked like a totally normal day.

Then I noticed a boy in the first row scratching his shoulder. He worked at the spot for at least ten seconds, stopped, then went at it again.

A couple rows behind him, a girl started coughing so loud I could hear her through the window. Someone else sneezed, and another boy laughed.

I turned around and started walking away, my legs shaky. Even the new me couldn't watch any longer.

As I was going by the parking lot, someone called my name. I was so startled I almost ran—as if some sick person was going to be coming after me. But I caught myself and looked around.

A woman was getting out of a car near the walkway. After a moment I recognized her. One of Dad's friends from the hospital, Dr. Something-or-Other, but I've always called her Nell.

"Kaelyn," she said again. She hefted a cardboard box out of the trunk and lugged it over to the edge of the parking lot. "I thought your dad had you staying home," she said.

"I didn't go to school," I said quickly. "I just needed to get out of the house for a bit. Taking a walk."

Dad will have a fit if she tells him she saw me.

"As long as you're careful," Nell said, shifting the box.

"Want some help with that?" I asked.

"No, I think Gordon would murder me if I took you in there," she said with a smile. "I'll be fine. It's just paper. We printed up informational booklets, how to stay safe during a potential epidemic. I'm in charge of going over them with all the kids here." She tipped her head toward the school.

It's probably the same sort of advice I've already looked up on the internet. Wash your hands lots. Stay home if you feel unwell. Avoid crowded public places.

"Do you think we're going to be okay?" I said. I didn't even know I was going to ask until the words came out. But I wanted to hear what someone other than Dad thought.

"I think we have to focus on keeping people informed without creating a panic," she said. "Often you end up with a real emergency more because of people who are afraid of getting sick than those who actually are."

Which is why Dad was so hard on Uncle Emmett, I guess. I nodded, and Nell said, "Well, take care of yourself, Kaelyn."

She headed into the school, and I decided I'd seen enough, so I'm here at home again.

I avoided crowded places. When I got back, I went right past washing my hands and took another shower. But I don't really feel any safer.

SEPT 18

Mackenzie called in the middle of dinner last night. Hell must have frozen over, because Mom let me talk to her while everyone else kept eating.

"I was afraid you wouldn't be there," Mackenzie said. "Everyone at school is talking about all those people getting sick, and I hadn't seen you since last week. . . ." She paused to take a breath, and then asked, "Are you all right?"

"Yeah," I said, which was true as long as we were defining "all right" as "I haven't yet succumbed to a deadly illness." "My dad's pretty worried," I added. "Seemed safer to stay home until they know for sure what's going on."

"Well, school definitely sucks even more than usual right now," she said. "Maybe I can talk my parents into letting me stay home too. How long is this is going to last? Does your dad have inside info?"

"He's been helping at the hospital," I said. "But they still don't know a lot. They're experimenting with different treatments. Some people from the Public Health Agency came in yesterday, and they're the experts."

"That's good," Mackenzie said. "So can we hang out after school tomorrow? I haven't had anything to do except homework and listening to people freak out."

I told her I'd try. I got away with sneaking out yesterday because no one else was home, but Mom doesn't work today. Since I knew what Dad would say, I waited until he left for work this morning before I talked to her.

"We won't go near anyone else," I said. "And Mackenzie sounded totally healthy on the phone."

Mom frowned, but thankfully she trusts me to look after myself more than Dad does. "Just make sure you're back before your father gets home," she said. "He's got enough on his mind without worrying about you too."

So a couple hours ago I met up with Mackenzie in Thompson Park. We sat on one of those benches near the pond, and Mackenzie threw chips to the ducks. The breeze is already getting that autumn chill.

"Guess they'll be heading south soon," I said, meaning the ducks.

Mackenzie nodded, and then hesitated. "I think we're going too," she said.

"What do you mean?" I asked.

"My 'rents are spazzing," she said. "Mom wants to go to the condo in L.A. until this blows over. There's not much to do around here anyway. They told us all to go home at lunch. School's closed."

I hadn't known. So the epidemic is really that bad. A chill crept down the collar of my windbreaker.

"Do you know if Rachel got this bizarro virus?" Mackenzie asked. "People are saying she did. She looked kind of sick the last day she was in school."

I wasn't sure if Rachel would want me telling Mackenzie or not. So I just said, "She did? I didn't notice."

"You probably didn't see her," Mackenzie said. "It wasn't until after lunch. She started coughing really bad last period. I mean, she couldn't have been feeling too awful, because she went to choir practice after. I figured she'd come down with a cold."

Choir practice. I remembered Drew telling me about the girls he'd noticed in his classes—were they in choir too? Maybe they'd stood next to Rachel, and she'd coughed, and that was that.

Maybe last Tuesday was the luckiest day of my life, that I didn't catch the virus when I was visiting her.

Mackenzie shifted impatiently and said, "Anyway, if she is really sick, it's not like there's anything we can do. It'd be stupid for anyone to stay here if they could leave. Not you, of course—I mean, they need your dad and all. But he'll make sure you're all right. Anyone who isn't helping..."

I considered telling her Dad's theory about why no one should leave, not without proper precautions. But the way Mackenzie gets off on breaking rules, she'd probably see that as one more reason to ditch us.

Before I could decide what to say, she turned her head, and her face brightened.

"Hey," she said. "It's them!"

I looked over. A bunch of guys from our school were standing on the other side of the pond. There were a couple from our grade and a couple younger, but most of them were seniors. I didn't see anything special about them.

"What?" I said.

"You know Gav?" she said. "The one in the red T-shirt?"

I don't know all of the senior guys by name, but the one in red looked familiar, particularly the curly light brown hair. I thought

I'd seen him hanging out on the field outside school more than once.

"Shauna heard from Anne, who heard from her brother, that he—that Gav guy—he's started up this whole *Fight Club* thing," Mackenzie said in a rush. "They get together secretly and beat each other up. That's got to be them! I wonder if they do it out here in the park?"

"Pretty hard for a fighting club to stay secret that way," I pointed out.

"True," she said. "But still. On the island! Pretty insane."

As if people only do crazy-stupid things in places like L.A. I'm surprised Drew never heard about this. Maybe he did and just didn't mention it.

"I guess that's what guys like to do," I said, trying to put a rational spin on the idea. "Work out aggression? Like football and wrestling."

Mackenzie giggled. "Obviously football isn't tough enough for these guys," she said, and glanced at her watch. "Crap! I told Mom I'd be back by five. I should get going or she'll totally freak."

She gave me the usual good-bye hug, which reminded me of the rib-crushing squeeze I got from Rachel that last time, and the horrible thought came into my head that I might never see Mackenzie again.

As she was walking away, I saw her reach to scratch the back of her neck. And then she rubbed her left wrist. Out of nowhere, I had the urge to scream after her, tell her to stop.

But people get itches for no reason. Five minutes ago I scratched my chin. It doesn't have to mean anything.

And even if it did mean something—what could I have done?

SEPT 20

Six more people have died. The Public Health officers are barring visitors and all patients who aren't in critical condition from the hospital unless they're showing symptoms of the mystery virus. Dad says the building's almost at capacity as it is. And one of the doctors has come down with the disease now.

Dad brought home a box of face masks yesterday. "If you absolutely have to go out," he said, "make sure you're wearing one of these. The transmission is almost definitely respiratory."

"So you're closer to figuring out how to deal with it?" I asked.

"Hard to say, with Public Health running everything now," he said. "They take records without making copies and run tests without sharing the results. How they expect the rest of us to work..." He trailed off with a huff of breath, and added, "The World Health Organization is getting involved. I just hope they have more to contribute than adding to the confusion."

I asked him about the contained area on the mainland that was supposed to be set up so people like Uncle Emmett and Meredith could leave, and he said it's not in place yet. I wish they'd hurry up.

Mom's still doing her shifts at the café, but she's taking a mask with her to work. She says she's seeing a lot more people than usual coming into the gas station to fill up their tanks. "Worried we'll end up closing soon," she said, but I wonder if they aren't all loading onto the ferry and driving as far from the island as they can go. I got an e-mail from Mackenzie late last night, from L.A. They caught the first ferry yesterday morning and headed straight for the airport.

And this morning, right before Mom was supposed to leave for work, a white van with the logo for one of the Halifax TV stations came down our road. It parked on the other side of the street, and a couple of guys got out, one with a mic and the other with a video camera. "Media vultures," Mom muttered as we watched from the living room window. "Looking for a story in other people's pain."

When they knocked on the door, we moved into the dining room and ignored them. Mom waited another fifteen minutes before she finally left. From what Dad's said, both the town hall and the Public Health people would rather keep the epidemic out of the media, to hold off a total panic. So far I've only seen a few mentions on the news about a "health concern" on the island, with brief interviews with regular islanders who don't know much about the situation. I don't know if the American stations have picked up the story at all.

I wonder if your parents have told you anything, Leo. They wouldn't want to worry you, your first month in a new city and a new school. You probably have no idea. Somehow that makes it feel like you're even further away. But right now I'm just glad you *are* away from here, and safe.

SEpt 21

I've been so cautious the last few days. It's not fun hanging around the house all the time, but now that I know what a close call I had with Rachel, I figure I shouldn't push my luck. Since I saw Mackenzie on Wednesday, I haven't gone any farther than the backyard. What with school being closed and the only two people I could call friends out of reach, there hasn't been much to go out for. Mom or Drew are around if I really need to talk to someone, and Uncle Emmett brought Meredith over for a little while yesterday.

But today I was by myself. Mom and Dad were working, and Drew snuck out in the morning to go who knows where. The house was empty. The feeling started to creep over me that it was going to stay that way. No one was coming back.

And then I thought about you way off in New York, Leo— probably not knowing there's anything *to* worry about. I wasn't even sure how your parents are doing. When we were kids I used to see them every other day.

Suddenly I was terrified they might have caught the virus, that they might already be in the hospital and neither of us had a clue. Maybe I just wanted an excuse to get out of the house, but it worked. I put on one of the face masks and set off.

Outside, a couple of chickadees were chattering on the phone wires like it was any other day. I started to breathe a little easier.

When I got to your street, I saw your mom in the front yard, trimming the hedge. I stopped by the corner and watched. After a few minutes, your dad came out with a glass of water, and they talked a bit. No scratching, no sneezing, no coughing. They're okay.

I didn't go over, because I didn't know what I could say to them anyway. That can wait until after I've sorted things out with you. When they went back inside, I headed home.

On the way, some of my edginess came back. Hardly anyone was out, but it was warm enough that people had their windows open, and every now and then I heard a faint cough or sneeze. I started walking faster, and decided to cut across Main Street instead of going the long way around. I figured getting home faster was worth the extra chance I'd run into someone.

As I was passing the old theater, Tessa came around the corner farther down the street.

She was walking along as if nothing was wrong in the world. Hadn't even bothered to wear a mask. I almost hurried on without stopping, but then I remembered hearing her say her parents were going on a trip the other week. I don't know if they're back yet. How lonely would that be? Maybe she didn't realize how dangerous it is to go out.

What kind of person would I be if I walked on without saying something because one time she didn't sit next to me?

So I jogged to catch up with her. "Hey, Tessa," I said.

She paused and glanced around, and I had a flashback to that day in biology, when she breezed right by me. But she nodded and said, "Hi, Kaelyn."

"Are you okay?" I asked. "Pretty much everyone's staying home these days."

"I'm fine," she said. "I'm just picking up a couple things."

She sounded so calm that I felt awkward, like I was hassling her, even though I was trying to help. My tongue started to trip over itself. "Because, um, it's really not safe to go out unless you have to, you know," I said. "You could run into someone who's sick." I realized I wasn't setting the best example, so I touched my mask and added, "Even though I have one of these, I'm on my way home right now."

"Oh, I won't be out long," she said.

"Okay," I said. "Well, be careful."

She gave that brief nod again, and then she walked off. A block farther down, she crossed the street and went into the garden supply store.

So, I tried. If your girlfriend wants to risk her life for fertilizer or a spade or whatever, that's up to her.

SEPT 22

I've been thinking about you a lot lately, Leo. When I get lonely
stuck here at home, or freaked out about what'll happen if they
don't find a cure for the virus, I make my mind wander back to
before everything got screwed up. And since we were best friends
for ten years, I guess it's not surprising that you show up in a lot
of my memories.

What I've been going back to the most is my ninth birthday
party. Remember that?

A few months before, you'd asked me to practice the waltz with
you because Ms. Wilce didn't have any other students for you to
work with, and you were worried she'd stop teaching you if you
didn't pick up the steps fast enough. The best I could do was clomp
around in my sneakers, but you loved dancing so much that some
of your enthusiasm couldn't help rubbing off on me.

And then my party came, and Shauna showed up with her
new puppy. Everyone was petting it and talking about it instead
of doing the treasure hunt Mom had spent all morning setting up.

Even then, Shauna was one of those girls who just shine, whatever they do, and so people like them. Which was why I'd invited
her. *I* didn't shine. I was the weird girl whose mom and dad were
different colors and who was just as likely to spend recess watching
anthills as playing Red Rover. Mom's family has been on the island

as long as anyone, so most of the time the other kids included me if I wanted to join in, and if they didn't, I didn't care. But standing there seeing all of them huddled around Shauna, I felt like I might as well disappear.

Then you said, "Hey, let's show them what we can do." And you pointed to the computer, where you'd brought up our practice song.

I thought I'd trip over my feet and everyone would laugh, which would be even worse than being ignored. But you looked so sure that I took your hand.

I didn't trip. I felt like I was floating, gliding over the floor. Everyone stopped and watched, and someone said, "Wow!" And I wasn't nervous anymore. People were looking at me and wishing they could do what I was doing. For a few minutes I was shining, because of you.

If I could, I'd snatch that feeling out of the memory and keep it here in the present. I could use it right now.

I thought the worst was last night. After dinner, this sound came from outside. First I assumed it was a raccoon—they can really screech when they're angry. But I started to hear words in there too.

Without thinking, I went straight to the front door. Mom says she called my name, but I didn't hear her. I stepped onto the porch, and there was Mrs. Campbell, the old lady who lives three doors down, standing in her front yard ripping up clods of grass and throwing them at her house. She was wearing nothing but her nightgown. Her bare feet were already brown from the dirt where she'd torn up the lawn.

She was the one screeching. In between the wordless bits she was saying things like, "You won't take me!" and "Get away, get away!"

I couldn't move. I couldn't even breathe. It feels like I stood there for hours watching her, but it was probably less than a minute before Dad came out and took my elbow and said, "Come inside, Kae."

Mom was already calling for an ambulance, but the hospital must have been overwhelmed. She dialed five times before she got through, and Mrs. Campbell was out there screaming for a whole hour before they finally came.

"Isn't there anything you can do?" I said to Dad, but I realized even as the words came out that I wasn't being fair. It's not like he's got a supply of medications stashed in the house.

"I think we'd better just keep our distance," he said.

"Right," Drew said. "Of course there's no way to actually help her."

Then Mom started crying, because Mrs. Campbell had called her over to visit a couple days ago. "I thought she was just lonely and frightened, with everything she must have been hearing," she said. "And you know she's had that cough for so long. I had no idea she was sick. If I'd known . . ."

My stomach flip-flopped and I blurted out, "Were you wearing your mask?"

Mom blinked, as if she hadn't considered her own safety. Her voice shook a little when she answered: "Yes. Yes, I was."

"There isn't much the hospital could have done for her even if you'd realized at the time," Dad said, and Mom asked, really sharply, "Why not?" She apologized right away, but we were all on edge for the rest of the evening.

But that's nothing compared to today. Even though it's Sunday, Dad went in to the hospital again. About a half hour ago he called and asked to speak to Mom. I could have gotten her—she was only in the backyard mowing the lawn—but I could tell from his tone that what he had to say was important. And I'm tired of being the last to hear the news.

"She went out for a minute," I said. "What is it?"

He sighed, and for a second I thought he wouldn't tell me. Other voices were babbling in the background, but I couldn't make out any of them. "Dad . . ." I started.

Then he said, quickly and quietly, "I don't know the details yet, and everyone here is begging to use the phone, so this is all I can say right now. The government's decided the area's too high risk. They're closing off the island."

SEPT 22 (LATER)

Leo,

When I started writing in this journal, I was doing it for me. But now I feel like I have to keep writing for you too. So there's some record of what's happening. You won't be able to come back, not for a while, and when you do you'll want to know everything. Maybe I'll be able to show you this someday.

Hopefully.

After Mom came in from the backyard, I told her what Dad had said about closing off the island, and we called Drew down and turned on the TV. Our story made the six o'clock news. The camera zoomed in on the harbor—on soldiers wearing masks that looked like scuba gear who were marching across the docks. "Government sources haven't confirmed the reason for this military operation," the reporter said. "But it seems clear their presence is related to the recent medical emergency on the island."

What Dad had told me didn't feel real even then. The harbor they'd shown looked like ours, but it had to be somewhere else. Or footage from a movie someone had filmed here. It couldn't actually be happening.

Dad got home just before midnight. He ushered us into the living room, and then he got right to the point. "Public Health has decided to quarantine the island," he said, his voice flat. "At least until we've isolated the virus and developed a successful method of treatment."

"What does that really mean—quarantine?" Drew asked. "We're all confined to our houses?"

Dad shook his head. "It means no one except government medical and military personnel are allowed to come to or leave the island, for the time being," he said. "The ferry's docked until the quarantine is lifted, and the military will be patrolling the harbors to make sure no one tries to sneak off on a private boat."

So we're trapped here. The uneasiness in my gut solidified into a rubbery ball. Then I thought of Uncle Emmett and Meredith.

"What happened to setting up a containment area on the mainland so people who aren't sick have a chance to leave?" I said.

"They've decided there's too much risk involved in moving people around," he said. "I'm sorry."

All the schools will stay closed. If possible we're supposed to continue working from our textbooks, but the year will resume where we left off—classes just might run a little into the summer holidays. All nonessential businesses are advised to stay closed. Mom agreed she'd forego her shifts at the café until the epidemic is over.

"They said they'll make sure we have everything we need," Dad said, while my head was spinning. "There'll be a boatload of food and medical supplies every week."

"They think the quarantine's going to last longer than a week?" Mom said. Her hands were clasped together on top of the table.

"A lot of progress still needs to be made," Dad said, which obviously meant yes.

That news took a moment to sink in. Thanksgiving's in three

weeks. I had my brilliant plan to talk to you when you came home then, Leo. Now I don't know if I'll ever see you again.

We could all die. If no one finds a cure, the government will just hold us here until the virus has infected every person on the island. Until we're all screaming in the streets like Rachel's dad, like Mrs. Campbell.

"How can they do that?" I said. "All because a few people died? What about the rest of us?"

Dad looked even more tired than he had a minute ago. "We lost twelve more patients in the last twenty-four hours," he said, and paused before going on. "One of them was Rachel."

For a moment I just sat there frozen. It didn't make sense. Rachel's dead? Rachel, who was perfectly healthy before any of this happened. I still can't believe it, not really. It seems so impossible.

And all of a sudden I was furious. At the government for imposing the quarantine. At Dad for not having found a cure in time. At Mom for making us move back here. At everyone. I stood up and walked out of the room, because I knew if I stayed any longer, I'd either throw something or burst into tears.

I managed to get to my bedroom before I started crying.

How could Rachel be dead? A couple weeks ago she was laughing, dancing. And now that girl just doesn't exist?

We should have left. I don't care about Dad's reasoning. We all should have followed Mackenzie's family and gotten out of here when we could. Because now it's too late.

SEPT 23

I'm sorry I freaked out last night, Leo. I don't really think we're all going to die. Of course we can beat this. It's not like new diseases have never sprung up before. There are three different sets of experts helping us—one of them has to find a cure. And I have to keep reminding myself the quarantine's in place for a good reason: to make sure the virus doesn't get to you in New York, or Gran and Grandpa in Ottawa, or anyone else outside the island.

When I woke up this morning, I was tempted to pull the covers over my head and just wait until it was safe to come out. But when I started writing here, I didn't want to be the kind of person who hides away anymore, and I still don't. Yeah, there's a lot more to be scared of now. But if I'm doing something to make our situation better, maybe I won't feel so hopeless.

So I got up in time to catch Dad before he left. "I want to help out at the hospital," I said. "There's got to be something useful I can do. I could run errands, or you could show me how to use some of the equipment in the lab."

Dad shook his head. "I don't want you anywhere near the hospital or the research center," he said. "Those are the most dangerous places on the island right now."

I'd sort of figured he'd say that. "What about outside the hospital, then?" I said. "Everyone there's busy dealing with the virus, but someone should let the rest of the island know about the quarantine, right? Stick notices in people's mailboxes or something? I could take care of that."

"Kae…" he started, and then paused. "There is a plan in place to notify every household by phone, but I'm not sure we've even gotten started. I suppose you could take that on. Let me talk to the Public Health representatives—they have an official statement they want used."

Which meant I had to wait until he came back this evening. So I found another way to keep busy. When I came down later to grab lunch, the first floor of the house was full of this buttery vanilla smell, so good I closed my eyes and just breathed for a few seconds. Mom was in the kitchen baking chocolate chip cookies.

"A little treat to cheer us up," she said, but the worry lines around her eyes looked twice as deep as they did a few days ago.

Suddenly I wondered how the hospital workers are managing to get together meals for all those people who've been catching the virus. They must be just as overwhelmed as the doctors. There wouldn't be much time for baking.

"Is there enough to make more?" I asked. "Maybe we could cheer up a bunch of patients too."

We ended up baking six more batches. By the time Dad got home, we had the cookies packed into the tins left over from Christmas. I'd been worried he might have forgotten our conversation, but he handed me a bunch of papers as soon as he'd taken off his shoes.

"Here's a copy of the master phone list we're working from," he said. "The people who have already been contacted are marked. And here's the script you're supposed to use. There's an extra section for anyone who sounds as if they're sick—we'd like you to ask them to stay home, and make a note so someone from the hospital can pick them up."

"Sounds good," I said.

"I can set up a database for you," Drew offered. "To keep track of who you've reached, and so you can generate reports on the people showing symptoms."

"And since you volunteered," Dad said to me, pulling a small package from his coat pocket, "I've got another job if you want it. The virus appears to be attacking nerve cells, but the standard medications are barely slowing it down. Before the quarantine was announced, I'd started looking into experimental treatments, and I found a chemical used in some areas of Asia. The compound hasn't been approved here, but I ordered seeds for the plant that produces it. Our priority has been isolating the contagion, so no one's looked into growing them yet. What do you think?"

"I'll give it a try," I said.

"The family that moved here a few years back," Mom said. "The Freedmans, isn't it? I remember hearing they had a greenhouse built on their property. They must be interested in gardening. Maybe they'd have some tips."

The suggestion sounded fine for the five seconds before I remembered Freedman is Tessa's last name. But obviously Mom was right about her family—I just saw her shopping at the garden store, didn't I? I figured even if Tessa didn't think I was worth her time, her parents would help. So after dinner I looked up their number.

Tessa answered the phone. I recognized her level voice.

"I'm calling on behalf of Dr. Weber and the St. Andrew's

Hospital," I said, feeling I should try to sound official. "May I speak with one of your parents?"

"Sorry," Tessa said. "They're not available right now."

My heart stopped. I'd been so focused on the job, I hadn't considered that they might not be okay.

"Are they sick?" I made myself ask.

"No," she said firmly, and even though I'm not sure I'd recognize her parents if I saw them, I was so relieved I almost laughed. But then she said, "They still can't talk right now. They're busy. We're already aware of the quarantine and the precautions to take. You really don't need to call again."

She sounded like she was about to hang up on me.

"Look, Tessa," I said quickly. "It's Kaelyn Weber, from school. I'm not calling to give you the standard message. I need to talk to your parents about something important."

"What is it?" she asked.

"It's kind of complicated," I said. "Can't I just speak to one of them?"

She hesitated, and then she said, "You can't. They didn't make it home."

"What?" I said.

"They were supposed to get in on Saturday," she said. "But there was a thunderstorm, and their flight was delayed. By the time they made it down, the ferry had stopped running."

"Oh," I said. My mind slipped back to that moment the other day when I was alone in the house and felt like no one would ever come back. That yawning loneliness. Tessa's been on her own for more than a week, and who knows how much longer the quarantine will last? That must be terrifying.

"So what's this important issue?" Tessa said evenly. Obviously she's not so easily terrified.

I explained what Dad had said about the plants, and Tessa asked a few questions. "You wouldn't be able to throw something together very easily," she said finally. "If you want to make sure the seeds germinate, I mean. Why don't you bring them over here tomorrow, and I'll take care of them in the greenhouse. I've had a good success rate with rare plants."

I couldn't see why not. I've never had much of a green thumb. Better to leave the seeds in the hands of someone who knows what she's doing.

"Just . . . don't mention to anyone about my parents, okay?" she said. "One of the neighbors found out, and she keeps coming over to check on me, even though I refuse to let her in. She sounds like she's sick."

I promised I wouldn't. So I lied to Mom when I was convincing her that I needed to go over to Tessa's place. "I talked to her and both her parents—no symptoms," I said. That's true in Tessa's case, anyway. And I swore up and down that I'd take off right away if I saw the slightest sign that they were sick.

"All right," Mom said. "I know you're taking this seriously. I want you to drive the car over; you don't know who might be on the streets."

"Sure," I said, and then, because it felt right, I hugged her. She looked a little surprised, but she squeezed me back.

Whatever else might go wrong, at least I've got her and Dad and Drew.

SEPT 24

Well, that wasn't what I expected.

I headed over to Tessa's place right after breakfast. It seemed strange to be driving when she only lives a ten-minute walk away, but having those steel walls around me did make me feel safer, like I had this impenetrable shield against the virus. I don't think Mom needed to worry, though. I only saw one person on the way—a man sitting on his porch, who grinned and waved as I drove by.

I was almost at her house when a helicopter whirred overhead. A news chopper, probably. Trying to get the scoop the only way they can with the quarantine in place. I imagined some reporter or cameraman up there, peering down at us, and all of a sudden I felt really small. Like an ant in some kid's ant farm. My hands clenched the wheel and wouldn't relax until the sound of the propeller had faded away.

Tessa opened the door as I came up her front walk, and hurried me in. She led me through the house to the backyard, talking about soil zones and sun ratios and other gardening terms that went right over my head. When we stepped outside, she stopped, and we both looked at the greenhouse.

I hadn't realized it was going to be so big. They have a good-size yard, and the greenhouse fills up almost the whole thing except the little patio area right by the house.

But of course you already know that, Leo.

"Wow," I said. Part of me was impressed, and part was wondering what the effect on the local bird population has been. It's like one huge window.

"We had a smaller one when we first got here," Tessa said. "But it was always getting cramped. This was my sixteenth birthday present."

She was smiling like it was a Ferrari or a trip to Cancún. And I realized then that I'd gotten a hold of the right person after all. Tessa's parents aren't the gardeners—she is.

Inside the greenhouse, the air was heavy and humid, and the sun felt somehow brighter filtering through the glass. The heat and light combined with all the green smells made me kind of dizzy. But I liked it. It was this warm, peaceful space removed from the craziness happening outside.

"Have you been able to talk to your parents?" I asked as Tessa set up what she called a seedling tray.

"They phone every day," she said. "They're trying to get an exception made to come back."

She sounded way more calm than I'd have been in the same position. I looked around and noticed a bench near the back of the greenhouse, by a bush with pink flowers. Suddenly I had an image of you and her sitting there, your arm around her, and the words just popped out: "How about Leo?"

"Oh, we e-mail back and forth a couple times a week," she said. "He's really busy, and I told him I'd rather get two good messages than short ones every day."

I remembered how you and I were when I first moved away —sending photos and jokes and random things eleven-year-olds say. For a second, my voice caught in my throat. I swallowed and asked, "Have you told him what's happening?"

"Of course not," Tessa said. "He hasn't asked about it—either the American news hasn't picked up the story, or he hasn't had time to watch—so why bring it up? There's no way he can help. Leo wanted to get into that school more than anything else in the world. I don't want to distract him."

She had a point. But if your parents haven't said anything to you either . . . And your mom wouldn't, would she? She'd be afraid you'd insist on trying to come back and make sure they're okay.

It feels wrong to me. To keep you in the dark, when people you care about are in danger. Shouldn't it be your decision what you do?

No matter what Tessa or your parents think, I know you'd want to know. So just a few minutes ago, even though it made me feel ridiculously nervous and sneaky at the same time, I sent a short message to your old e-mail. It bounced back. I guess you switched to a new address sometime in the last couple years. I tried! Maybe I can come up with an excuse to ask Tessa for your current one— I'll definitely be seeing her again.

After she planted the seeds, she ushered me into the house and got us both glasses of lemonade.

"I think it'll take a couple weeks for the plants to start sprouting," she said. "But you can come by and check on them whenever."

"I'll call first," I said. "So you know I'm not sick."

She shrugged. "You don't have to," she said. "I know you wouldn't come over if you were. You were the one trying to make sure *I* was okay the other day."

She said it as a simple statement of fact, but my face heated up, remembering, and I looked away. That was when I noticed the board of keys on hooks by the fridge. Tessa must have followed my gaze.

"My dad does maintenance on a bunch of the summer houses," she said. "Checking for leaks and other problems during the winter."

Then her eyes lit up, and she said, "You know, I bet the owners have all sorts of medications in those places. They always talk about taking pills for their nerves or their blood pressure. If the hospital starts running out . . . I could get in, no problem."

"The government's going to be sending meds over from the mainland," I said. "We should be okay."

"Well, if anything goes wrong, think about it," she said. "The summer people don't need whatever they've left here."

When I got home, I asked Mom if Dad had mentioned anything about the hospital's inventory. Apparently the hospital got a good supply of medication before the quarantine started, and he said not to worry. If even Dad doesn't believe the situation's desperate, we must be all right.

But I'm going to keep Tessa's idea in mind anyway. Maybe we're okay for now, but who knows what'll happen tomorrow?

SEPT 25

Drew transferred his custom database file to my computer yesterday afternoon. It amazes me how easily he can bend programs to his will. If he wanted to, I'm sure he could get a big-money computer job right out of high school, but he's still set on becoming a lawyer. "One of the few not-corrupt ones," as he says.

Of course, that's assuming we even get to finish high school.

"You sure you're going to be okay with this?" he said as I was entering the phone numbers.

"Sure," I said. "All I have to do is read the script."

"Well, yeah," he said. "But not everyone's going to be happy to hear from you. A lot of people are angry about the quarantine. You call them up and sound like you're partly responsible, they might really tear into you."

I hadn't thought about that, but he was right. And what if someone picked up who was going crazy like Mrs. Campbell did? My chest started to get tight, and I took a deep breath.

"I'll just be glad they're on the other end of the phone line, nowhere near me," I said.

"Okay," he said. "Let me know if you want me to take over any time." He paused, and then added, "It's really cool to see you getting involved, Kae. I was kind of worried you'd be so freaked out you'd just hole up in your room and let whatever happens happen. Guess you're braver than I thought."

He said the last part with a half smile, and then poked me in that ticklish spot on my side before I could stop him, like he couldn't let me forget I was his kid sister even while he was giving me a compliment. But it was still kind of nice to hear. Drew's got high standards, and I have the feeling I don't live up to them very often.

There've been at least a dozen times last night and this morning when I've wanted to throw the phone across the room, but I haven't asked Drew to save me yet.

A few people do sound happy that someone's looking out for them. They thank me and promise they'll take all the precautions. But lots of others start ranting about the quarantine as if it was my idea.

The worst ones, though, are the people who're coughing and sneezing while they're on the phone with me. The ones who haven't been sick very long ask me if they should be worried, and what medicine they should take, and I don't know what to tell them other than that someone will come by from the hospital to pick them up. And the ones who've been sick for a while chatter away, gossiping about people I don't even know or telling me all sorts of details about their lives, until I've said five times that I need to get off the phone and end up just hanging up.

Actually, those aren't the worst. Because there are also the calls where I get no answer at all. Where people either took off early or have gotten so sick there's no one to answer the phone.

I'm trying not to think too much about that.

SEPT 26

I don't know what to do. I was sitting here reading what would have been this week's history chapter, and all of a sudden I got this tickle in my throat. No actual coughing, but this itchy, scratchy feeling. I just drank a whole glass of water and it's still there.

What if I caught it? What if Rachel gave me the virus, and the symptoms have just taken ages to show up?

No one else is home. Maybe I should go to the hospital? Or am I safer staying here until I'm sure? I don't want to get

Never mind. I coughed a few times, and now I feel fine. I must have gotten something stubborn stuck in my throat. Wow. I don't think I've ever felt this relieved in my entire life.

Thank you, thank you, thank you, any higher powers that happen to be listening!

SEPT 27

Over the last few days I got through almost all of the phone list. Then yesterday, after my little panic attack, I decided it was time to take a break, and did some more baking with Mom and Drew.

We used up all the flour in the house, but Mom didn't seem concerned. By the end of the afternoon the entire house smelled like a bakery, doughy and sweet. I don't know how much bread and rolls and cookies are going to help anyone, but even if they just put a smile on the patients' faces and distract them for a minute, I guess the work was worth it.

Dad seemed impressed, but he's probably less happy now that he's carried all the bags we filled to work. His fault for insisting on leaving the car with us in case there's an emergency.

I made the last few calls this morning: sick, angry, angry, really sick, and no answer. After that I couldn't take another moment of being stuck in my room. I went downstairs and saw Mom standing by the living room window, looking out at the street.

There was no one there. She was just gazing at the outside, like animals do at the zoo, remembering when they had a whole world that wasn't caged in. It made my heart ache.

"Let's go to the park," I said. "The ferrets could use a walk."

I expected her to argue, but she smiled.

"That's a good idea," she said. "We've got to give ourselves a moment to stop being scared every now and then. It can't be healthy staying cooped up inside all day. Go see if Drew wants to come. I'm going to call your uncle."

No one answered when I knocked on Drew's bedroom door, so I peeked inside. His computer and his unmade bed and his sci-fi movie posters were all there, but he wasn't. He's been sneaking out for an hour or two most days. I wonder where he's going? Just to hang out with friends, to prove the virus isn't going to run his life? I hope he's remembering his mask, at least.

I put the leashes on Mowat and Fossey more slowly than I needed to, because I could hear Mom's voice carrying up the stairs. The quarantine's really pissed Uncle Emmett off, no surprise, and he's been taking his frustration out on Mom. I didn't come downstairs until she'd gotten off the phone, and by then she looked calm enough.

"We'll take Meredith along," she said. "It'll be good for her too."

"Drew wasn't interested," I told her.

We drove the two blocks to Uncle Emmett's house, and then the five blocks to the park. Mom's eyes kept flickering back and forth when we left the car, as if she expected some maniac to come leaping from the shrubbery. But all we saw were a few fall birds hopping through the trees. After a couple minutes she relaxed. I pulled down my face mask so I could taste the fresh air, and she didn't say anything.

"Can I take one of them?" Meredith asked, practically bouncing, and I handed over Mowat's leash. She raced with him to a patch of tall grass, giggling. She must have been dying to get out.

Fossey decided she wanted to take a dip in the pond, so I let her tug me over to the edge. She slipped in and then scurried back out, shaking herself with her fur all puffed up. I glanced around to call Meredith over, and then I saw we weren't the only people in the park after all.

About thirty feet off, through the trees, a group of guys was standing around, a couple of them passing a bottle of beer back and forth. None of them had masks. I recognized most of them from school—Quentin was there, and the guy with the tawny hair that Mackenzie pointed out when we were here last time. Gav. The fighting club. I couldn't remember exactly who'd been with him before, but I was pretty sure it was the same group.

Right then, Quentin turned my way. His expression didn't change, but he said something to the others, and a few more of the guys looked over. My fingers tensed on the leash. They were being really careless about the virus. If just one of them had been exposed, he could pass it on so easily. But I had my mask, and maybe they'd heard things we hadn't found out through Dad.

While I was debating whether to go talk to them, Fossey managed to tangle her leash around the branches of this brambly bush. I had to crouch down to work it loose. By the time I'd gotten her free, the guy with the tawny hair was walking toward me.

I stood up with Fossey on my shoulder. I had the urge to yank my mask back over my face, but that seemed incredibly rude. At least he wasn't scratching or coughing.

He stopped when he was a few steps away. Like he knew I'd want him to keep a little distance. "Hey," he said. "You're Kaelyn, right? Can I talk to you for a sec?"

There wasn't anything threatening about him. He just stood there waiting, his eyes intent on me. I felt awkward, especially with Fossey squirming across the back of my neck, and I lowered my gaze. The cuffs of his shirtsleeves were rolled up, and he had a brownish-yellow blotch from a fading bruise by his wrist. His forearms were wiry with muscle. Possibly from pummeling his friends on a regular basis.

I made myself look at his face instead, and tried to sound normal. "Sure," I said. "What about?"

"I hear your dad's some sort of expert on diseases," he said.

"He's a microbiologist," I said. "So, yeah, he's studied bacteria and viruses and that sort of thing."

"So you must know more than just about anyone what's really going on," he said. "What's he told you? How bad is it really?"

"Pretty bad," I said. "They still haven't found an effective treatment. People are dying. The people who haven't died aren't getting better. My dad's really worried."

"So this quarantine isn't going to get lifted anytime soon," he said, jerking his hand in the direction of the mainland. "They're saying to hell with us."

"Well, if the doctors find a working treatment, everything could be okay in a few days," I said. "And the government hasn't abandoned us. The health agency's here, and they're going to be sending food and supplies." All the same things I've been telling myself over and over.

He smiled crookedly. "Right," he said. "As long as helping us isn't too much trouble. First time one of them gets sick, it'll be 'Sayonara!' and we're on our own."

One of the other guys called out, "Hey, Gav, come on!" before I had a chance to answer. He gave me a nod.

"Thanks," he said. "Stay safe." I watched him stride back across the lawn toward his friends, a weight sinking deep in my stomach.

The government would never *totally* give up on us, would they? I mean, how would Gav even know how they work? He's just freaked out like the rest of us.

Maybe for some people it's easier to be angry. But if I couldn't keep believing we'll get through this, I'd probably end up hiding away in my room like Drew expected.

SEPT 29

I tried to put that conversation with Gav out of my head. Told myself I had enough to worry about already. But it's starting to look like he was right.

The first shipment from the mainland came today. The government was supposed to be making sure the distribution was done fairly and safely, with people going door to door so everyone got some of the food without having to go out and risk being exposed. It sounded decent of them. They could have dumped the supplies at the dock and taken off, but they were going to make an effort instead.

So Mom and Drew and I were at home waiting for the doorbell to ring. I was trying to figure out what exactly the government would consider essential foods, and wondering whether the grocery store had any Cheetos left and if I might have to go the whole quarantine without them—as if cheezies really mattered right now. And then the bell finally sounded.

It wasn't the food delivery, though. It was Uncle Emmett. He glowered at Mom, who'd gotten to the door first. I saw Meredith sitting in the truck behind him, peering at us through the window. Her shoulders were hunched and she was nibbling at her thumbnail.

"I know Gordon's got you brainwashed into agreeing with the

quarantine," Uncle Emmett said. "But I thought I should at least try. There's a protest at the dock. We want them to see just who they're killing here. If you come now, we can get there on time."

"Emmett, you're smarter than this," Mom said. "Come in and have lunch with us. Who knows what could happen down there? Think about Meredith!"

He nodded sadly. "I am thinking about Meredith," he said. "Think about what could happen to her—to your kids—if we let those government bastards leave us here!"

Mom tried to stop him, but he stomped to the car and peeled off. Her mouth went tight.

"I can't just let him go," she said. "Not when he's in a mood like that."

I imagined Mom being swallowed up in the protest. "I'll come with you," I said. "In case someone needs to keep an eye on Meredith." But mostly I wanted to keep an eye on her.

Mom didn't even stop to call up to Drew. She grabbed a face mask for herself, shoved one at me, and ran to the car.

For the first time in what seems like forever, there were people on the streets. Everyone was going to see the shipment come in. Some were carrying signboards with messages like END THE QUARANTINE NOW, as if that was going to change the government's mind.

Parked cars clogged the roads around the harbor, so we pulled over to the sidewalk a few blocks away and jogged the rest of the distance. My face mask made it hard to catch my breath. I heard coughing in the crowd, and we passed a woman who'd stopped to scratch her knee. My lungs started to burn. All I wanted to do was go back to the car and leave. But Mom caught sight of Uncle

Emmett's truck and hurried on. I was afraid if I took my eyes off her for a second, I'd lose her.

A boat had just pulled in—our ferry. Several men and a couple of women in military uniforms stood in a semicircle on the asphalt between the crowd and the dock. A few more leaned against the railing of the ferry. They all wore the bulky masks I'd seen on the news, and each carried a rifle. I wondered if they were going to escort the government people through town to make sure no one tried to hijack the food. Or maybe the soldiers *were* the people who'd come to distribute it.

The crowd surged forward as the boat docked. So many people were shouting, I couldn't make out a single word. They were waving their signs and their hands, but they parted when the soldiers motioned for them to clear a way.

Then Uncle Emmett lunged out in front, dragging Meredith by the hand. Mom pushed through the crowd even faster. The bodies pressed harder and harder against us as we forced our way forward. A cold breeze came off the water, but sweat was trickling down my back.

There was still so much yelling around us I couldn't hear what Uncle Emmett was saying. He gestured to himself, to the mainland, and to Meredith, who just looked terrified. The soldiers shook their heads and said something back. You could tell they wanted Uncle Emmett to move. But he stood firm, his voice rising until I could hear a few phrases: "killing children" and "live with yourselves" and things like that.

The soldiers didn't seem to care. One of them grabbed Uncle Emmett's arm to pull him off to the side. He wrenched away and shoved the soldier hard enough to send him stumbling backward.

A gunshot snapped through the air, so sharply my ears started ringing. And Uncle Emmett fell too.

Mom gave a little gasp and reached toward him. At the same moment, the people around us shifted forward, the yells getting louder, the voices more furious. I lost sight of Uncle Emmett and Meredith as the crowd rushed past them. I heard another shot, maybe two—it's a blur in my mind.

When we reached them, Mom almost tripped over Uncle Emmett's leg where he was sprawled on the ground. Blood soaked the front of his shirt. Meredith huddled against him, her head bent next to his, saying, "Daddy, Daddy, Daddy," over and over. A gray undertone was creeping across his dark skin, and a bubble of spit quivered on his lips.

For a second, the world seemed to spin. I closed my eyes and opened them again, and the scene in front of me looked just as awful as before.

Mom grabbed Uncle Emmett's shoulders. "Help me carry him," she said, her voice shaking. "We have to get him to the hospital."

I leaned over to help, but a couple of men nearby realized what we were doing and hurried over. "Just show us where your car is," one said, taking Uncle Emmett's feet. I slid an arm around Meredith's shoulders, and we squeezed back through the mass of bodies, which were weaving back and forth as if they no longer knew whether they wanted to go toward the ferry or away from the guns.

I glanced back once. All I saw was the ferry pulling away from the dock.

Uncle Emmett's truck was blocked by the vehicles parked around it, so we had to carry him all the way to our car. The men who'd helped us eased him into the backseat. He wheezed, and Meredith shivered against me. Mom looked at the two of us and said, "Can you take her back to the house, Kae? I'll call as soon as we know how he is."

I brought Meredith home in such a haze that I'm surprised we made it here so quickly, and I've done my best to distract her. She's playing the new Mario game, though she's staring at the screen like she isn't really seeing it, and sometimes she lets the Goombas walk right into her. I don't know what to say to her. Someone in the harbor—*our* harbor—one of the soldiers who was supposed to be bringing us food and medicine so we can stay alive, shot Uncle Emmett. And other people too, I think.

And then they just left us.

Please, please, please, let Uncle Emmett be okay.

SEPT 30

Mom got home about a half hour after I finished writing yesterday. She wanted to be with Meredith when she told her.

Uncle Emmett was dead when he got to the hospital. The doctors did everything they could to revive him, she said, but the bullet nicked his heart. There was no way he could have survived.

That's not true, though. If he hadn't gone down to the harbor, if he hadn't pushed that soldier, he wouldn't have gotten shot. He was so concerned about making sure he survived the epidemic that he got himself killed. It's so stupid. It shouldn't have happened.

He was so worried about Meredith, and now he's gone and left her alone.

Is it awful that I want to punch him almost as much as I want to cry?

Every time the floor creaks, I expect him to walk into the room to pick up Meredith. But I'm never going to see him again. *Meredith* is never going to see him again. He's gone. Because of one stupid decision.

Now I'm getting the pages wet. I'd better stop.

OCT 1

This morning Meredith, Drew, and I went over to Uncle Emmett's house to pick up her things. Mom didn't feel up to it. She's spent a lot more time in her bedroom than usual the last couple days, and when she comes out her eyes are always a little red.

When we got there, Meredith just stood in the middle of her room, looking dazed. So I picked out the clothes I thought she liked best, and some books and toys. Then I stopped and gave her a hug, and she started to cry with short, gulping sobs. I patted her back and said the things you say when there's nothing that would make what's happening any better. The whole time a lump was filling up my throat and I was fighting the urge to join her.

After she'd stopped, Drew came upstairs with a pair of binoculars he'd found, and we peered out the window.

"Hey, check that out," he said, and pointed down. On the spit just a little south of the house, a few figures in bulky plastic-looking suits were setting a boxy contraption by the water. They disappeared from view, then came back, each carrying more metal boxes. We watched them for a few minutes, passing the binoculars back and forth, but neither of us could figure out what they were doing. I started eyeing the mainland instead.

I couldn't make out much, even with the binoculars, but I thought I saw a couple of figures moving around in the harbor over there. Between us and them, a few patrol boats were sitting in the strait, watching for quarantine breakers.

The ferry hasn't come back. Dad said the government is trying to arrange something else, that they've decided delivering supplies at the dock is too "inciting." It feels like they're punishing us. As if shooting people wasn't punishment enough. Uncle Emmett was the only one who died, but there was a woman and an older man who were injured. Are the soldiers going to be punished for murder and assault? Or is the army going to say the shots were justified, self-defense?

At this point, I doubt they'll ever tell us.

Drew must have been remembering that day too, because he frowned and said, "I wish Uncle Emmett had told us about the protest ahead of time. I could have talked to him."

"You really think you could have changed his mind?" I said, lowering the binoculars. "He wouldn't even listen to Mom."

"I wouldn't have told him not to protest at all," Drew said. "I'd just have told him there are better ways. The government was never going to give in and end the quarantine because of a bunch of islanders shouting—everyone on the mainland would have been pissed, for one thing. But everyone who wanted to leave could have started demanding a way for those who aren't sick to be moved, like we were originally promised. If we'd gone on the internet, gotten the whole world aware of how we were screwed over, reached out to the media— Hey, did they have cameras down there yester..."

He turned toward me as he started the question, and his voice petered out. Meredith was staring at the floor, her arms crossed tight in front of her and her whole body quivering.

"Mere!" I said, squatting down beside her. She leaned into me, and the shivering slowly stopped. I squeezed her, my stomach churning and my eyes tearing up.

"Daddy was trying to keep me safe," she said. "He told me that."

"I know," I said. "I know. And he'd have wanted you to have all the stuff that makes you happy, right? Let's go downstairs and find your favorite movies. We should watch one of them as soon as we get back to my house."

Drew came down a few minutes later. He followed me into the kitchen when I went to get a bag for the DVDs.

"Sorry," he said. "I got carried away—I shouldn't have said that in front of her."

I sighed. "Maybe your way would have worked," I said. "But it's not like we're ever going to know. How can you be criticizing him when he just *died*?"

"I don't know," he said, rubbing his forehead. "That's just how I think. It doesn't even seem real yet, you know?"

"Yeah," I said softly.

As we walked back to the living room, I felt him hesitate, and then he said, "Kae, if we could convince the government to start letting people off the island, if there was a safe way . . . would you leave, even if Dad wouldn't?"

We'd just come through the doorway, and Meredith looked up at me with the faintest hint of a smile. I didn't even have to think to answer.

"If it meant I could get Meredith out of here?" I said. "Yeah. For sure."

We gathered up her bags, and I kept my hand on her shoulder on the way out to the car.

While we were putting the suitcases in the trunk, this girl who looked twelve or thirteen came wandering down the street. I noticed her as soon as she stepped onto the road. She was scratching her wrist. Every muscle in my body tensed.

"Get in the car," I said to Meredith. She stared at me for a second, but she did it without asking.

"Hey!" the girl said, and then sneezed and wiped at her nose. "What's going on? You going on a trip or something?"

"Kind of," I said. "We're, um, in a bit of a hurry. See you around!"

I had the keys, so I dove into the driver's seat. Drew hopped in while I was fumbling with the ignition. The rattle of the girl's cough sounded like it was right beside me. I told myself we were safe, the windows were closed, the virus couldn't get in, but it still took me three tries to start the engine. The girl tapped on my window, and I hit the gas.

"Why didn't you want to talk to Josey?" Meredith asked as we roared around the corner. "She's really nice. She babysits me sometimes."

"She was sick," I said. "If you see someone who seems like they have a cold, or like they're really itchy, you have to get away from them fast. Okay?"

"Oh," she said, so quietly I could hardly hear her.

"We're fine," Drew said. "Kaelyn did the right thing. We got out of there, and we're okay now."

His saying that made me feel better, but you know what? None of us knows what the right thing is. Uncle Emmett thought the right thing was pushing around soldiers to protest the quarantine.

Dad figures the right thing is for us to never leave the house. Maybe I should have told that girl to go to a hospital, or tried to find her parents. Instead I just drove away.

At least I kept Meredith safe. That's the only thing I know for sure was right.

OCT 3

So the government figured out another way to get supplies to us. Last night a military helicopter flew in and dropped the packages. Of course, with an air delivery there was no one to bring the food to people's houses. A few volunteers took it to the town hall and put up flyers telling people to come there if they need anything.

And one of the packages broke on the landing, so some of the medication they sent is unusable.

Dad looks exhausted. Even when he's home, he's mostly in his study, still working.

I didn't say anything to him or Mom, but after I've finished writing here I'm going to head back to Uncle Emmett's and grab whatever food is left in the fridge and the cupboards. We might as well leave what the helicopter brought for the people who really need it.

I did ask Dad about the people with the big suits we saw on the spit the other day. He nodded when I described them.

"The World Health Organization wanted to trap a sample of the island's wildlife," he said. "Most viruses have a reservoir in the local animal population—a species they live in without killing. If we can find the reservoir, we can isolate the virus more easily, which will help us develop a means of eradicating it."

"Any kind of animal?" I said. If you count insects and fish, there have to be thousands of species that have contact with the island.

"For the virus to have jumped to humans, we're probably looking for a mammal," he said. "Or a bird—as we've seen happen with viruses like avian flu."

A bird. I remembered the dead gull Mackenzie almost stepped on, when we were at the beach on Labor Day. I can't believe that was only a month ago.

"Sounds like a long shot," Dad said, when I brought it up. "The virus wouldn't generally be killing the reservoir species; they'd have more of a symbiotic relationship. But I'll tell the WHO people to make sure they catch a few black-backed gulls to test."

I thought to ask then, "What are they going to do to them? All the animals they catch? Take a blood sample?"

Dad's expression went grave. "They have to kill them, Kae," he said. "A blood test isn't enough."

I felt sick to my stomach. I probably just condemned a bunch of black-backed gulls. Isn't there enough dying already?

The right thing or the wrong thing? I wish there was an easier way to tell.

OCT 4

At least some of those animals didn't die in vain. Dad called this afternoon to say the WHO people have isolated the virus, which means they can start working on a vaccine. When Mom told us, we all cheered.

The bad news is, it looks like the quarantine wasn't totally successful. I've had the TV news on more than is probably good for my sanity, watching those helicopter views of the island. A couple of stations have reported a "virulent strain of the flu" going around on the mainland. Maybe it's not even the same disease. As far as I can tell, no one's died there so far. But if even one of the islanders who took off before the quarantine was carrying the virus, the mainlanders aren't any safer than we are.

"If you feel a cold coming on, do the responsible thing and take a sick day," the reporters are saying. As if skipping work is going to do any good once people get to the extra-friendly stage. Our virus is a lot smarter than the ones you see in zombie movies. It doesn't make its victims stagger around slobbering and moaning so anyone in their right mind would run the other way. It gets you cozying up to people so you can cough and sneeze it right into their faces.

We just need the vaccine. Then we'll be okay.

I wanted to e-mail Mackenzie to find out what's happening in

L.A. But when I tried to go online, the browser kept giving me an error. None of the computers in the house worked.

I went to check Drew's last. He was already staring at the monitor.

"I can't get the internet going," I said. "Is it connecting for you?"

"We lost service some time this morning," he said. "The issue's not at our end. I'm working on it."

I don't see what he can do if the problem's not here, but with Drew's computer skills, who knows?

I figured I'd give Mackenzie a call instead, since she gave me the number for their condo before they left in the summer. No luck there either. I tried the L.A. number twice, and then I tried Gran and Grandpa in Ottawa, and all I got was a recording saying, "This service is no longer available."

The local numbers still work. I called Uncle Emmett's house and listened to the phone ring until the answering machine picked up.

The internet and phones have gone down before, but always after a storm messed up the equipment. The weather's been fine the last few days, and I can't think of anything else that would have caused a problem.

Why did they have to go down *now*? Until we've got either long distance or internet working again, there's no way I can find out what's happening to Mackenzie or Gran and Grandpa or anyone else outside the island.

And there's no way they can find out what's happening to us.

Maybe Dad will know what's going on when he gets home. Maybe the technicians are fixing it right now.

God, I hope so.

OCT 6

The internet and long distance are still down. Turns out there was an "incident" at the communications building. One of the workers there got sick and started freaking out with the hallucinations, and ended up damaging the cables that come in through the strait. Dad says the technicians—the ones who are still healthy, anyway—are trying to fix them, but they don't know if they can without parts from the mainland. Which, of course, we can't get right away.

Drew lent me his cell phone, after warning me that the reception's really bad on the island. I got through to Gran and Grandpa's number, but there was so much static I couldn't tell if I was talking to a person or an answering machine.

At least at the hospital and the town hall they've got satellite service, so we're not completely cut off. Dad's going to check in with Gran and Grandpa as often as he can.

Drew snuck out again this morning while Mom was in the shower. It was the first time he's done it since Uncle Emmett died, and this time he was gone for most of the day. After a few hours I started glancing out every window I passed, hoping I'd see him coming home. We're so shut off from everything now, even our neighbors, it feels like he could get lost on the island somewhere —fall into the ocean, get shot—and we'd never know what happened to him.

Finally, just before dinner, I looked up from the book I was trying to distract myself with and saw him climbing over the backyard fence. I caught him as he came in through the mudroom.

"What are you doing?" I said.

"Just getting a little fresh air," he said, as if he'd only been hanging out in the yard. That must be his official story.

"No," I said. "Where are you going? You keep taking off. Don't lie to me, Drew. I've seen you."

"It's not important," he said, looking away. "I just need to get out of the house sometimes, and I want see what's going on around town. I'm careful." He poked at the mask he had jammed in the pocket of his cargo pants.

"If that's all you're doing, why don't you tell Mom and take the car?" I asked. "I've been covering for you, you know. She and Dad are going to be so pissed if they—"

"You can't tell them!" he said before I could finish. "I need to do this, okay?"

He sounded so desperate, so unlike the Drew I'm used to. "Okay," I said. "I wasn't going to anyway."

"Thanks," he said, a little more calmly. "For covering for me and everything."

As he brushed past me, I got a whiff of salt and seaweed. He'd been down by the shoreline, somewhere.

Whatever he's up to, it's obviously about more than stretching his legs. He's *doing* something out there. Something that's important to him. And I'm stuck in here playing board games with Meredith.

The frustration ate at me all through dinner. And then Dad

came home, looking weary, and I heard him say something to Mom about running out of one of their medications.

I didn't even think. I went up to my room and dialed Tessa's number.

"Hey," I said when she picked up. "Let's do it. Let's check out those summer houses."

So it's settled. We start tomorrow.

OCT 7

Tessa Freedman and Kaelyn Weber, medical burglars at large. I bet you never could have imagined that, Leo.

The story I gave Mom was that I was going over to check on Dad's plants. By the time I parked in front of Tessa's house, I was so jittery I had to take a few deep breaths before I got out, and my hands were sweaty from squeezing the steering wheel. But I reminded myself that the new Kaelyn wouldn't let nerves stop her, wiped my palms on my jeans, and marched up to the door.

It seemed like ten seconds later we were already in her parents' car, the board of keys heavy on my lap. The wind picked up as we neared the ocean, hissing past the windows.

You remember the time we snuck onto one of the private beaches, the first summer I came back to visit the island after I moved? Ten minutes of being battered by the ocean-side waves and we were never tempted to go back. But most of those "cottages" have their own pools, and the view of the ocean *is* nicer than looking across the strait, so I suppose it works out fine for the summer people.

When we parked in the driveway of the first cottage, which looked about twice as big as my house, I got cold feet for real.

"Are you sure no one will be home?" I said.

"Most of the summer vacationers leave by Labor Day," Tessa

said. "Starts getting too cold for them. I asked my dad the last time he called, and he said no one told him they were staying late. The houses should all be empty."

She acted so cool. I wanted to see she was nervous too. To know there are a few chinks in her armor.

"I guess it's been a few days," I said, "since you've been able to talk to him. They are trying to fix the long distance."

"I know," she said. "I talked to someone at town hall. It hasn't been that bad. I mean, I know they're okay. It must be so much harder for them." She shook her head, and then she said, "Well, let's do this."

I felt so strange walking up to the door and unlocking it as if the place was ours. That first house had a big wraparound porch with a hot tub in the corner. Inside, the hall was wide and airy. We took off our shoes, and I could have skated across the floor in my socked feet, the wood was so polished.

Can you imagine spending that much money on a place you're only using as a vacation home? It's crazy.

"Where should we look?" I said.

"Wherever people keep medicine, I guess," Tessa said. "Bathroom, kitchen?"

"The bedrooms too," I suggested.

"Okay," she said. "So we'll check all the bathrooms and bedrooms, and the kitchen, and then we move on."

We crept from room to room, opening cabinet doors and drawers, like a bizarre Easter egg hunt. Finding a bottle of Advil or a bag of throat lozenges started to give me a little thrill. Everything went into the paper bag Tessa had brought with her. Even if we couldn't tell what something was for, if it looked medicinal, we tossed it in.

"Better to have too much than too little," Tessa said.

After the first few houses I didn't feel so odd anymore. You wouldn't believe everything the summer people have—and this is just what they left behind! One house was a total jackpot: Tylenol 3, Xanax, Valium, Ambien, Ritalin, a couple of tubes of what Tessa thought was an antifungal cream, plus a whole bunch of nonprescription pills.

We hit twenty houses, which gave us two big bags full. Tessa wrote A FRIENDLY DONATION on them with permanent marker and we dashed them up to the hospital doors. Tessa looked so serious hitting the gas as we took off that I started laughing.

I imagined how weird we'd look to you, the two of us together, partners in crime, and then I thought that you'd be proud of Tessa for coming up with the idea, and my stomach dipped as if we'd gone over a pothole. The question just popped out:

"How was Leo the last time you talked to him?"

"Good," Tessa said. "He's excited about a new partner he's working with. The school's exactly what he thought it'd be, and he loves the city too. I'm so glad he's not here in the middle of this."

And I felt guilty, as if it said something awful about me that I'd been going to interrupt your happiness by telling you what's happening here. I just think you have a right to know. I still want you to stay safe.

I'm not sure what I said. Something vague like, "That's good," and then we were back at her house. She smiled at me, and my stomach untwisted a little.

"I've got lots more keys," she said. "Let me know when you want to go out again."

You know what? I think I'm looking forward to it. Now that's strange.

OCT 9

When I opened my eyes this morning, I just wanted to lie in bed until the sun went down again. Maybe I should have. It would probably have been a better day.

But I got up. I was picturing another fifteen hours of watching depressing news reports and reading more and more ahead in my books for school, which may never open again for all we know. Then I saw Meredith huddled on her cot beside my bed, silently, with tears streaming down her face.

How can I complain about my life when she has it so much worse? I'm lucky, really.

I sat down beside her and hugged her, and when she stopped crying we went downstairs and I made breakfast for both of us. The whole time she looked so solemn. Every now and then her lower lip would wobble and I was afraid she'd start crying again.

I didn't want her to be sad. I wanted to make her feel better. But even *I* still feel torn up inside when I think about Uncle Emmett. The best idea I could come up with was getting her mind on something else, something happier.

"You want to go outside for a bit?" I asked her. "Let's get out of here."

I figured we'd stop by the grocery store and buy a treat. Most of the shops have been closed since the quarantine started, but it was still open the last time I drove past. And we'd only be going a couple blocks, so I figured we'd be safe enough walking, getting a little exercise. I made sure Meredith had her mask on tight, and we set out.

"Where is everyone?" Meredith said after a minute. The streets were so dead, our footsteps practically echoed.

"They're all staying home," I told her. "Like we do most of the time. They want to keep safe, away from anyone who might be sick."

When we came around the corner onto Main Street, she perked up. "Look," she said, pointing. "It's not just us!"

A delivery truck was parked in front of the grocery store, and a couple of guys were hanging out by its open back end. The store's door was propped open with a rock.

A little jolt of excitement shot through me, at the thought that maybe the ferry had come again and brought more food and medicine and the parts to fix the cables, and we just hadn't known. But right away the feeling fizzled out. That didn't make sense. Why would the government suddenly switch back from helicopters to boats; and if they had, why would a couple of teenage guys who didn't even have masks on be bringing the food around? I stopped walking and grabbed Meredith's hand.

At the same moment, a couple more guys and a girl came out of the store. They were carrying cartons of food, and the girl was hefting a huge package of bottled water. They came around to shove their haul into the truck, and I realized they all looked familiar. One of them I knew for sure—it was Quentin.

I eyed the others more closely. Gav wasn't there, but I recognized the guys from his group. So he and his friends figure the right thing to do is hoard all the food left on the island for themselves? I can't believe him! He goes off on the government for not helping us enough, and then turns around and does something ten times more selfish.

"What are they doing?" Meredith whispered.

"Just getting some food," I said, and started to tug her away. "I don't think they'll want to share. Let's go home. We've still got some ice cream."

Her fingers curled around mine. "They're stealing!" she said.

Then Quentin turned in our direction. I froze, hoping he wouldn't see us there under the awning of Keith's Fish Mart as long as we didn't move. It seemed to work. He sauntered a little ways toward us, but didn't look at us, only the storefronts. He stopped in front of Maritime Electronics, tapping a board he was carrying against his leg.

"Hey, Vince," he shouted. "There's no reason we can't have fun too, right? We could have the best sound systems on the island!"

The guy named Vince looked skeptical. "I don't know," he said, heading back to the grocery store. "Gav said just to grab the food. I'm gonna stick with that."

"Wimp," Quentin called after him. Then he raised the board and slammed it into the store window.

Back in Toronto, nothing would have happened. The glass would be super-reinforced or fitted with bars. But you know the shops around here: most of the buildings were built before our grandparents were born, and still have the same glass. People just don't go around breaking into places. At least they didn't before.

The window shattered. Meredith and I both flinched. Thankfully, Quentin was so busy ogling the merchandise we could have been tap-dancing and he wouldn't have noticed. I was waiting for him to step inside so we could make a run for it, when Meredith yanked her hand away from mine and marched toward him.

"You can't do that!" she yelled, sounding way too fierce for a seven-year-old. "Nothing in there belongs to you! Leave that store alone!"

I'd known she was sad, but that was the first time I realized she might be pissed off too.

I caught up with her as Quentin spun around. For a second he looked uncertain, and then he sneered at us. I could almost see his hackles rising, like one of the ferrets when they're startled.

"You got a problem?" he said, waving the board. "You want to talk about it?"

"No," I said, clamping my hand around Meredith's elbow and backing away. "Do whatever you want."

"Good," he said. "'Cause otherwise I might have to smash a few more things."

"But, Kaelyn," Meredith said, and I squeezed her arm so tight it must have hurt. I dragged her around the corner and halfway down the next block before she started walking fast enough to keep up.

"If you meet someone bigger and stronger than you who starts looking mean," I said, "you get away as fast as you can. Understand?" Every animal knows that rule of survival. We've got to start thinking like that. About surviving.

"But they're not supposed to steal," Meredith said. "Isn't it wrong to just let them?"

"If there are still police around, they'll take care of it," I told her. "It would be way more wrong if you got hurt because you tried to do their job."

"Were those people sick?" she asked a couple minutes later, as we reached the house. "Is that why they were acting so mean?"

I didn't know what to tell her. I went to school with Quentin all the years we lived on the island, and he might have been a jerk, but he never seemed dangerous. You remember fifth grade, Leo, when I said I was going to punch him if he kept teasing you about your dancing? He got all scared and ran to tell the teacher. I can hardly believe that's the same guy we saw today.

So I said to Meredith, "It's not just sick people you have to watch out for. My mom and dad and Drew and me, you're safe with us. Anyone else you shouldn't trust."

I wish I could have blamed the virus. I wish the virus hadn't put us in a position where I needed to explain any of this to her in the first place.

OCT 10

Mom came over while I was making lunch today and gave me a hug, out of nowhere. I hadn't realized how wound up I'd been until I let myself relax into her.

"You've been doing a really good job looking after Meredith," she said.

I thought about the trouble I almost got us into yesterday, and my chest went tight.

"I don't really know what to do," I said. "Do you think she's okay?"

"I hope so," she said. "I think Emmett would be really pleased to see how you've been there for her." She paused for a moment, blinking hard, and swallowed audibly. Then she said, "I just wanted you to know how proud I am of you."

They were only words, but I've felt lighter all afternoon.

OCT 12

I can't stop thinking about it. Maybe if I write it down I can get it out of my head.

Tessa called this afternoon and said some of Dad's seeds had sprouted, so maybe she should bring a couple by and then we could check out more of the summer houses. I said sure. After seeing Quentin the other day, I had trouble feeling any guilt about taking medications from rich people who aren't even living here and giving them to the hospital. At least we were stealing to help.

The plants she brought were just little tufts of leaves, but they're a start. We left them on the porch and headed out.

It was kind of calming, going into those "cottages" with their gauzy curtains and shiny appliances, everything clean and tidy. Like no one had ever been sick there. They felt safe.

The third house we pulled up to had a satellite dish mounted on the front lawn. As soon as I saw it, I didn't care so much what medicine we might find. I was hoping I could get on the internet, to finally write to Mackenzie and find out what's been happening in L.A. She must be wondering why I haven't e-mailed her for so long.

If I hadn't been so focused on that, maybe I'd have noticed something was off right away. There were a few dishes sitting on the kitchen counter. Someone had left a sweater slung over the banister. But I assumed these owners just weren't as tidy as the others.

Tessa headed for the downstairs bathroom while I hurried upstairs. I opened one door and found the master bedroom, which was about the size of our entire second floor and had a big flat-screen TV, but no computer. There was a crumpled tissue on the floor. If nothing else, that should have warned me. I should have gotten Tessa and left.

But I didn't. I opened the next door.

The first thing I saw was the blood.

It had seeped across the carpet almost all the way to the hall from where the woman was lying. She was curled on the floor by the foot of the bed, facing toward me. Her eyes were closed, but her mouth was pulled back in this grimace like she'd been snarling when she died. Her arms were wrapped around a toddler, who was staring at nothing, his face pale and blue. His pajamas were soaked red. It looked like she'd sliced herself open from wrists to elbows and held him while she bled out.

It couldn't have happened that long ago. There wasn't even any smell yet.

All I could do was turn around, and then I was throwing up all over the polished hardwood. My legs gave out. I crouched there for a minute or two, heaving. Then somehow I made it to the top of the stairs. Tessa was there. She must have heard me.

"Are you okay?" she said.

I blinked and blinked to keep the tears from leaking out. My throat was burning. Tessa looked at me and then down the hall, and started to go to see, but I grabbed her arm. I don't know if I managed to say anything intelligible. I remember shaking my head a lot.

But she went anyway. Then she came back and sat beside me,

close enough that our sides touched, and waited until I got a hold of myself.

"Let's go," she said. I thought she meant go home. It wasn't until we'd been back in the car for a minute that I realized she was heading for another cottage.

"Can you take me back?" I asked. "To my house?" I can't remember what she said, but she did. I thanked her when I got out. Then I went upstairs and lay down and pulled the blanket over me, and hoped Meredith wouldn't come in and ask how I was.

I've tried to tell myself that what happened is obvious. The little boy got sick and died, and the mom killed herself out of grief. But if he was that sick, why wouldn't she have taken him to the hospital?

What if she was the one who got sick, with no one there to tell her to see a doctor, no one nearby to hear her if she went crazy? It could have happened like that. The hallucinations taking over, her imagining someone or something was after her, the kid started crying and making a fuss, and she hit him or grabbed him around the neck, and

But it doesn't matter how it happened. I don't care why she did it. I just want this to be over. I want the stores to be open and people to be able to talk to each other without masks over their faces and no one to ever die again.

OCT 13

We were supposed to have Thanksgiving dinner today. Mom surprised us by showing us the turkey she started thawing in secret yesterday. She must have bought it before Gav's group ransacked the grocery store.

"We've got a lot to be thankful for," she said. "The five of us are still healthy, and your father's making progress with the vaccine."

Honestly, we have way more to complain about than to celebrate, but it was a relief to see her smiling. So I said I'd help with the cooking, and Meredith volunteered too. Drew begged off, claiming he was busy with something on the computer, but I caught a glimpse of him slipping out the back door a few minutes later.

We started getting dinner ready a little after lunchtime, even though Dad said the earliest he'd be home was six. Mom was preparing the turkey over by the oven. I was peeling potatoes by the sink. Meredith was setting the table.

I was telling her to just use the regular knives and forks, that we didn't have anything fancy for holidays, when Mom suddenly went still.

Before I had a chance to ask her what was up, she walked right out of the kitchen. The turkey was sitting there on the cutting board, with half the stuffing still in the bowl. I figured she must have needed to go to the bathroom. But when I'd finished with the potatoes and washed the slimy feeling off my hands, she still hadn't come back. Meredith wanted to know what she could do now that the table was set.

"Why don't you take a break?" I said. "You can play Nintendo if you want."

Mom wasn't anywhere downstairs, and the bathroom was empty. Her bedroom door was closed. I knocked.

"Don't come in," she said right away.

"What's going on?" I said. "Do you need anything?"

"No," she said. "I'm just feeling a bit off. I need a little time by myself, okay?"

She hadn't sneezed or coughed, but all of a sudden I understood. She was afraid she had the virus. My whole body tensed up.

Mom must have sensed I was still standing there. "Don't worry, hon," she said firmly. "Go downstairs. I'm sure you and Meredith can get the rest of dinner together. I'm going to take a rest."

I turned and started down the stairs, my heart pounding so loud I could hardly hear anything else. I have to tell Dad, I thought. It was all I could think. Over and over, *Get Dad, get Dad*. He'd know what to do.

Telling Meredith would just have scared her, so I said I was going out for a bit and she should keep playing her game. It wouldn't take more than half an hour, I thought. Drive to the hospital, grab Dad, drive back. I took the keys off the hook and went to the car.

The whole way there, my heartbeat chased my thoughts through my head. Mom couldn't really be sick. She didn't have any symptoms. She was just nervous and being extra careful. Dad would see that. He'd tell her she was fine, and she'd calm down, and we'd have a normal Thanksgiving dinner. But then I'd remember the way she'd stiffened up and walked out without a word, and my pulse would thump even louder, and I had to tell myself the story all over again.

I figure it's a miracle I managed not to drive into a telephone pole or a fire hydrant. But I reached the hospital in one piece. The parking lot was jammed. I wove back and forth along the rows twice, searching for a space. I've never seen the lot even halfway full before. Some of the cars had a fine layer of dirt all over them, like they'd been there a month without being used.

Which maybe they had. Maybe the people who had driven them there to get help had never come back out.

I had to park a block away. I ran from there to the hospital doors.

I hadn't been inside the hospital since those couple of days during our summer visit last year, when I got that bad fever. Usually there's a nurse or an orderly at the desk in the reception room, and a mom or a dad with a crying kid, or one of the elderly islanders who's come in for a checkup. Never more than a couple of people. It's quiet, almost peaceful, in a disinfected, artificial-light sort of way.

Today it was crazy.

The reception room was so packed I couldn't make out the desk, only a crowd of people shifting restlessly. Voices were echoing off the walls. I hadn't made it two steps from the front door when Mrs. Stanfeld from fourth grade came in behind me with a little girl who was skipping and chattering between her sneezes. They rushed past me into the room.

"My daughter needs help!" Mrs. Stanfeld shouted, and someone yelled back, "Everyone needs help! Wait your turn!" And someone else started sobbing. All around, people were coughing and sneezing and rasping their fingers over their clothes to get at some itch they couldn't quite scratch away. The disinfectant smell was still there, but overwhelmed by sweat and something sour that made my stomach turn.

I'd been in such a panic when I left the house that I'd forgotten my face mask. I felt like I'd walked in there naked. But no way was I turning back and going home and starting over. So I held my sleeve up to my nose and squeezed into the room.

A nurse with a mask, a plastic gown like a thin raincoat, and long plastic gloves was drawing a blood sample from an older woman who couldn't stop rubbing her chin. The nurse had a cart of labeled samples behind her—probably for testing to see who really had the virus. They all have it, I thought. For a second, I couldn't breathe. It felt like the virus had to be all around me, clouds of it in the air.

Dad wasn't in that room, and obviously the nurse was too busy to help, so I pressed my arm to my face as tightly as I could and pushed through the crowd to the hall at the other end.

Another nurse hustled by. She ducked into one of the exam rooms, which I saw held six patients crammed in on cots and a couple on mats on the floor. "They're coming, they're coming!" one of them started to whisper in a hoarse voice.

"No one's coming," the nurse said. She injected something into his arm, and his eyes went glassy. She stood watching him for a moment, looking like she might be blinking back tears.

"Excuse me," I started to say as she came out.

"Back to the reception room," she said briskly. "Blood test, then you're admitted."

Before I could explain, she'd hurried on to the next room.

Maybe Dad was upstairs, but there was a bunch of people already standing around the elevator, and I didn't know where the stairwell was. As I walked on, an orderly marched past me with a bunch of feverish, coughing people from the reception room in tow.

"Where are the new ones going?" he asked a nurse in an anxious voice. I couldn't hear the answer.

Around the corner, mats lay on the floor along the wall, some occupied, some vacant. The orderly gestured to them.

"What?" a woman said. "You're leaving us in the hall? Where are the doctors? We need proper treatment!"

I turned the other way, searching for the stairs, but there was only a short hall lined with patients, and a dead end. In one of the rooms nearby, someone started shrieking.

I stepped back against the wall and sank down, my sleeve still pressed against my nose, trying to take deep breaths through the fabric. I just needed a moment, I told myself. Just a minute or two, to pull myself together. But with each breath I felt like I was shaking more, not less.

I'm not sure how long I was there. It was a blur of voices and people rushing by, until I felt someone stop in front of me.

"Kaelyn?" she said. It was Dad's friend Nell. She looked like she'd been on her feet since the night before. Her hair was frizzing out of her bun, and brown and yellow stains spotted the plastic gown she was wearing over her lab coat. Her smile was hardly more than a flat line. But it was something. I stood up.

"I need to find my dad," I said. "My mom thinks she's got it. He needs to come home."

Her trace of a smile disappeared. "Oh, Kaelyn," she said. "I don't know where he is. He's been going back and forth between here and the research center."

I must have looked totally helpless then, because she touched my arm with her gloved hand and said, "Is she bad?"

I shook my head. "I don't even know if she's really sick," I said.

"Okay," she said. "Then you don't want to bring her here. She'll be better off at home, where she's comfortable. I'll give you a couple of drugs we've found help with the symptoms. Stay right here."

She pulled her mask back up over her face and hurried off. A few minutes later she came back with a couple boxes of sample pills, and a mask for me. I slid it on gratefully. "I'm sorry I can't give you more—we're running low again," she said. "If she takes one of each, it should help at least a little. You get out of here now, okay? As soon as I see your dad, I'll let him know."

"Thank you," I said. A few pills didn't seem like a very good trade for Dad, but that wasn't Nell's fault.

She walked me out the front door, even though she must have had a million other more important things to be doing. When we got there, I blurted out, "Does anyone get better?"

Her jaw tightened, and she looked outside. "We have a few cases that look promising," she said.

A few cases. How many people have already died?

When I got home, Meredith was still jabbing away at the controller. I went upstairs and stood outside Mom's room, but I didn't hear any coughing or sneezing. So maybe she really is okay. I showered and changed and threw my old clothes into the wash. Then I went downstairs to the kitchen, to figure out if I could do anything with all the food. That was where Drew found me.

"Where've you been?" he said the second he walked into the room. "I wanted to talk to you, and Mom said she didn't know where you were, and all Meredith knew was you'd gone out. You can't just wander off without telling anyone!"

My nerves were way too frayed already. How could he seriously think *he* had any right to complain about me? "What are you talking about?" I said. "You sneak off all the time!"

"I have good reasons," he said. "I've never—" He cut himself off and shook his head. "Look, I don't want to argue right now. You're back, that's what's important. We'd better get started."

"Get started on what?" I said. "What's going on?"

"I found a way to leave," he said.

Which was so not what I was expecting to hear that I just stared at him and said, "Leave where?"

"The island, of course," he said, lowering his voice. "I've figured some things out—I'd have gotten a plan together faster if the internet hadn't gone down. I know Dad won't go, but I bet we could convince Mom if she thought it'd protect us and Meredith. We're all still okay, so it shouldn't be— Kae, what's the matter?"

I wiped at my eyes before any more tears could leak out. "Mom thinks she's sick, Drew," I said. "That's why I went out. I went to the hospital to try to find Dad."

"She's sick?" he said. "She sounded fine when I talked to her —she just wanted to take a nap."

"I don't know," I said. "I could tell she's worried. She wouldn't even open the door to talk to you, right? I guess Dad will do a blood test or something to find out. When he gets here."

Drew frowned. "She can't be sick," he said, sounding like he was talking to himself more than to me. "She hardly ever goes out. How could she have caught the virus? She's just on edge, like the rest of us. Dad'll say she's fine. Then we'll talk about leaving, okay?"

"Okay," I said.

I should feel relieved he thought the same thing I did. That Mom isn't really sick, just nervous. But Mom isn't normally the kind of person who lets her worries get the better of her. And we still don't know for sure all the ways the virus might be passed on. We've all been out of the house. Any one of us could have brought it home.

OCT 13 (LATER)

I was going past Mom's room to the bathroom a few minutes ago, and I heard her coughing.

It still doesn't mean anything. Lots of things make people cough. It could even be her nerves making her imagine a tickle in her throat. That happens. Psychosomatic symptoms.

I tried to talk to her, but she said she's resting and not to worry. So I told her I was leaving the pills Nell gave me outside her room, and she should try taking one of each. She opened the door to get them as I was going downstairs.

We never ended up making dinner. The turkey's still lying on the counter half stuffed. It's eight thirty and Dad's not home. Where the hell is he? The people at the hospital have other doctors. This is Mom. He should be here.

Happy Thanksgiving.

OCT 15

Leo,

Sometimes I envy you for getting out of here before all this started. But it must be almost just as awful for you, being stuck out there not knowing what's happening to your parents or your girlfriend or any of your friends.

I wonder if you worry about me at all?

I hope you're okay in New York, at least. I know from TV that there've been a few deaths off the island that the reporters say are related to the virus, and now there's a segment on precautionary measures on every news broadcast, but the government hasn't tried to quarantine Halifax or Ottawa. So the situation can't be that bad—not as bad as here, anyway.

There is some good news. Another helicopter delivery of supplies came this morning. And Dad got in late on Thanksgiving because the team he's been working with finally figured out how to make a potentially usable vaccine. Some of the WHO people took it off the island for testing—and hopefully mass production, if it's working. Which is great, except a vaccine isn't going to do anything for someone who's already sick. Like Mom.

Dad took a blood sample to the hospital yesterday to confirm. Mom still hasn't come out of her room. I haven't seen her since we were getting Thanksgiving dinner ready. But I hear her coughing and sneezing through the walls. Dad gave her a little of the emulsion they've made from Tessa's plants, and he says her symptoms eased off a bit.

I've been talking to her through the door. "You just look after yourself and Meredith," she says, "and I'll do everything I can to get better. We'll get through this." But if she talks for very long she starts coughing so hard she can't speak, so I haven't tried as much as I'd like to.

God, what if I never get to hug her again?

I can't think like that. It'll just make me crazy.

At least I did something useful today. Dad said they'd gotten everything they could from the two plants Tessa gave us, so I called her up. She said the others had sprouted and were looking good. I went over this afternoon to pick them up.

When she opened the door for me, I suddenly felt awkward, because the last time I saw her was the day I found that woman in the summer house. Maybe she could tell, because she said, "I thought about calling you, but then I thought, if it were me, I probably wouldn't want to be reminded of it. But if you want to go out again..."

Even considering going into one of those houses made my stomach clench. "No," I said. "I don't think I will." But in a weird way it was nice to know that she'd bothered to worry about me. It also made me feel guilty for maybe not worrying enough about her. I just never feel like she wants anyone's help.

We carried about a dozen pots out to the car, and this youngish man, maybe in his twenties, came sauntering down the street toward us. "Pretty ladies!" he called out. "Just what I've been looking for."

Then he sneezed, but we'd have gone inside and shut the door even if he hadn't been sick.

"And that's why I spend most of my time inside or out back," Tessa said.

She made lunch for both of us. I protested until she pointed out that she had more food than she could eat on her own before it spoiled.

"Normally I'd give the extras from the greenhouse to the neighbors," she said. "I should send you home with some. There's lettuce that's about to go to seed, and tomatoes ready to burst, and I think some beans that are ripe too."

"I didn't know you grew vegetables," I said. Somehow when I was in there before I only noticed the big exotic plants.

"Oh," she said, "the showy flowers and things are just for my mom. She said if I was going to take up most of the backyard, I'd better make the greenhouse look nice. But my focus is common crops. Do you know the big farming companies have been decreasing the diversity of the genetic pool for almost every one? Which means if some plant disease comes along that attacks one type of corn, or broccoli, or whatever, we could lose all of it."

She had a bunch more opinions to share about farming corporations and plant genetics while we went into the greenhouse to harvest some of her "crops." It was strange seeing her so intense. A dead toddler doesn't faze her, but corn and broccoli she gets worked up about.

"Wow," I said at one point. "You must have done a ton of research."

She nodded. "I want to help reverse the process," she said. "I've been working on different strains of certain vegetables. Someday

I'm going to have a whole farm, maybe here on the island, and start providing new seeds to other farmers."

When she was talking, I sort of got why you fell for her, Leo. The way she feels about her greenhouse, it's like you and dance. You both have this passion that most people wouldn't understand.

My biggest goal has always been to go off into the wilderness and study arctic wolves and mountain lions. Tessa's planning on saving the whole world.

I guess that's how she manages to stay sane, living there alone, not knowing when she'll see her parents again. But as we were standing in the front hall, me with my armful of vegetables, she glanced at me with those dark blue eyes, and for a second she looked lost. I had to say something.

"You know," I said, "I'm sure my parents would be okay with you coming to stay with us. There's not a whole lot of extra room, but at least..." *At least you wouldn't be on your own all the time*, I wanted to say, but it seemed insulting to imply she couldn't look after herself. And then I remembered—I'd actually managed to forget—Mom.

"Oh," I said. "Except, my mom's gotten sick, so maybe—she's staying in her room, she wouldn't be coughing on you or anything —but if you thought it wouldn't be safe—"

I'm surprised she could follow what I was saying. I hardly could. She waited until I stalled, and then she said, "Thanks, Kaelyn. Really. But I'd rather be here. Not because of your mom or any-thing. I have to look after the greenhouse, and I want my parents to be able to find me as soon as the phones start working again, or if they finally get permission to come over."

She paused. "Your mom," she said, "is she going to be okay?"

Those words were all it took for my eyes to prickle with tears. I closed them for a second and dragged in a breath. "I don't know," I said.

She looked at the floor, and then at me, and said, "Well, I hope the plants help. And she's got the best chances of anyone, doesn't she? Your dad can be her personal doctor, and you must have realized and started treating her early on, considering you're all so careful. If anyone's going to get better, it should be her."

It wasn't a hug or an outpouring of sympathy, but that's not Tessa's style, is it? As I was driving home, with her words running through my mind, I felt a little more settled than I have since Mom first shut herself in her room. If Tessa the Ever Practical can be hopeful, I should be too.

OCT 16

It feels like there's this wall of fog getting thicker and thicker between us and the mainland. You can't trust what you see on the TV. There's always spin, as Drew likes to say. On the internet there'd be real people talking about what's really happening to them. I was hoping when the government helicopter came again, we'd get the equipment to fix the long distance and the internet, but I guess there was so much going on that the message got lost, and the parts didn't come with the other supplies.

When I asked Dad, he looked almost surprised, like he'd forgotten we ever had internet. Probably because the hospital has a satellite dish and never lost service.

"I've managed to talk to your grandparents every few days, and they're fine," he said. "I can't call more often because the hospital needs to keep the line open in case something important comes through."

Which makes sense. For half a second I wondered if the hospital has the same restrictions on the internet, but it's not as if Dad would allow me to hang out there just to surf the web.

He's been spending most of his time in the bedroom with Mom, wearing one of those plastic gowns all the staff had on in the hospital, to keep from spreading the virus when he leaves the room. So even though he's been home, I haven't had much chance to talk to him.

Mom hasn't gotten any worse. When he left for a quick trip to the hospital today, I sat beside her door and told her some of Mackenzie's best famous-people stories, and she didn't seem to be coughing quite as much as before. And she laughed at some of them as if she really felt okay. That's got to be a good sign, right?

After a while she said she was feeling hot and she thought she should go lie down. Before I left, she said, "I love you, Kaelyn. You always remember that, all right?"

She's said it plenty of times before, but it's different now. I got choked up after I told her I loved her too.

The rest of the time I've been on Meredith duty. The ferrets are exhausted from getting so much playtime. We're halfway through Drew's *The Simpsons* DVDs. I started showing her one of my nature series, since she was interested in the coyotes, but after the first episode I decided that wasn't such a good idea. I never realized before how depressing those shows can be. Something's always getting hunted down, or struggling against the elements. It reminded me too much of how we're living right now.

This evening we were getting ready for bed, and a horrible screeching sound came from outside. Thankfully this time it actually was raccoons. Two of them, dueling by the hedge next door.

"Why are they so angry?" Meredith asked.

"I don't know," I said. "Probably one's defending what he considers his territory. Sometimes they sound like that when they're looking for a new, um, girlfriend. But it's the wrong time of year for that."

We kept watching until they scrambled around the hedge and disappeared. Strange to think that for the raccoons, the world is continuing on as usual.

OCT 17

So obviously we're not trying out Drew's secret plan for getting off the island, since Mom's sick. The last few days he's spent most of his time in his room or wandering off outside. He hardly needs to sneak now—Mom's not in any position to notice he's leaving, and Dad's attention is all on her. I don't know what Drew is up to. Maybe making sure everything's in place in case she gets better and we can go.

He must have realized it's been tough for me to keep Meredith busy all day, though, 'cause this morning he offered to teach her how to play this computer game she's asked about before, that he used to say was too complicated for her.

I tried watching one of my Hitchcock movies, but as soon as the first dead body appeared, my stomach clenched and I had to turn it off. I got out my math textbook, which seemed safer, and went down to the dining room to tackle the next chapter. I've been avoiding algebra, but I know I'll forget the formulas and have to learn them all over again if I don't practice. Even if life never gets back to normal here on the island, I have to assume eventually I'll be going to classes again somewhere. Believing anything else feels like giving up.

Once I got going, there was something comforting about switching the numbers around and teasing out the answers. I could hear the classical music from Mom's radio through the floor, and it all formed a weird sort of rhythm.

I'd gotten through a couple pages when the doorbell rang. My head was so full of numbers, I got up to answer it automatically. I had my hand on the doorknob when it occurred to me that I shouldn't open the door to just anyone.

Since the front door doesn't have a window, I leaned close and said, "Who's there?" I hoped it was Nell bringing something for Dad, or Tessa with more plants. Or anyone, really, as long as it wasn't an overfriendly neighbor with an intense desire to chat and sneeze on me.

"Kaelyn?" the voice on the other side said. "It's Gav. We talked at the park a couple weeks ago, about your dad?"

The first thing I thought of was the grocery store. The way Quentin had smashed that window and then threatened me and Meredith. Panic jolted through me before I had a chance to think. Then I realized it wouldn't make any sense for Gav to come looting our house when he probably had the contents of all the stores in town. And if he was going to, he wouldn't ring the doorbell first.

"What do you want?" I asked.

"I could use your help with something," he said.

"I don't think I'm interested," I said. I didn't know until the words came out of my mouth how angry I was. My hands had closed into fists.

"What do you mean?" he asked.

"I mean," I said, "I know what you've been doing, and the last thing I want to do is help. Just because the government delayed one shipment doesn't give you the right to start breaking into places and helping yourself to whatever you want."

There was a pause, and then he said, "It's not like that. I don't know who you talked to—"

"I didn't talk to anyone," I told him before he could keep going. "I saw. And then one of your friends threatened to hurt me and my seven-year-old cousin because she dared to say something."

"What?" he said, sounding startled. "Look, Kaelyn, that isn't . . . No one should have been doing that. And I can explain the rest to you. Can I come in, or would you come out?"

He hadn't been at the grocery store that day. I could believe he hadn't known everything. And I was starting to get worried Drew or Meredith would hear me yelling through the door. It was so hard to get a read on Gav when I couldn't see him.

"Go over to the window," I said.

He was already in front of it when I stepped into the living room. With the sunlight streaming in from behind him, he probably couldn't see much more than his reflection. But he just stood there on the porch, his expression grave and his hands tucked into the pockets of his hooded sweatshirt.

I'd somehow been remembering him bigger, but he's only a few inches taller than me. More important, he looked perfectly healthy: no rubbed-red nose, no fever flush, and no scratched-raw skin. I hadn't heard any coughing or sneezing through the door, so I figured he was safe as far as the virus went. He had a fleck of what looked like motor oil on his forehead and a few speckles in his tawny hair, which was shaggier than it had been the last time I saw him. After a moment he turned his pockets inside out as if to say, *Look, I'm not hiding anything.*

I walked back to the door, unlocked it, and leaned out. "Okay," I said. "You can come in. For a few minutes."

He was very polite, taking off his shoes on the mat, scanning the house to see if there was anyone else he should acknowledge. He had this watchfulness to him, like a wild cat—calm but wary at the same time. It made me feel better that he thought he needed to be as cautious with me as I did with him.

I pushed aside the math books on the table, and we sat there. "All right," he said. "Who was threatening you?"

I told him about seeing the guys with the truck, Quentin breaking into the electronics store, and Meredith accusing him of stealing. Gav listened silently. The only time he reacted was when I repeated what Quentin had said to us. His jaw tensed, and one of his hands folded over the other on the table.

"I'm going to talk to Quentin," he said when I was done. "He'll bring back everything he took. And maybe he'll have to find someone else to hang out with."

He spoke with this certainty, like it would be nothing to make Quentin do what he asked, as if the other guy didn't have a few dozen pounds and at least a couple of inches on him. I wondered what exactly Gav had done to become the leader of the group.

"That still doesn't make it okay for you to hoard all the food," I said. "The hospital's struggling enough trying to keep people alive without having to worry that they'll starve if the next shipment's late. Why should you get the extras?"

"We aren't," he said. "I'm trying to help. After what happened at the docks, it looked like people were starting to go kind of crazy. I figured before too long somebody would panic and start trashing places and grabbing whatever they could."

"So you figured you'd grab everything first," I said.

"Well, sort of," he admitted. "But the food's not just for us. For all we knew then, the government wasn't going to send another shipment. For all we know now, the one that just came is the last. And the people at the town hall are handing supplies out to whoever shows up—what about the people who are too scared to come out? We have a better plan. We moved all the nonperishables into one of the warehouses by the wharf that Vince's dad has access to. And we've been going around in the truck every other day, checking at all the houses, making sure people have enough to eat, giving them more if they need it. I was even here last week—I talked to your mom. The whole idea is to make sure everyone gets some of the food."

His explanation was so far from what I'd expected, it took me a little while to find my voice.

"Seriously?" I said. "You stole all the grocery store's food just so you could give it back to people?"

He shrugged and said, "Anytime you read about a disaster like this, it's the same. The people in charge look after themselves first. The military's more concerned about staying out of danger than making sure the food gets to everyone. No one at the town hall can be bothered. The rest of us can either fight each other over what's left, or try to do something good. I figure the more people help, the more likely we'll get through this."

I wasn't sure he was being completely fair, considering the government has mostly kept their end of the deal, and I'd imagine anyone with any authority on the island has their hands full dealing with the hospital crisis. But what he was doing wasn't so different from Tessa and me with the meds, really.

"So what is it you think I can do?" I asked.

He gave me a little smile, which could have come off as cocky, but instead seemed like he was glad I was even listening. "Well, you're the best person I know right now to get the scoop on what's really going on, because of your dad," he said. "But specifically today I'm here because your mom mentioned working at the gas station when I came by before. We've got the truck and a few cars between us, and they're all getting low on fuel. I was hoping you could ask her to open the station for a few minutes so we can fill up."

I opened my mouth, and closed it again swallowing hard. If I told him why Mom wouldn't be going anywhere, it'd make the situation all awkward and I would get teary, and that wouldn't help anyone. He didn't need her—she'd left the key to the café by the front door after her last shift, in case one of us needed to gas up the car and she wasn't around.

"If you want," he said when I didn't answer right away, "I can show you. So you can see what we're doing. It's only a ten-minute walk."

That was when the stairs creaked, and Drew poked his head through the doorway. "Who are you talking to, Kae—" he started, and stopped when he saw Gav.

"Weber," Gav said with a nod.

"Reilly," Drew replied, his voice stiff. "Didn't know you two were friends."

They weren't quite at the point of lunging for each other's throats, but they didn't look too friendly either. I stood up. "We were just about to head out," I said. "I'll be back in a bit."

Once we were outside, I wished I'd brought a thicker jacket. The fall chill has settled in, and my windbreaker only took some of the edge off. Gav shoved his hands into his pockets and didn't seem particularly bothered.

"You got some problem with Drew, or him with you?" I asked.

"It's nothing to do with him," he said. "He seems like an okay guy. Just one of his friends and I don't get along so well—so, you know."

I had to wonder if in this case "don't get along so well" was a euphemism for "beat each other up on a regular basis." The words fell out before I could catch them: "I heard you have some sort of fight-club thing going on. With Quentin and those guys."

"Well," he said, and ran a hand through his hair, "that just sort of happened. A few of us clean pools and mow lawns and other odd jobs at the vacation houses in the summer. There was this one guy around our age who came with his family every summer and liked hassling us. Trying to get us riled up, prove how much tougher he was. I always just ignored him, but last year he pissed Warren off so much that he took a swing at him, and the guy just pounded him. Broke his nose, knocked out a tooth, totally bashed him up. And to top things off, the guy's parents tore a strip off of Warren the next time they saw him, for not finishing the job that day."

"That's awful," I said, shuddering.

"I know," Gav said. "So this summer I figured one of us should stand up to him, and since Warren wasn't enthusiastic after the last time, it might as well be me. I started watching videos on fighting techniques online. You wouldn't believe what you can find. I got Warren to help me practice some of the moves, and then he told a couple of our friends, and we were all practicing together on each other. Someone must have been talking about it, 'cause some guys I didn't really know, like Quentin, started coming around asking about joining in. After a while there were about ten of us who'd get together. It might sound stupid, but you get to blow off some steam. And what could be wrong with knowing how to defend yourself, right?"

"Nothing, I guess," I admitted. "I wouldn't have a clue what to do if someone attacked me."

It hadn't occurred to me before that I might need to. But what would I do if I was out of the house and someone in the middle of a hallucination came at me? Or if a guy like Quentin really did try to take a board to my head? I'd like to feel I could protect myself, and Meredith, if I had to.

"If you want," Gav said, "sometime I could come by and teach you a few things."

"Sure," I said. "That'd be great."

Then I realized he'd never finished his story. "Did you get to show up that summer guy?" I asked.

"Didn't have the chance," he said. "He stayed home this year."

The wind rose as we approached the wharf, colder and damp and slightly fishy-tasting. Gav pointed to a row of warehouses up ahead, the ones used for storing fishing gear during the winter. Even though the buildings didn't look like they were in the greatest shape, Gav was probably right that the food was more secure there than in the store. Their paint might be peeling and their clapboard siding cracked, but the warehouses have only a few small windows and big sturdy doors.

The truck I'd seen at the grocery store was parked around back. A figure with dark hair was sitting in the cab, his head bent over a pad of paper.

"Hey, Warren!" Gav called, and jerked a thumb toward me when the guy looked up. "Meet Kaelyn."

Warren stepped down out of the cab, tucking the pad under his arm, and shook my hand like we were at a business meeting. He was taller than Gav, and broader in the shoulders, but at the same time softer, more panda bear than grizzly. His voice was soft too.

"Good to meet you," he said.

"You fixing up the charts?" Gav asked, and then said to me, "We're heading out this afternoon to do another round."

Warren nodded, his hair falling into his eyes as he showed us the pad he'd been working on. It was graph paper, divided into a grid of days and addresses, boxes crossed out or checked off beside notes like *4x soup, 1 peas* or *wait 1 week* in tiny handwriting.

"I crossed off all the places we've tried at least three times with no answer," he said. "Should cut down on the time."

"Wow," I said, looking from him to Gav. "You've really gotten organized." It looked like they were doing a better job of figuring out who was still around and who needed what than I had with my official phone list.

"It's Warren who put it together," Gav said, with that little smile he'd given me before. "I'm the idea guy, but he's the real brains."

"Hey, ideas come from brains too," Warren said, raising his eyebrows, but his cheeks had gone a bit pink at the compliment.

Standing there, with the sun shining down and the two of them leaning against the side of the truck, for a moment I felt like everything was all right. We didn't need the government's help if they stopped giving it. We could look after ourselves and get through the epidemic just fine. Even if our heroes were a bunch of teenage guys who spent their free time coming up with new ways to knock each other out.

"Okay," I said. "Let's get you some gas. Can you bring the truck and whatever else over to the station in, say, an hour?"

The pumps worked just like Mom had said. Warren brought the truck around, and Gav and a couple of his friends showed up in cars, and I watched through the café windows as they filled them up. When Gav came over to thank me, I made him take a few of our spare face masks.

Then they went off to bring food to the desperate, and I headed home.

When I got there, I folded up Meredith's cot, dragged her into my room, and turned on some old dance music I haven't listened to in ages. Because if we don't celebrate the things that are going right, what's the point in hanging on?

OCT 18

No dancing today. Mom's gotten worse.

Dad must have suspected it was coming. He told me he was only going in to the hospital to check in, and he'd be back in a couple of hours. He's been wearing this old pager he dug up sometime last week, and he reminded me about ten times that I should page him if we needed him for any reason.

At the time, I assumed he was just having one of his paranoid moments. But his mood infected me too. After he left, I was cleaning up the dishes from my and Meredith's lunch, and I started wondering how safe our kitchen is. I mean, Mom was in there when she first realized she was sick. Even if she wasn't symptomatic yet, in any way we could see, could she have left the virus somewhere in the house? Why hadn't I thought to ask Dad about that before? It could be anywhere.

Somehow the worrying got me thinking about turkey vultures. They pretty much never get sick, even though they're standing on dead animals all the time, because they have this super-acidic urine that kills off any bacteria that try to come creeping up their feet. Which is gross but also kind of cool. It would be awfully handy if all we had to do is pee on ourselves and, voilà, protected!

I started giggling kind of hysterically, picturing it, which is probably why I didn't hear Mom coming down the stairs.

She swept into the room, out of nowhere, and threw her arms around me. Her favorite perfume prickled in my nose, vanilla and berries, but too strong, like she'd sprayed it all over. I returned the hug tentatively. I hadn't done anything more than talk to her through a door for days. How could I push her away?

As she squeezed me, the full realization of what this meant washed over me in an icy wave. She wouldn't have come down if she was still in her right mind. She'd gotten worse. None of the treatments had stopped it. The virus was digging its way deeper and deeper into her brain, and there was nothing I could do.

"Kaelyn! It seems like forever since I've seen you, hon," Mom said. She pressed her cheek against my forehead. Her skin was hot. Then she turned away to sneeze, and coughed a few times into her elbow the way Dad always taught us to. I guess some habits stick, even with the virus in your head.

I wanted to call for Drew, for some sort of backup, but he was in the living room playing a video game with Meredith. The most important thing was keeping Meredith away. If she knew Mom was downstairs, she'd want to come see her. And if I reminded Mom that Meredith was here, she might get the idea that she needed to hug her niece too.

I was terrified. For Mom, for me, for Meredith. But at the same time I felt . . . relieved, to see her. Like part of me had started to believe she didn't exist at all anymore, except as a voice behind a door, and now I had proof that wasn't true.

"It's good to see you too, Mom," I said, hoping if I pretended to be calm, maybe I'd start feeling more calm. "Let's go talk upstairs."

She screwed up her face. "I'm tired of staying upstairs," she said. "Do you know how long I've spent up there? I'd be perfectly happy if this whole house burned down and I never had to see that bedroom again."

"Then we'd have nowhere to live," I said. "Come on. We'll run you a bath. With that oil you really like. When was the last time you used it?"

She huffed, putting her hands on her hips. "You're just like your father," she said. "Speaking to me like I'm a child."

"I'm just trying to help," I said.

"You probably didn't even mind that I was stuck up there all this time," she said. "I don't know how my daughter turned into such a cold person. Talking to you the last few years has been like pulling teeth. You think you'd be better off if I died and never bothered you again, don't you?"

Tears sprang into my eyes, and my plan to stay calm went out the window. I couldn't believe she could say that, even now, even sick. "Of course not, Mom," I said. "I want you to get better."

"I've tried to be patient," she said, shaking her head. "I've tried to give you your space. And the thanks I get is, 'Mom, go back up to your room and leave me alone.'"

"I never said that," I started, but then she looked toward the living room and I panicked. I pushed in front of her, trying to motion her in the other direction. "Let's go in the backyard, then," I said. "You'll feel better if you get some fresh air."

She might have shoved right by me if a coughing fit hadn't doubled her over. I took a second to wipe at my eyes, and then I eased her toward the other end of the house with my hand on her back. "It'll be okay," I said. "Dad will be home soon, and he'll bring you some more medication that'll help you feel better."

"I don't want any more of his medicine," she said hoarsely. "It never does anything. Why isn't he here? I want to talk to him. Is he at the hospital? I'll go get him."

She hustled past me before I could stop her. But as she stepped into the front hall, with me hurrying after her, Dad came in the door.

"Gordon!" Mom cried, and threw herself at him the way she'd done with me a few minutes before.

"Here, Grace, I brought you something," he said gently, but his voice wavered a little.

As he guided her toward the stairs, I heard her whisper, "I'm so scared."

I don't know what else he said to get her back into her room, but the second I heard the door close, I bolted up to the bathroom and jumped into the shower with my clothes on. When the water was steaming hot, I scrubbed soap everywhere, then stripped off the wet clothes and scrubbed again. And then, after I'd gone over every inch but the inside of my mouth and the undersides of my eyelids, I really started crying.

I touched my mother for the first time in a week, and it made me absolutely petrified. That's how warped my life is now.

Dad said the virus breaks down people's inhibitions. He didn't mention whether the things they say without those inhibitions are necessarily true. I mean, Mom doesn't really want the house to burn down, right? So she can't be *that* angry at me, can she? Yeah, I haven't talked to her about half of what I've gone through since we moved to Toronto. I never let on that I was lonely, or how hard it was to fit in, or that I'd fought with you, Leo. But what teenage girl doesn't keep secrets from her mom? It's not fair. How could she expect me to tell her everything?

How could she think I'd want her to die?

OCT 19

Dad put a new lock on the bedroom door. He gave Mom something to help her sleep last night, but she's spent all day jiggling the knob and calling to us, one after the other, begging someone to let her out, or at least come in and talk to her. Meredith tried to open the door once. Thankfully, Dad's holding on to the key, to make sure no one can.

"But she sounds so sad," Meredith said to me when I caught her.

"I know," I said. "But she's really sick, and we're all safer if she stays in one place—her too. We wouldn't want her to go wandering outside, right?"

I say that, but I feel awful too. It's like hearing a cat or a monkey clawing at the bars of its cage in one of those anti-animal-testing ads. Except a million times worse, because the animal is *Mom*, and just a couple of days ago she was talking to us like a rational human being.

I haven't said a word to her since yesterday. I can't. I've been doing my best to pretend I can't even hear her. I know it's not really her anymore. She's there, but she's already gone.

And maybe I'm a little scared of finding out what else she might have to say about me. Which really does make me an awful daughter, doesn't it?

Drew sat by the door and talked to her for a bit this afternoon, and when he passed my room afterward, his hands were clenched and he was blinking fast. He took off a half hour later, and he hasn't been back since.

Dad stayed home since she got like this, but he slept on the couch last night, and he only went in to see Mom for a little while in the morning. She was yelling when he left, so maybe she's had some angry words for him too.

He spent most of the day at the dining room table with his laptop, scrolling through files and rubbing his face. His hair's getting scraggly because he hasn't had it cut since the summer. He used to look young for a dad, with his sandy blond hair that hides whatever gray he's got, but his skin has gotten so pale and washed out, it's like he's fading.

I made him tuna on crackers while I was putting some together for myself, because I don't know how much he's been eating. And we're out of bread. I sat across from him, and we both ate without saying a word. He hardly glanced up from the computer. When I couldn't stand the silence anymore, I pushed my plate aside and forced out the words: "She isn't going to get better, is she? The special plants, the medicine, none of it works."

He looked at me then, like I'd slapped him, and I wished I hadn't said anything. But the thought had been rattling around in my head since yesterday, getting louder and louder. I needed to know.

"We don't know that," he said quietly. "We've had a couple people recover at the hospital. And we're doing everything we can."

"A couple," I repeated, my gut knotting. "All those people who've gotten sick, and only *two* have gotten better? What makes you think Mom's going to be that lucky?"

"The alternative is giving up," he said. "I'm not going to do that."

I didn't say it, but I wonder if it wouldn't be easier to give up. Easier than putting all your heart and energy into fighting an impossible battle. Because he looks half dead himself already.

But a couple hours ago, when Meredith leaned against me on the couch and asked, "Is Aunt Grace going to be okay?" I said, "Of course she is. No puny little virus could beat her."

So I am an awful daughter and a liar.

OCT 21

This afternoon it was so sunny, we all went out in the backyard. At least that's why we said we went. I suspect it was mostly because we can't hear Mom at all back there.

Dad sat on the swinging chair with his laptop, and Drew and Meredith and I threw a Frisbee between us, and then Drew, in a rare show of benevolence, told Dad he was going to go brain-dead if he didn't take a break, so why didn't they toss around the baseball for a bit. They haven't done that since before we moved to Toronto, and I don't think Drew's asked Dad to do *anything* with him since the boyfriend discovery. So Dad got up and dug out the gloves.

Around the same time, one of those news helicopters passed overhead, close enough that I could see the shape of the cameraman peering down at us. Meredith looked up, frowning at the noise.

"What are they doing?" she asked.

"Checking to see how we are," I said. I suppressed the urge to raise my hand and let them film my middle finger. They come and take their footage, and then they zip back to the mainland like they were filming some sporting event, not people's actual lives. I hope they drop their cameras in the strait on the way back.

To distract both of us, I found a bag of stale peanuts to throw to a couple of squirrels that had crept over the fence.

"You hear how that one's chattering right now?" I said. "He's trying to tell the other one to back off, this is his yard. But the other one knows he's bluffing, so he'll keep sneaking down the fence whenever the first one's back is turned. Look, here comes another that heard there was food."

I kept talking about squirrels until my throat started to feel scratchy, pulling up every fact I've ever learned or guessed from watching them. At least Meredith seemed sort of entertained. Dad and Drew were throwing the ball back and forth with a satisfying thump as it hit their gloves.

And then the shrieking started.

At first I figured it was another neighbor, someone down the street. My voice hitched in the middle of whatever I was saying, but I kept going. Then the shrieking got a little louder, so you could make out a word here and there, and Dad froze. He dropped his glove on the grass and hurried into the house.

My throat closed up, and Drew looked at me wildly, and Meredith sucked in a breath. I think we all realized at the same moment it was Mom.

Her voice peaked for a minute. "No, I won't, I won't, I won't," she screamed. And then she was quiet. We waited silently, listening. After a bit, as long as it took Dad to get her downstairs after he'd given her whatever medication he had to keep her calm, we heard the car engine rumble.

"Where's he taking her?" Meredith whispered.

"To the hospital," Drew said. "Where the doctors will continue to be totally useless." He hurled his glove at the fence, and the squirrels scattered.

Meredith started to sob. I wrapped my arms around her and tugged her closer. "Don't say that," I said to Drew.

"Why not?" he said. "Because it's true? Why shouldn't we talk about what's really happening? The whole island is dying and it's been weeks and they still have no idea what to do about it! Which one of us is going to be next?"

He stomped into the house, and Meredith's crying turned into little gasps. I hugged her as tightly as I could and blinked back my own tears. "It'll be okay," I said. "It'll be okay." Even though I can't imagine how anything will be okay ever again.

OCT 22

I made it through last night. I felt kind of stiff and cold going through the motions, but I calmed Meredith down, and cooked us dinner, and got us to bed, and even when the lights were out and she was breathing softly, I didn't let myself cry. I was afraid if I started I wouldn't be able to stop, and I'd wake her up.

What's the point of crying anyway? I know I'm sad. Why does anyone else need to see it?

Dad didn't come back all night. Over breakfast, Drew said he was going down to the hospital. I would have gone too, but I didn't want to leave Meredith on her own—and I can't stand the thought of bringing her into the hospital the way it is now.

So instead I put on *The Little Mermaid*, her favorite, and we were halfway through when the doorbell rang.

I assumed either Drew or Dad had forgotten to take their house key with them. We never used to lock up. I was so sure, and I guess in a bit of a daze, that I opened the door without checking.

Gav was standing outside. His shoulders were hunched like he wasn't sure how he'd be welcomed. I stared at him, and he stared at me, and then he straightened up and gave me that little smile. "No interrogation this time?" he said.

"Hi," I said. "I . . ." And then I stopped, because I had no words. It was like all the walls I'd put up to keep me from falling apart were getting in the way of thinking too. My brain switched to autopilot.

"Come in," I said.

He stepped inside and I shut the door. "Are you okay?" he asked.

"Sure," I said. "What's up?"

"I told you I'd show you some of those self-defense techniques," he said. "If it's a good time for you."

"Sure," I said again. I didn't really see the point right then. But I thought, I said I'd do this; I'll just get through it, no problem.

Then he glanced around and said, "House seems quiet today." Which reminded me how much I'd wanted Mom to just be quiet the last few days, and now she was quiet because she wasn't even here, and probably she was never coming back. It was the first time I'd let myself think that far, and before I could stop it, this sob burst out of my throat. I sank down and wrapped my arms around my head and pressed my face against my knees, as if I could hold myself together if I squeezed hard enough. But I'd already lost it. Everything spilled out. Tears, snot, I don't even want to know what I sounded like.

After a while I registered a pressure by my arm, and a while after that I realized it was Gav's hand on my shoulder. Like an anchor, bringing me back into place. There was a floor under my feet and a wall behind me. I was home. I wasn't alone.

The sleeve of my sweater was totally soaked. I wiped at my face and at my jeans, which were pretty damp too. Gav took back his hand, but I could still feel him crouched down in front of me. I didn't want to look at him.

"Sorry," I said. "My dad had to take my mom to the hospital yesterday."

He let out a strangled sort of laugh and said, "Why are you sorry? *I'm* sorry. I should have figured out something was wrong. Why would you want to be practicing headlocks when you're dealing with that?"

He didn't move, though, and he didn't say anything else, so after a moment I raised my head. He was watching me, both concerned and nervous. Like I was a fox with my leg in a trap and I might bite him if he tried to help. I remember noticing, inanely, that his eyes were sort of green, even though I'd thought they were brown, but maybe it was just because he was wearing a green shirt today. Then he started talking again.

"My mom's sick too," he said. "My dad'll probably be soon if he isn't already, considering they're still sleeping in the same bed. I've been crashing at Warren's. Mostly I'm worried *he'll* get it. He was sick a lot when he was a kid."

"Make sure he wears one of those masks I gave you when you go around with the truck," I said. "And you too. If you want, I can give you gloves. My dad's been wearing protective gear at the hospital and when he was looking after my mom, and he's still fine."

"Yeah," Gav said. "We've been using the masks. And sure, I'll take some gloves if you have extras. Thanks." He looked down at the floor and then at me again. "Do you want me to go?" he asked. "Or...I mean, I can stay if you want."

Him leaving would mean going back into the living room with Meredith and pretending everything was fine. I wasn't sure I could do that.

"Actually," I said, "maybe a little fighting practice would be good. Blowing off steam, right?"

Which is how we ended up having a martial arts class in my

living room. I asked Gav if he could teach Meredith too, and he said sure, so we paused the movie and pushed the ottoman off to the side. "This isn't professional or anything," he said, but he seemed to know a lot. When you're actually trying techniques on other people, I guess you figure out what works and what doesn't pretty fast.

He showed me how to break a hold on my arm, and what to do if someone grabbed me from behind, and quick moves you can do that cause enough pain to buy you time to run away. Even Meredith could handle most of those. At one point she jabbed at his eye a little harder than she meant to, and he ended up sitting on the couch holding it and wincing while I wrapped an ice cube in a napkin for him.

"I think you've got that move down," he said to Meredith. "And see, it works!"

Meredith was kind of shy at first, but after poking Gav's eye, I think she felt she owed it to him to be friendly. By the time he'd shown us everything useful he could come up with, she was talking to him like he was her new best friend. She hasn't seen any of her real friends since she moved in with us, maybe not since school shut down, depending on how paranoid Uncle Emmett was. She must get bored having just me and sometimes Drew for company.

Then I wondered if any of her friends are even still alive. Another awful thought to add to an already long list.

But depressing as I sound right now, it was good. I even laughed once. Gav was putting on his shoes, and Meredith said, out of the blue, "What's your real name?"

"What?" he said.

"Gav isn't a real name," she said. "It's a nickname, right? Like my mom used to call me Mere, and I call Kaelyn Kae sometimes. So what's your real name?"

"Oh," he said, and waffled while he tied his shoelaces. "It's Gavriel."

That's when I started laughing. He shot me an evil look, smiling to show he didn't mean it.

"That's like a Knights of the Round Table name," I said. "No wonder you think you have to save everyone. Trying to live up to it."

"That must be it," he said.

He asked how we were for food, and I said we were fine, because we have everything I grabbed from Uncle Emmett's house too. It doesn't seem

Oh god, Leo. I don't know what to do. I stopped writing for a sec because I had an itch, but when I scratched it, it didn't go away, and then it moved, it was on my hip and now it's my stomach. I told myself I just had dry skin and put on some of the expensive cream Dad uses for his eczema, but it didn't help. What if

No. I won't think that. I'll go make dinner, and that'll distract me, and then the itch will go away. I'm just extra nervous because of everything that's going on. That's all.

OCT 23

Now I know how Mom must have felt. She looked like she was fine, but she sensed it, creeping under her skin until she couldn't ignore that something was wrong. So she shut herself away from us before she got any worse.

I went downstairs to cook dinner yesterday, like I intended, but then I saw Drew and Meredith playing Connect Four on the dining room table. And I thought, What if I am sick? I'm the last person who should be touching anyone's food. The spot on my stomach was still itching. For a minute or two it would ease up, and I'd started to feel relieved, and then my skin would start tickling even worse than before.

I gave it an hour, because that seemed scientific somehow, and then I put on my mask and some gloves from the box Dad left in the hall. Even with the mask on, I tried not to breathe as I was moving Meredith's things out of my bedroom. I dragged out the cot, but didn't know where to put it. Maybe they'll set it up in the living room? I left it by the top of the stairs so they could decide. Then I got the suitcases she's been living out of even though I told her there was room in my wardrobe, and a few books and toys she's left scattered around, and piled those beside the cot.

The itch was killing me. Just as I was about to pick up the shirt she'd left on my computer chair, my hand got away from me and went for it. I had to toss out that glove and grab another.

But it was still just an itch, and part of me believed there could be another explanation, like I was the one person in the history of the universe to get chicken pox twice, or I'd managed to contract some new form of measles, either of which, honestly, would be better.

My door doesn't have a lock, so I sat on the bed listening for the creak of the stairs, and when I heard someone coming, I stood by the door in case they tried to open it. Thankfully, the first person who came up and noticed the cot was Drew and not Meredith. I'm sure he figured out the most likely explanation right off.

"Kaelyn?" he said, just outside the door.

"Yeah," I said. "I think..." I didn't want to say it out loud, so I settled for, "I'm worried. Can you make sure Meredith doesn't come in? And when Dad gets home, I want to talk to him."

He said he'd tell Meredith, but just to be sure, I shifted my bed over so it would hold the door shut. Then I lay down and tried to sleep. But my thoughts kept jumping around, and the itch wriggled over to my armpit, and I felt too hot when the blanket was on and too cold when it was off. I might have dozed somewhere in there.

Around midnight, there was a light knock on the door and Dad's voice asking softly, "Kae? Are you awake?"

I sat up and said, "Yeah, just a second," so I could move the bed. He came in with his mask in his hand instead of on his face, so I put mine back on. Maybe he assumed that if I wasn't coughing or sneezing, I wasn't contagious, but I wasn't going to let him take that chance.

He sat on the computer chair with his hands clasped in front of him, and said, "Drew says you're not feeling well."

He sounded exhausted, and like he was trying incredibly hard to sound calm and optimistic. I knew what he really wanted was for me to say I'd been wrong, or to show I was just being paranoid. And suddenly I felt guilty, for doing this to him on top of whatever is happening with Mom, as if I had any choice in it. But lying wouldn't fix anything.

So I told him about the itch that wouldn't go away, and how I couldn't sleep, and he nodded and said it was too early to tell and he'd take a little blood in the morning so we could find out for sure. He went out and came back with a glass of water and a pill to help me sleep. When I got up to take them from him, he set them on the desk and hugged me.

It wasn't the safest thing he could do, but in that moment I didn't care. I hugged him back until the itch got so bad I had to step away to scratch at it.

The whole time I felt like I was being so levelheaded, so mature. I think somehow I believed if I stayed calm it'd go away.

But this morning, right after Dad left for the hospital, I got a tickle in my throat. I had to call Drew through the door to bring me another glass of water, which I made him leave outside and took after he was gone. It's been half an hour, and I'm still coughing, off and on.

What the hell else could it be? I've got the virus.

I can't see Meredith or Drew or anyone except Dad again.

I'm going to be stuck in this little room until I get so sick Dad has to drag me away.

The virus is going to eat away at my brain until I can't control what I say or what I think, until I'm blathering all sorts of horrible things, like Rachel's dad did, like Mom, until I'm screaming at people who aren't even there, and I won't even know how crazy I am. God. I've got to

Leo, if somehow you're reading this, if you've come back and you were trying to figure out what happened and you found this journal, burn it. Burn it now. I've just coughed on it and I've been breathing on it, and the virus is probably crawling all over every page.

It's not like I'll have time to write much more anyway.

OCT 24

You know how people in books and movies make deathbed confessions? They realize they're about to go, and they just have to get those long-held secrets out while they still can.

I've been thinking about that, since I don't have a whole lot to do other than think—and cough and sneeze and try not to scratch any one spot too much. Dad offered to keep me company the way he did with Mom, said we could play cards or something. But every time I look into his eyes it's like I can see his heart breaking no matter what face he puts on, and it reminds me of what's going to happen to me, and mine breaks too. I know he wants to be with Mom at the hospital, and doing more research, and a lot of things more important than playing cards. So I told him I'd rather be by myself, and he's mostly let me.

At least his meds are helping keep the fever down. And he must have given me something to help me stay calm. I feel a little woozy. Like I'm not totally here.

But, getting to the point, I was wondering whether there was anything I should tell Dad, or Drew, or Meredith, before I can't control what I'm saying anymore. And there isn't. Not that I've been totally honest with them my whole life, but I haven't hidden anything big.

The only real secret I've kept has to do with you, Leo. I've been holding on to it so long, I haven't even wanted to write it down. But I might not get another chance.

It happened the summer I was fourteen, before I started high school in Toronto, before we had our fight and stopped talking. Dad and Mom and Drew and I were visiting the island for a week, like we had every July after we moved. The last day of the trip, you came over and we went down to West Beach, eating homemade blueberry ice cream from the Camerons' shop and ambling along the sand. A totally normal day.

Around dinnertime, I said I should head back. As we were walking down the street, there was a kid riding his bike up and down the road, the training wheels rattling away. I wonder if you even remember that?

He passed us a couple times, and then he braked a little ways ahead of us and narrowed his eyes.

"I've seen you around before," he said to you. "Shouldn't you be living in China?"

He hadn't even looked at me, but I stiffened up right away. You just cocked your head and shrugged.

"Nah," you said, like it was no big deal, and held up a finger. "First, I was born in Korea, not China." Another finger. "Second, my parents wanted me *so much* they went all the way over there to get me, which I think was a pretty good reason to come back with them." One more finger. "Third, how old are you?"

"Six," the kid said, wide-eyed.

"Well, there you go," you said, smiling. "I've been an islander more than twice as long as you!"

So many people must have treated you like you didn't belong here, for you to come up with an answer that good, that you could roll off your tongue in a second. So many times you must have had to pretend you didn't care. But right then, all I saw was how cool and confident you were. The way you always were. The way I pretty much never was, no matter how much I wanted to be. I'd seen it thousands of times before, of course. But this time, as I stood there looking at you, it made me want to kiss you.

Maybe the moment would have passed, just a brief urge that seemed ridiculous a minute later. Except then the kid looked at me and said, "So what country are *you* from?"

"Um," I said. "I'm not. I mean, I was born here."

"And if I had my way, you'd quit leaving," you said to me, like the kid wasn't even there, and you grabbed my hand. I let you pull me past him because the second your fingers brushed against mine, every other thought emptied out of my head. My face got hot, and I was afraid to look at you the whole way back to Uncle Emmett's house, in case you'd notice.

I don't think you did. You let go of my hand when we got there and gave me a quick hug good-bye and told me to write and call lots when I was back in Toronto, the same as always. But everything was different for me. I didn't want to let you go. I wanted to believe your heart skipped a little when you looked back at me one last time before you went around the corner, like mine did. When I got on the ferry that evening, I felt like something inside me was tearing, knowing it'd be months before I had a chance to see you again. And the feeling never went away, not when we got to Toronto, not when we moved back here.

I wanted you to be more than my best friend.

Maybe if I hadn't felt that way, we wouldn't have had the fight to begin with. But hanging on the fringes in that enormous high school while all the city kids gossiped and laughed and flirted, I started to wonder if you could ever fall for a sort of weird, kind of awkward girl like me. Every time I complained about them to you, I wanted you to tell me I was fine the way I was, that they were just boring snobs. Which is why it hurt so much when you said it was my fault I didn't fit in.

Maybe if my feelings were less confused I would have called you up the next time we came to visit. But the thought of hearing your voice made my stomach do somersaults, and I chickened out, telling myself you should be the one to apologize first.

And maybe if I'd gotten over it, we could have made up right after I moved back. I knew we had to talk. But I walked up to the school my first day back and there you were on the steps, your arm around Tessa's shoulders, your head bent so close to hers your faces were almost touching. And the little piece of hope I'd been holding on to died. I couldn't even look at you. Every time you glanced my way, I pretended I couldn't see you. Every class we shared, I sat at the opposite end of the room. Like the ten years we were best friends had never happened.

I'm sorry for making you think I must have hated you when you hadn't done anything wrong. I'm sorry for all the petty thoughts I had about Tessa. And I'm especially sorry you'll never get this apology. You're going to spend the rest of your life believing our friendship meant nothing to me, when really the problem was I cared too much.

OCT 25

Drew brought me some chicken soup for lunch a little while ago, but instead of setting the bowl down and leaving, he hesitated on the other side of the door. I waited for the creak of the floor to tell me he'd gone. It didn't come.

"I'm not letting you in," I said.

"I know," he said. "I just wanted to—"

His voice cut off awkwardly, and for a minute he was silent. I could feel his presence through the door. His head would be tipped forward, his jaw clenched.

"I acted like it was wrong to be scared," he said. "I encouraged you to get involved, to go out there."

My chest got tight. "Don't," I said.

"What?" he said.

"Don't try to make this your fault," I said. "It's not."

"But—" he started, and I didn't let him go any further.

"You know what probably happened?" I said. "How I caught it? I've worked it out. I went to the hospital when Mom first got sick, to find Dad, and I was there without a mask. And when Mom came downstairs the other day, when she wasn't thinking straight anymore, I didn't have my mask on then either. Those are the only times I've been near anyone sick in weeks. And neither of them were because of you or anything you've said, Drew."

He paused for another few seconds, and then he said, "I was trying to get all of us out of this safe. That's all I wanted."

"I know," I said. "Me too."

He left, and I brought in the soup, but I haven't got an appetite anymore. It's sitting on the desk, getting cold.

Maybe if I'd picked up my mask before I ran off to the hospital that day. Maybe if Dad had thought to lock Mom in her room before she started wandering. I could blame any of us. But what's the point? None of it changes where I am now.

OCT 26

I started reading the third act of *Hamlet*, and I got about two pages in when I realized there's no point.

I am never going back to school.

I am never going to university.

I am never going to watch wolves stalk through the northern forests or elephants graze the savanna. I am never going to have sex or get married or raise a family. I'm never going to have a first apartment, a first house, a first car. I'm never

OCT 27

I've found the trick to staying sane. Just don't think about it. Play games and watch videos on the computer, tussle with Mowat and Fossey, re-read my favorite books one last time, and *just don't think*.

The meds Dad's bringing are helping. Sometimes I feel like my head is floating off somewhere near the ceiling. I'm not sneezing as much as before, which is nice. Nothing left to worry about except the ferrets, so I made Drew promise he'd look after them.

Everything taken care of.

Writing makes me think too much. Back to the computer.

No one will talk to me. Why won't anyone talk to me? It's like they've all gone off and left me here. That would be horrible. It has to be child abuse or something if you leave a teenager with no one to talk to except for her journal, doesn't it?

You'd think at least my friends would come over to see if I'm okay. Oh wait. Rachel can't come, she's dead. That was dumb. Well maybe Mackenzie will. She could be a good friend sometimes, when she wasn't obsessing about how much cooler she is than everyone else on the island, I mean. Does she know I'm stuck here? I couldn't tell her because of the stupid phones getting broken. She really should come and take me out to L.A. with her. I'll meet all the movie stars. What do I need Mom and Dad and Drew for, anyway? Drew has all his plans and Dad does all his medical stuff. They think they're so brilliant, but did either of them manage to get rid of the virus? Nope. I don't need any of them. I should have hopped on the ferry when I could and

Dad brought me lunch. Or maybe that was dinner. Mac and cheese! I told him he should stay and have lunch or dinner or whatever it was with me and he sat for a while, but he has that stupid plastic coat that squeaks whenever he moves and that stupid white thing on his face so I can't even see his mouth moving when he's talking, which is really creepy. I told him I wanted him to talk to me without it and he said then he'd have to leave the room, and I told him how stupid that was and then he got kind of upset and left. What the hell Dad? I wanted to go out and see what's up with Meredith but he's gone and locked me in here. My own dad! I yelled and yelled for someone to help me open it but no one's listening and no one cares and the window is here but it's too high up to jump. I wonder if there's

Hey! I saw someone in the backyard across from ours! I opened the window and tried to talk to her but she got a funny look on her face and went into her house, which is very rude don't you think? I mean I just wanted to talk. It's awful being alone in here. Why is everyone being so horrible to me? What did I do wrong?

Funny when I first saw that woman I thought it was Tessa except she was too old and it wasn't even the right hair color it was brown not red. I couldn't really see well until I got the window open. Not that Tessa would come anyway. She never liked me really I know that she doesn't like anyone. She just wanted someone to find the dead bodies in houses for her right we saw that hell yes. Would you still want to be her boyfriend if you knew that Leo? She lied to you about what was happening on the island and I would never have lied to you. I don't see

*   *   *

Why did you go anyway? The one thing I really missed on this awful island was you and you had to go and leave me here with no one. I miss you. If you come back I absolutely promise I will forgive you for every

It's here I have to get away I have to

I'm alive, Leo.

I don't really get it. I woke up, and I wanted to go right back to sleep because I'm sooo tired. But the space felt wrong, too wide to be my bedroom, and something weird was on my arm. I opened my eyes and saw that I was hooked up to an IV. Dad was sitting by the bed. The second I saw him he lunged for my hand and said, "Kaelyn?"

I wanted to ask him who else I could possibly be. Then I remembered being sick. Being in my room, not letting anyone in. The rest is kind of fuzzy.

This is the end, I thought. They gave me something to stop the hallucinations for a bit so I can say good-bye. I felt ready to die. I feel like I've been mauled by a shark from the inside out. Which I guess is almost true. It was a huge school of really tiny sharks.

"How long?" I asked Dad. That other doctor, his friend Nell, she came in and smiled, and Dad said, "More than a week." Which seemed like a lot of time.

"I've got a whole week?" I said.

Nell looked like she was going to cry suddenly, even though she hadn't stopped smiling, and she said, softly, "She thinks she's still sick." That made Dad squeeze my hand so hard it hurt.

"You've been in the hospital for a little more than a week," he said. "But you're all right now. You're recovering."

I still don't totally believe it. Maybe they're saying I'm okay so I can be happy the last little while I'm around. But they did seem happy too. And even if I do feel like crap all over, I'm not coughing or sneezing anymore. My throat's kind of sore. I wonder if I've done a lot of screaming? And I'm a bit itchy. Dad started talking about residual nerve damage needing longer to correct itself, but I was too foggy to follow everything he was saying.

I can tell there are other people in the room because I can hear rustling and breathing, but they have me in a corner with the curtain closed. I guess I was given extra space because I'm getting better and they want to make sure I stay that way? Or because I'm Dad's kid?

As I was checking out the room, Dad handed me this journal. "I thought you'd want to have this as soon as you woke up," he said. "You wouldn't let go of it the whole way here when I brought you in." And then he told me I should rest some more. Which is probably a good idea, because even though I was sleeping up until half an hour ago, my eyes are so heavy I might as well have just pulled an all-nighter.

But it seemed important to write something down first. There was a pen on the clipboard at the end of the bed. Because of the IV, I had to grab it with my toes. That was fun.

So it's taken a while to get this down. I don't even know what day it is. No one else has come. What does that mean? I wish I could remember more. The last entries I wrote in here are a jumble. I have no idea what I said when I got really sick. Maybe I pissed Drew off so much that he's decided not to talk to me?

Oh god. What if no one else has come because everyone except Dad is sick? For all I know, Drew's on the other side of the curtain, or Meredith, or I

NOV 10

Apparently I pushed myself a little too hard yesterday. Passed out in the middle of a sentence. Dad says the virus really took it out of me.

They unhooked the IV this morning. It's a lot easier to write without a tube in my arm.

Dad made me take a couple more pills. I don't know what for, but I got kind of foggy again. Not so much that I forgot all the questions I needed to ask, though, which maybe he would have liked.

"We'll talk later, when you're further along," he said, and then rambled about delicate balances and additional stress until I grabbed his wrist.

"Dad," I said, "I'm already as stressed as I can get, imagining the worst that could be happening. Talking will help. Okay? Get it over with." But then I had to stop and swallow before I could ask, "Mom?"

He lowered his gaze, which was all the answer I needed. "She didn't make it," he said, and caught my fingers as they slipped off his arm. He rubbed his thumb over the back of my hand while I stared at the ceiling.

I knew. I mean, if Mom had gotten better, she'd be here with me. I knew that. But hearing the words, I felt like someone had reached into my chest and torn my heart in half. I dragged in a breath, and another one, and still my lungs felt ready to burst. I didn't even get to see her. I didn't even get to see her one last time. I should have been there.

For a while, I couldn't speak. Finally I wiped at my eyes and took the tissue Dad handed me, and said, "Meredith?" Bracing myself.

"She's fine," Dad said. "She's staying with your friend Tessa right now. I was trying to decide what to do with no one else at the house, and Tessa came by to ask about you, and she offered. It seemed like the best solution."

My stomach flipped over. "No one at the house?" I said. "Where's Drew?"

Dad looked down at his hands again. "I don't know exactly," he admitted. "When I came home after you were . . . settled in here, he was gone. He left a note saying he was heading to the mainland, that someone there had to have something that would help, and he was going to get it and bring it back. Some of my old scuba gear's missing—he must have planned on using it to avoid the patrol boats."

Absurdly, the first thing that came out of my mouth was, "He was supposed to look after the ferrets."

"I think he felt it was more important to do whatever he could to try to save you and your mother, Kae," Dad said. "The last few days you were with us . . . he couldn't sit still. He wouldn't talk to me, but I could tell he was getting more and more frustrated not being able to help. If I wasn't needed here, I might have done the same thing."

I would have expected Dad to be pissed off, but instead he just sounded worried. And maybe a little regretful, like he thought if he'd been able to do more, Drew would never have taken that risk. But even if Dad could have slipped away to the mainland to look for help, I doubt Drew would have been content to sit and wait.

I hope he's okay. Please let him be okay. Let him come home safe.

"*Have* they found a working treatment on the mainland?" I asked. "Why didn't they send us the vaccine, or new medication, if they have some?"

"We're not sure what's happening outside the island," Dad said. "The day after I brought you to the hospital, a nor'easter blew through, and you know what those are like. Cable went down, and the satellites were damaged. We haven't been able to reach anyone who can fix them. Only the local phone service is still working."

"So we're totally cut off," I said. No way to call anyone on the mainland, no internet at all. Not even TV now.

Dad nodded. "We tried to establish contact via the military," he said. "One of the men who's been helping here volunteered to go talk to them. But a couple of the soldiers stationed in the harbor have gotten sick, and the rest must have panicked." He hesitated and then went on: "They shot him before he got within twenty feet of the docks."

"Like Uncle Emmett," I said. The weight of all that information made me sink back down on the bed.

"We still have a couple of the Public Health and WHO doctors working with us," Dad said. "Most of them left before the weather started getting bad—I suppose they take the perspective that the island's already contained, so it's more important to focus their efforts on the mainland. They may have made more progress there. So a vaccine or a new treatment might be on the way. We just have no way of knowing when. One of the volunteers has been monitoring the best radio we can find, but so far we haven't been able to make contact."

"What about supplies?" I asked. "Are the helicopters still coming?"

"There've been some difficulties," he said. "We're working it out. We have enough food, but we're low on several medications. Honestly, most of them weren't having any effect, so I'm not sure it makes a great difference. And the same with the experimental plants Tessa was growing for us, unfortunately. We need the sedatives the most, to help people stay calm through the later stages."

"Until they die," I said. I thought of Mom again, and my eyes prickled. I crossed my arms over my chest, hugging myself.

"Not always," he said, trying to sound cheerful but only managing pained. "You're our fifth patient to make a full recovery. The woman who's sharing this room with you looks as though she'll be the sixth."

And how many didn't recover? I remembered the crowd in the reception room the day I came in to find Dad, the patients lining the halls. But I didn't think Dad would tell me if I asked. I didn't want to see the expression his face would make. So instead I just said, "Why? How were we different?"

"The best we can say is luck," he said.

I've been lying here for a while since Dad left, letting it all sink in. This is the part where I'm supposed to be celebrating that I survived. But all I want to do is burrow into the mattress until the devastation is finally over.

What difference does it make that I'm still alive? It didn't stop everything else from getting worse. Why me and not Mom, or

Rachel, or Mrs. Campbell? What did I do to deserve to live, when they're all dead, and gone, and

I didn't do anything at all.

NOV 10 (LATER)

Gav came to see me this afternoon. Somehow that changed everything.

"Hey," he said as he nudged aside the curtain. He looked more worn out than before, and his hair was windblown and messy, but he had the same intensity in his eyes and, when he pulled down his face mask, that little almost-cocky smile.

I was still feeling low and useless, but I made myself smile back. "Hey," I said, and pushed myself up so I was propped against my pillow. "What are you doing here?"

"I heard you got better," he said. "Took me a while to find your room, but everyone's too busy to notice some random guy walking around."

"Well, you found me," I said. "Come in."

He sat down on the stool Dad's been using beside the bed, but he didn't say anything else. He looked around the room, glancing back at me every few seconds as if he was afraid I might disappear if he wasn't paying attention. It occurred to me that I probably looked sort of a mess—I got to shower in the morning, but I'd lain down with my hair wet, so it had to be sticking out funny. And the tears and the sniffling all morning wouldn't have helped.

Then I thought how ridiculous it was to agonize over how I

looked when the alternative was being dead, and shoved those worries aside.

"How's the food drive going?" I asked.

He frowned. "It's, well, it's gotten kind of screwed up," he said. "You don't want to hear about that."

"No, I do," I said, even though I'd really wanted to hear it was going great. "What happened?"

"I don't know," he said, looking down. "Everything seemed to be working. But then . . . one of the guys got sick. Kurt. And then Vince. And the other guys weren't so sure they wanted to keep doing the rounds. And then Quentin and a couple of them started talking, and I guess I wasn't paying enough attention. This group of older guys has started going around town the last few weeks, breaking into houses and stores and grabbing stuff, and Quentin and his friends decided to buy their way in with them. By bringing them the warehouse key."

For a second I couldn't speak. "They got everything?" I managed.

"No," he said. "We were lucky. Warren figured out what was going on, and we headed over there and caught them in the act. It was kind of crazy, because they have a couple of guns and it's not like they'd hesitate to use them. But they must have decided they'd taken enough, so why waste bullets? They hot-wired the truck, so we lost that too, but we've still got about half the food that was left. Had to move it, of course. And now just me and Warren and Patrick are showing up to make the rounds by car. I feel like we should be doing more—we keep seeing sick people at the houses, and I think in a few there are only kids left with no one looking after them, but it's just the three of us."

His voice petered out.

"You should talk to someone here," I said. "If you asked—"

"No, I know how that conversation would go down," he said. "I'd get bawled out for taking the food and trying to run the operation on my own, and they'd stick someone in charge who'll ignore everything we've already sorted out. There's no point."

He sighed and rubbed his face with his hands. "I'm sorry," he said. "I shouldn't be putting this on you. I really just wanted to let you know how glad I am that you're okay."

At the same time, a hopeful feeling was creeping over me. Maybe Gav thinks it couldn't happen, but I know he's wrong. Earlier today, I saw Mrs. Hansen, who worked in the school office, bringing a meal to the woman I'm sharing the room with, and Mr. Green, the mailman, passing by the door, and other volunteers who never worked in a hospital before. But they are now, because they want to help just as much as Gav does. No one's worrying about who's in charge, as long as it's someone who's headed in the right direction.

Gav needs people, and the people are here. We just have to bring them together.

So when he was leaving, I said, "Would you come back tomorrow morning? It was good seeing you." And he grinned and said he would.

I can do this. I beat the virus—that's who I am now, someone who survived. I have to *prove* I deserved to.

I have to make it matter.

NOV 11

I hoped having a plan of action would make the pain easier to get through. But I woke up in the middle of the night wanting Mom, her hand against my cheek, her steady voice. For a second I didn't know. And then I did, and I remembered how Drew was gone and maybe dead too, and I never got to say good-bye to either of them. I started sobbing so loud I must have woken up the woman in the room with me, but I couldn't stop. The tears just kept coming, until my chest ached. I was still choked up this morning when Dad came in.

But I did what I'd planned. I told him what Gav has been up to—I could tell from the comments he made that he'd already known bits and pieces—and how he needed more people helping, for the food and the sick people and the kids. When I was done, he looked at me for a long moment, and then he said, "We're talking about a lot of work, Kae."

"Of course," I said. "But Gav can handle it, and his friend Warren's really good at organizing everything. And I'll help too."

He gave me a bit of a smile, and I started to think we were set.

Gav showed up a half hour later. And I realized it might be harder than I'd expected. He stepped inside, saw Dad fiddling with something on his laptop, and stiffened.

"I guess I'll come back later," he said, already backpedaling.

"Wait!" I said. "Gav, this is my dad. I wanted you to talk with him."

He stopped, eyeing Dad warily, and it occurred to me that he's probably lumped Dad in with the government and the town hall and all the other people in charge who've let us down. Dad's a scientist, a specialist, and he didn't catch the virus in time.

But Gav trusts me. He came to me when he wanted to know what was going on, when he needed help before.

Dad stood up slowly and bobbed his head in greeting.

"Gav," he said. "I've heard a lot about what you've been doing for the town. It's impressive."

"I've been trying my best," Gav said. His shoulders were still tensed, but he stayed where he was in the doorway.

"There are a bunch of volunteers already helping out at the hospital," I said, figuring the sooner he understood what I wanted to do, the better. "At least a few of them would be happy to take the time every couple of days to distribute food in town."

"We can arrange for you to have more vehicles, too," Dad said. "As many as you need."

"Just like that?" Gav said, sounding skeptical. "No strings attached?"

"Everyone at the hospital has been just as worried about the rest of the island as you are," Dad said. "The only reason we haven't done more is our hands have been so full here. Anything we can give you to make the job easier, we're more than happy to offer."

"You and Warren would still be running everything," I said. "You'd just need to tell everyone how they can help."

Gav eased into the room. His eyes flickered between us and settled on Dad. "Is that true?" he said. "No one here's going to suddenly decide that because you gave us a couple cars, you get to start calling the shots? We've been doing this for weeks—we've got a system that works."

"You might be offered a little advice now and then," Dad said. "If the hospital staff notice something that could be done more effectively. But frankly, we don't have the time to take on something this big, even if we wanted to."

They faced off for a moment, Gav's mouth tight, Dad watching him calmly, and then Gav's expression broke into an awkward version of his usual smile. "Okay," he said. "That sounds all right." And I started grinning.

We talked a while longer, about what could be done for the infected people still at home and the kids who'd lost their parents. Even though the hospital is overcrowded, it's still the best place for anyone sick to be if we want to stop the virus from spreading.

"With the extra cars, we could pretty easily drive people back here when we find them," Gav said.

"We wouldn't want the healthy kids here," I pointed out. "But if they were all together, we'd need fewer people to look after them."

"I might know someone who'd be willing to set up a home for the children who've been orphaned," Dad said.

By the end of the conversation, Gav was sitting easily with us, as if he'd never been concerned. He got up and nodded to Dad and said, "We'll see if we can get this thing started, then."

He paused, and then he squeezed my shoulder, with a look on his face like he wanted to say thank you but didn't know the right words.

"I'll see you, Kaelyn," he said instead.

Dad watched him go, then turned to pick up his laptop.

"Dad," I said, "will I have to stay here much longer? I don't want to just lie here while everyone else does the work."

"We'll see how you're doing over the next couple days," he said. "I don't want you to push yourself too hard."

"But I'm definitely okay, right?" I asked, and a terrifying thought hit me. "I can't get sick *again*, can I?"

Dad sat down beside me. "Well," he said, "your immune system should be able to fight off the virus if it encounters it again. But we don't know what might happen in the future. The virus could mutate, and then your defenses wouldn't necessarily be enough. So we're going to keep being careful, all right? All the same precautions as before."

So right now I'm safe—as safe as a person can be. Maybe I'm not invincible, but I've got a lot less to be worried about than anyone else. The sickest patient in the hospital could sneeze in my face and I'd be fine.

I have to see the fact that I survived as a gift, whether I deserved it or not. And I'm going to do everything I can with that gift. Today was good, but it was just a start.

NOV 13

I'm free!

Dad decided today that I'm doing well enough to leave the hospital. Gav had just stopped by when I got the news, and he offered to drive me over to Tessa's.

I hadn't realized how much I'd gotten used to the pretty-much-quiet of my room. In the halls of the hospital, people are sitting on blankets or pillows or whatever else the volunteer staff have been able to find, coughing and sneezing into their face masks. They watched me as I walked by with Gav as my shadow. My face mask only filtered out some of the sour-sweat smell, and made each breath thick and humid. I pulled it down when we stepped outside, to gulp the cool air.

On the street, it was quiet again. Dead leaves were blowing across the tops of all those cars no one is ever going to claim. Almost all the trees are bare. Litter drifted on the road, and the windows across from us were dark.

I shivered and pulled my jacket closer around me. There's no way to look at this town and believe our lives could flip back to the way they were two months ago.

Gav had tugged down his mask too. "You all right?" he asked.

It's going to get better, I told myself. We're going to make it better.

"Yeah," I said. "Just, you know, haven't been out in a few weeks."

Gav's car—or, as it turned out, his parents' car—is a Ford hatchback that used to be white but now is more gray, with rust creeping along the edges of the frame like lichen. The inside stank of cigarette smoke. I wrinkled my nose reflexively, and Gav noticed.

"My mom," he said. "I've tried to air it out, but I guess that takes a while when the smell's had fifteen years to sink in."

"She doesn't mind you using it?" I said cautiously.

His voice stiffened. "She's not really in a position to care," he said.

He said she was sick the day he came by to teach me and Meredith those self-defense moves. Which means she was probably dead by the time I woke up in the hospital. He never said anything.

"How's your dad?" I asked.

"The same as her," he said, in a tone that suggested he'd rather not talk about it, and turned the key.

The engine rumbled to life more smoothly than I expected, given the look of the car. It seemed terribly loud in the stillness as we cruised toward Tessa's house. The only sign of life I saw was a cat scampering through a pet door as we passed.

"Doesn't look like I really needed an escort," I said, not because I minded, but because talking made the situation feel a little more normal. "Pretty quiet out."

"For now," Gav said. "You've got to be careful. That gang Quentin got in with, well, they're pretty rough. The last couple helicopter drops, they grabbed all the supplies, and I heard they shot at the people from the hospital who came to collect it. And . . ."

He hesitated, and shut his mouth. Something he'd decided not to say. Something even worse?

I felt colder than I had outside in the wind. "They're taking all the food and the medicine?" I said. "Then how are we managing?"

"The last shipments the hospital got, your dad says there's some left over from those," Gav said. "And we've got the food we held on to from our stash. And there just . . . aren't so many people left still needing to eat."

He said the last bit quietly, as if that would make it less true. I remembered the list Warren had made, all those houses. How many do they still stop at? How many have anyone left to open the door?

"I know," he went on, when I didn't say anything. "I should have been paying more attention. I should have caught Quentin and them before they took off on us. Then we'd have twice as much food, at least. And if they didn't have the truck, maybe they wouldn't be able to take *everything* from the drop-offs."

"It's not your fault," I said. "You had a lot going on."

"It is," he said. "I was in charge. I was supposed to be keeping an eye on everyone. And look how things ended up. We were managing the whole operation by ourselves, and now we have to go begging for help because of my screwup."

He pulled over in front of Tessa's house with a jerk of the steering wheel. His hands were tight and his eyes dark as he stared through the windshield.

"You can't really think you screwed anything up," I started.

"Of course I did," he said before I could finish. "If I hadn't—"

"Listen!" I said, so loud I startled both of us. His mouth snapped shut and he finally looked at me.

"Quentin's a jerk," I said. "He's been one as long as I've known him. I bet there wasn't a single thing you could have done to stop him from joining that gang. And if he hadn't gone to them with the key, they'd have broken the warehouse door down, and you wouldn't have had any warning, and they'd have taken everything instead of just half. So even if we *totally* ignore all the things you've been doing to help, even if we pretend none of that counts just because it didn't go exactly the way you planned, in what universe could you have made sure not one piece of food got stolen?"

I hadn't meant to give a huge speech, but once I got going I couldn't stop until all the words had spilled out. It's just so ridiculous that Gav, who's been doing so much, is beating himself up over one little thing he probably couldn't have changed anyway. Let Quentin beat himself up for being a selfish asshole!

When I finished, Gav was still watching me, and still looking kind of startled.

"I don't know," he admitted.

"Well, there you go," I said. "That's because there wasn't anything you could have done to stop it. So give yourself a break, okay?"

He let out a breath, long and slow, and then he smiled for the first time since we'd got in the car. "Right," he said.

It seemed like the conversation was over, so I reached to open the door. Then he said, "Kaelyn," and I turned back toward him, and something in his expression made my heart start thumping.

He was looking at me, but he'd been looking at me already. It just felt like his focus had sharpened, like before at least a little of his attention had been on other things, and now every single thought in his head was centered on me. He'd shifted forward, and his hand was resting on the side of the passenger seat, a few inches from my shoulder. His lips were parted like there was something he was going to say once he figured out the words.

I don't know what I thought he was going to do.

No, that's not true. I thought he was going to try to kiss me. I don't think I realized in the moment, and I don't know if I wanted him to, but I braced myself, and my heart kept pounding.

And then it didn't matter, because he didn't. His hand dropped to his side and he glanced out the window, and when he turned back to me, his gaze wasn't half as intense.

"Thanks," he said.

It took me a couple seconds to remember what he was thanking me for, and then I shrugged and smiled like there hadn't just been this potentially awkward moment. "Happy to help!" I said, way too brightly. I reached for the door again, and he didn't stop me.

One of us said something like, "See you around," and the other one agreed, and then I was standing at Tessa's door, hearing the Ford's engine growl as Gav drove away.

Tessa is probably the only person who could look totally composed while the world is falling to pieces. When she opened the door, she had her hair pulled back in a smooth ponytail, and even though a few smudges of dirt marked the knees of her jeans, otherwise her clothes were clean and unwrinkled.

"Your dad called to let me know you were on your way," she said. "We were just making some lunch. Are you hungry?" Totally calm, like I hadn't almost died since the last time she'd seen me. It was kind of nice not to be treated like a miracle.

That lasted about five seconds, because then footsteps came charging down the hall and Meredith flung herself at me.

"You're really okay!" she said. "I was really, really worried, Kaelyn. Are you going to come stay here with us? Tessa says you can. I wanted to bring your stuff so I could set it all up for you, but Uncle Gordon wouldn't let me go in your room. I'm sorry."

I hadn't heard her say so much all at once since Aunt Lillian left. I got a lump in my throat, and for a minute I couldn't say anything. So I just hugged her and kissed her forehead.

"I'm glad *you're* okay," I said, after a bit. "My dad was right— you've got to be really careful. I need you to stay healthy."

She nodded. "I know," she said. "I'm staying inside where it's safe. And I've been looking after the ferrets for you!"

She grabbed my hand and dragged me over to the guest bedroom, which was stuffed full of her suitcases and toys and the ferret cage. Mowat and Fossey scrambled up the bars to see me, nuzzling my fingers. They didn't look any worse for my absence. I opened the door and let them clamber over me.

"Tessa doesn't really like them," Meredith whispered to me. Once she'd gotten over her excitement, she was really quiet again.

"Why not?" I asked.

She looked at her feet. "I thought it'd be fun to take them into the greenhouse," she said. "But Fossey tried to dig under one of the bushes, and Mowat knocked over a pot."

"Don't worry," I said. "I'm sure Tessa isn't upset with you."

Tessa called us for lunch, which was canned ravioli. Meredith was almost silent, and Tessa was awkwardly polite, speaking to Meredith the way I might have talked to a friend of my parents I didn't know that well. I guess she hasn't spent much time around kids. She was trying, though; don't get me wrong.

So this is us now. We've formed some strange new sort of family.

I felt almost happy until I looked at the three empty chairs, and thought that Drew ought to be sitting in one, and Mom in another, and a familiar ache filled my chest.

Three weeks sick and I feel like I've missed a century.

NOV 14

So now I know what Gav didn't tell me yesterday.

This morning after breakfast, Tessa said she'd take me over to the house to grab my things. I wanted to go by myself, but I'm not sure where Dad has our car, and even if Tessa would let me borrow hers, it's a stick shift, which I don't know how to drive. Walking was out because I still get faint sometimes. We had a hushed discussion about Meredith, and in the end decided it was safer for her to stay in the house with the door locked, since we didn't know who we'd run into. God, am I glad for that.

"Are you sure you don't mind?" I asked as we drove. "That we're, like, moving in with you? Meredith and I could stay at my place now that I'm out of the hospital."

"Your dad said he didn't know how safe your house is, right?" Tessa said. "Because you and your mom were both sick in there? No one's been sick at my place. It makes sense for her to stay there and for you to stay with her. There's lots of room."

"But it's your house," I said. "You don't have to let us just because it makes sense."

She hesitated for a moment, and then she said, "I kind of like having someone else around. The house gets really quiet sometimes."

She always seems so unflappable, I forget to think she might be lonely. But of course it's been weeks now since she could talk to her parents, or to you, Leo—since the long distance and the internet went out. If it were me, I'd have gone insane by now.

"Okay," I said, "then it works for both of us," and she smiled.

As we drove, I noticed a couple houses that reminded me of the gang Gav had talked about. The doors were swinging open and the front windows smashed. When we turned onto my street, I was suddenly terrified my house would look the same. But it was fine, everything as it should be.

I told Tessa I'd rather go in on my own, both because the virus might be hanging around and because I wasn't sure how emotional I'd get. But when I went in and looked around, I didn't know what I'd been worried about losing. Tessa had told me they'd already moved all the food to her place, so I went straight to my bedroom. I stood in the doorway for a few minutes, wondering if I cared enough about any of my belongings to risk the virus traveling with them.

In the end I stuffed a garbage bag full of the clothes that seemed the most useful and sealed it up so I could throw them straight into the wash when we got back to Tessa's. I tossed my iPod into my backpack with my coyote notebook and a couple other journals I'd been writing observations in, a guide to surviving the wilderness I'd gotten as preparation for research expeditions, and the framed photo of the four of us, Mom, Dad, Drew, and me, that Aunt Lillian took down by the beach a couple years ago. I looked at Mom and Drew a little too long, and had to blink hard as I was putting the photo away. Then I hemmed and hawed over my computer and finally burned a disc of pretty much everything on the hard drive.

So there you have it. That's what my life comes down to now: some clothes, a few books, and a DVD.

"Okay," I said when I got back in the car. "Let's get out of here."

We were about halfway back to Tessa's house when a woman ran in front of us.

Tessa hit the brake so hard I jolted against my seat belt. The car stopped just a few inches away from the woman, but she didn't seem to notice.

"It's so good to see someone!" she said. "Where are you going? Can I come with you? I don't think I can stand being alone another second!"

Her face was flushed, and she sneezed as she waited for us to answer, refusing to budge. Tessa backed up a little, and the woman followed us.

"No, no," she said. "Don't leave! I just want someone to talk to." And then she started crying—sobbing and coughing at the same time.

I realized right then that I could do something. I could get out and talk to her, and I'd be almost as safe as if she were healthy.

"I should take her to the hospital," I said. "I think I can get her to walk there. I'll meet you back at your place."

Tessa shook her head. At first I thought she was going to tell me not to bother, but then she said, "We can drive her. We've both got masks—it should be okay, right?"

To be honest, I didn't really want to spend an hour or more cajoling this woman into coming with me as far as the hospital. I decided I'd get her into the back of the car and stay with her there, and put my mask over her face so the virus stayed more contained.

As I got out of the car, I heard another engine somewhere behind us, and I figured it was one of Gav's group taking food around.

The woman turned toward me, scratching at her scalp above her ear. A few strands of hair drifted to the ground.

"What's your name?" she said, beaming at me. "I'm—"

The air crackled, rattling in my ears. I flinched and ducked my head. When I looked up, the woman was falling. A circle of blood was spreading across her forehead. She crumpled onto the pavement.

Her body twitched, and then she was still.

A door slammed. I spun around to see a guy a few years older than Drew striding toward us from a pickup truck, a shotgun dangling from his right hand. He was wearing a face mask with the words "survival" and "strength" scrawled on it in blue pen, but I recognized him by his white-blond hair. He used to help out at the MacCauley's apple orchard, where we picked up a basket every fall.

Then Tessa called my name, and it occurred to me that I had better get back to the car.

"What the hell are you doing?" the guy said, stopping about ten feet away and cocking his head like he was making sure the woman was dead. "Don't you know what's going on? You want to get sick?"

"What are *you* doing?" I shouted back. "You just shot someone!"

"She already had it," he said. "She was dead anyway. I just made sure she didn't pass it on first."

"She wasn't dead!" I said. "She could have gotten better! I did."

I knew as soon as the words came out of my mouth it was a mistake. His eyes narrowed and he raised the gun. "You've had it?" he said. "Probably still in you then."

I threw myself at the car door, but I'm sure he would have shot me before I'd gotten inside if Tessa hadn't stepped out right then, between us.

He hesitated, and she started yelling.

"You have so many bullets it's worth wasting them?" she said, hands on her hips. "Did your friends tell you to go around shooting healthy people?"

He just stared at her. I did too.

"You're worse than the virus," she went on. "At least *it* lets a few people survive. You're out here trying to kill everyone."

"See if you're still saying that when your friend gets you sick," the guy said, but he'd lowered his gun. As soon as it was obvious he was walking away, I dove into the car. Tessa followed. She'd left the engine running, and she backed up just enough to swerve around the woman's body before she put her foot on the gas, so abruptly my shoulder smacked the window.

"Sorry," she said, sounding like her regular self again. "I didn't think we should give him time to change his mind."

"No," I said. "Oh my god. Thank you."

"Well, I couldn't let him shoot you," she said, like it was a fact.

But it's not. She *could* have let him shoot me. She could have driven away and not risked her life for some girl she wouldn't even sit next to a couple months ago.

I don't know what I would have done if our positions had been reversed. I want to think I'd have stood up for her, but I can so easily imagine my mind going blank until it was too late. I want to be that kind of person, though. The kind of person who saves other people.

I fought off a virus that's killed almost everyone who's caught it—I should feel stronger. I *am* stronger. I have to remember that.

NOV 15

When I went to take a shower this morning, the water coming out of the tap was brown. Enough that it looked muddy in Tessa's clean bathtub. I tried calling the hospital, but the line was busy like pretty much always, so I told Tessa and Meredith not to drink any water, and headed over. Thankfully Dad brought our car around last night.

I saw Nell as soon as I went in. "Something must have broken in the filtration system," she said. "We'll try to find someone who can fix it, but I think we're lucky it's only happened now. Anything mechanical will break down without proper maintenance. I'm surprised the electricity's held up this long."

So we have to boil the water before we can drink it now. I spent the morning filling up the hospital kitchen's biggest pots and letting them steam and then pouring the still-brown but at least safe to drink water into these jugs one of the volunteers found. The more they have on hand, the better. It seemed like a simple way to help.

After I'd topped up the last jug, I went looking for Nell to find out what she wanted to do with them all. I'd just spotted her in the hall and was calling her name when the elevator doors opened between us and a man with shaggy, graying hair came out, wheeling a wide gurney.

A sheet was draped across the top of the gurney, but that wasn't enough to disguise the lumps and bulges underneath. Feet and elbows, shoulders and foreheads. A hill of bodies. My stomach lurched as he pushed it past me, the wheels squeaking. The patients in the hall went quiet. When I managed to pull my gaze away, Nell was standing beside me.

"Where does he take them?" I asked.

Nell lay her hand on my arm, which was trembling, and I realized what I was really asking was, Where's my mom?

"I wish we could give them the proper respect," she said softly. "But after the first wave . . . There aren't enough volunteers and there isn't enough time. We've had to use the old quarry."

The quarry. I remember exploring it as a kid, slipping and skinning my palms on the gravel. It was like a big empty lake. Except it isn't empty now.

My lungs tightened, and I had to fight the urge to walk right out of the hospital and not stop until I was standing on the edge, until I could find Mom amid the jumble of bodies. To see her one last time. I know that sounds morbid, but I think there's some part of grief you just can't get past when all you have is other people's words. When you haven't looked at the body with your own eyes, or watched a coffin lowered into the ground. You can't shake the feeling that it could be some big mistake, like they might be wrong and no one died after all.

Animals honor their dead. Elephants stand vigil over fallen friends and family. Gorillas howl and beat their chests. Mom didn't even get that much. She was dumped into a pit with so many others, like the victims of a genocide. Like garbage. How could we do that to her?

In a way, it's not so different from what I saw yesterday. All it takes is one microscopic virus, and even the people who aren't sick start acting like mass murderers.

I closed my eyes and opened them again and swallowed down all the angry painful words I could have said. It isn't Nell's fault. Not really. And there are worse things to be upset about. Like the fact that Drew could be floating out in the strait or crumpled on the mainland shore somewhere, dead and lost. At least I know where Mom is.

I watched the man with the gurney disappearing through the front doors. "Isn't he worried about getting sick?" I asked after a moment, groping for something else to talk about. He was wearing a mask and a protective gown like everyone else, but being that close to so many bodies has got to be risky.

Nell smiled a little sadly. "Howard's like you, hon," she said. "He caught the virus early on, was our first to make it through. That's why he took the job."

Dad told me I was the fifth survivor, and the woman who shared my room would be number six, but somehow the idea hadn't quite sunk in until then. There are other people walking around who beat the virus. Who've shown that we can.

Dad also said we were lucky, but that's a cop-out. When it comes to science, luck just means you haven't found the reason yet.

A shiver of excitement went through me, like a flash of light in the darkness. "Nell," I said, "there are records for all the patients, right?"

"Of course," she said. "Though we haven't been able to keep them as organized as we used to. The file room's just off reception. Why?"

"Could you write down the names of the people who got better?" I said.

She frowned. "Kaelyn," she said. "You know your dad's already been over those records a dozen times. He hasn't found anything."

"I know," I said. "But maybe they need a fresh pair of eyes. Can't hurt for me to look."

So she gave me the code for the door and the names of the five other survivors, and left me to get to work. She was right about the disorganization—the cabinets are overflowing, folders left sitting on top of them or jammed into the wrong spots. But after a half hour I managed to dig out the files for the six of us who recovered. I sat on the floor looking them over until the tiny print started to give me a headache, and then I stuck them together in the space between two of the cabinets so I can find them right away next time I come.

I didn't see anything today that would connect us, explain why we lived and all those other people didn't. But I'm going to keep looking. There has to be something.

NOV 16

I went into town today, and no one aimed a gun at me. Small victories.

I'd run into Gav yesterday when I was heading out of the hospital, and he told me Dad had asked his group to inform people about the water problem while they're doing their next food run. Which makes sense. Everything will just get worse if people who haven't caught the virus pick up something else by drinking contaminated water.

"When are you going?" I asked right away. "I'll come with you if you need more people."

"We've got a bunch helping now," he said. "But the more we have, the faster the rounds get done. We're going out tomorrow morning—I could come by and pick you up."

He sounds, and looks, so much more confident than he did the last time I saw him, when he was beating himself up about what happened with Quentin. But he still watched me tentatively after he said it, as if he thought I was going to tell him to take a hike.

"That'd be great," I said, and smiled, and he smiled back. Right then, even though I hadn't found anything in the records, it felt like a good day.

So this morning he came by in the old Ford, and we headed to the hospital, where everyone was meeting. For an operation that a week ago only consisted of three guys, Gav and Warren got organized amazingly fast. As he was driving, he told me the details.

"Warren's divided the town into different areas," he explained, "and there's a list for each one. Plus another for the places on the outskirts, the farms and everything. The lists let you know which houses to skip, to save us time. You knock on the door, give whoever answers a bag of food. Today we'll also tell them about having to boil the tap water. And you ask them if anyone inside has symptoms. If they do, or we see someone who's sick, we do our best to convince them to let us take them to the hospital. One of the nurses is setting up a home in the church near the hospital for the kids who are alone, so if you see any, make a note and we'll hopefully have somewhere to bring them in the next couple days."

"Wow," I said, and he laughed.

"I know," he said. "It sounds like a lot. But once we get going, it's not that different from how we did things before. I still wish—"

"If you say you wish you could do more," I interrupted, "I will hit you. I really will."

"All right, all right!" he said, ducking his head. But I know he was thinking it.

When we got to the hospital, a cluster of people was waiting outside. I recognized Warren and another guy who'd been with Gav's group before, a middle-aged woman I'd see helping around the hospital, a youngish man who used to wait tables at the Seaview Restaurant, one of the orderlies, and a few other adults I only vaguely knew.

Gav's expression went serious. He nodded to them as he stepped out of the car, but I saw his shoulders hunch just slightly, as if he was a turtle fighting the urge to duck into his shell. Then he hurried over to Warren, who was sitting on the fringes of the group in the driver's seat of a car, the door open.

"Good to see you, Kaelyn," Warren said, and glanced at Gav. Something silent passed between them, and a second later Gav's face looked a bit more flushed than it had before. He shrugged and leaned on the car door.

"So what's the plan today?" he asked.

Warren shuffled through a bunch of papers that looked a lot like the ones he'd been holding when I first met him.

"We've got five cars today," he said. "I divided the lists up to fit. Each group should have to make about eight stops, except the outer area group, but they only need to do one house at a time. Patrick and Terry already loaded up the cars like you asked, so I think we're ready to go."

He handed the papers over to Gav, who eyed them and then the waiting group.

"You know," he said, "one of these days I'm going to make you stand up there and talk for yourself."

"And *you* know they listen to you better than they'll ever listen to me," Warren replied. "Just talk—they're all raring to go."

Gav pretended to scowl at him before he jogged over to the hospital steps. He hesitated for a second, then shouted for everyone's attention. Warren turned to me with a half smile.

"He liked the job better when it was just us guys," he said. "But he manages to get everyone working together anyway. And don't let him give you the impression he's taking credit where he shouldn't. This was all his idea. I just help make it work better, because he asked me to."

"You don't think this is important?" I said.

"I know it's important," he said. "Put me up there, though, and I'd freeze up. And he *feels* it. That's what gets people going."

We both looked toward Gav, who was gesturing in the air as he explained why everyone needed to know the water wasn't safe. Whatever nerves he'd been feeling before were gone. He stood straight and steady, and he had that familiar intensity in his eyes, like it was a matter of life and death. Which it was, after all.

"You seem like you've been friends a long time," I said to Warren.

"Yep," he said. "Since second grade. The teacher kept making fun of him because he hadn't learned how to swim yet. He wanted to get back at her, and I came up with the perfect prank. We have conspired together ever since."

I raised my eyebrows. "What did you do to her?" I asked.

His smile turned a little wicked. "I don't think he'd like it if I told you," he said, and tipped his head toward Gav, who was coming our way. The other pairs were ducking into their cars with maps and lists in hand. It looked like Gav had handed off his car keys to the orderly.

So the three of us piled into Warren's car, the guys in the front and me in the back with a heap of bagged food.

In some ways, it wasn't as bad as I'd expected. When we were driving and talking, I could almost believe we were just a group of friends out for a ride. And most of the people whose doors I knocked on looked healthy and relieved to see me, even when I told them about the problem with the water.

But then there was the woman who just grabbed the food from me and shut the door before I could say anything else. I heard a little boy's voice on the other side, chattering away with a sneeze here and there. And the man who couldn't stop coughing and had to be taken to the hospital.

"I'll drive him," I said, and Gav gave me a horrified look.

"I take the sick ones," he said. "I'm the one who wanted to start bringing them in—I'm the one who should handle it."

"Yeah," I said. "But I've already gotten sick, and you still can. It's common sense."

He couldn't exactly deny the facts, so in the end I got my way, even though Gav insisted on helping the man into the car. As I came around to the driver's seat, he touched my arm.

"Keep an eye out," he said. "If you see someone driving around who's not part of our group—"

"I know," I said. "I'll be careful. Thanks."

I made it to and from the hospital just fine, so that wasn't the worst part of the day. The worst was all the addresses we were already skipping, and all the ones I had to cross off the list because there hadn't been any answer the last three tries. In the end, we only found people at forty-three houses. Warren looked at the sheet I brought back at the end of the morning, littered with X's, and pinched the bridge of his nose.

"I'll redo them before next time," he said to Gav.

Gav nodded, like it was no big deal, but a minute later he swiped a can of beans from the trunk and hurled it down the street. It made a heavy clunk when it hit the pavement.

At least we're trying, I thought, but I didn't say it. I'm pretty sure that's not what he wanted to hear. I wish I could say something better.

NOV 17

They hit Uncle Emmett's neighborhood—that gang Gav says Quentin joined. I went down to the house this morning for one last look around, and I found the door wide open. The knob had been wrenched off.

I had a moment of panic and almost bolted for the car before it occurred to me that I could be at one of the safest spots in town. They've already taken whatever they wanted. Why would they come back? They're about as likely to loot the house a second time as I am to catch the virus again.

There wouldn't have been much worth stealing. The liquor cabinet is empty, and it looks like they rummaged through the bedrooms, searching for valuables. But Aunt Lillian took her jewelry box with her when she left, I'm sure, so they would have been disappointed.

For a few minutes I was worried they'd snatched the binoculars, which I'd really wanted to find, but I unearthed them in the mess by Meredith's bed.

The patrol boats were still anchored in the strait, keeping watch. Beyond them, the mainland looked the same as it always did. I caught little flickers of movement and the gleam of lights through the haze.

It's hard to imagine life continuing as usual over there. People going to school and buying groceries and hanging out with their friends without masks plastered over their faces. It's like a totally different planet, across vast distances of space, instead of a town just a few miles away over some water.

That might sound horribly pessimistic, but honestly, it's better than the alternative. Because the alternative is that life isn't continuing as usual, that they're falling just as fast as we are.

I've tried to imagine what you're doing right now, Leo. Sometimes I picture you in class, spinning and leaping while your teachers watch in amazement. It's a nice thought, but I know it's not true. Because you have to know what's going on now, and you wouldn't just continue on as usual. You might be over there at this exact moment, trying to negotiate with whoever's in charge to let you come home.

I wonder if Drew's with you. Maybe he got across all right, but his scuba gear was damaged on the way, and even if he's found something that would help us, he's stuck there. But someday, when the island's safe again, you'll both come back to us.

I wish that day didn't feel so far away.

When I left the house, I took the binoculars with me. I don't want to have to come back. As I was heading down the front walk I saw movement down the street and paused. A body was sprawled outside the house four doors down, half on the sidewalk, half on the road. Someone who had died of the virus or the water or was shot—I wasn't close enough to tell. A coyote was tugging at its arm. I looked the other way and got in the car.

I really can't judge, after all. Coyotes have to eat to survive too.

On the way back to Tessa's, I took a detour toward the harbor. Not too close, because I remembered Dad's story about the trigger-happy soldiers. But near enough that I could get a pretty good look with the binoculars.

I couldn't see anyone moving around on the docks. Then I scanned the boats, and my skin went cold. The ones in my line of view were half submerged, white bows or sides protruding from the water where they were tied to the dock, some with chunks missing from their rims or splintered holes in their hulls. It looked as if a giant had stomped through swinging a sledgehammer. I followed the bending lines of the docks, trying to spot Uncle Emmett's cruiser. The wreckage was too messy to make out any identifying details, but from what I saw, none of the boats escaped unharmed.

The big storm Dad mentioned couldn't have caused that much damage—I've never seen a nor'easter smash up boats that badly. So it must have been a person. Or people.

I started feeling so queasy I had to put down the binoculars and close my eyes. Every time I look around, something else is broken.

NOV 18

The hospital's been getting noisier the last couple days. Dad and Nell haven't said anything, but I suspect they're almost out of sedatives. You can hear the whole progression of the disease standing in the halls: coughing and sneezing and aggressively friendly chattering and shrieks of panic. It took me three tries to get a nurse's attention yesterday, and I realized why when she popped out an earplug to hear me properly.

The virus has a voice, and it doesn't sound very happy.

I'd meant to spend the afternoon in the records room, but after an hour of going over every detail of the treatments one more time, comparing the survivors to people who died, I put the files aside and walked out. I've checked and double-checked over the last few days, and there's nothing. Nothing special the six of us got and no one else did. No miraculous solution just waiting for me to stumble on it.

As I stepped out into the chilly air, I heard the buzz of a passing helicopter. It whirred by overhead, back toward the mainland. A reporter collecting news footage? Or another delivery that the gang will have snatched up? I pictured the bunch of them tossing all the meds the hospital desperately needs into the back of their stolen truck, and my hands balled into fists.

I went straight back to Tessa's. She was kneeling in the green-house, pruning one of the shrubs.

"We should start going out again," I said. "Scavenging. We never finished all the summer houses."

"I did the rest on my own," Tessa said.

"Then we'll do regular houses," I said. "We can start with your street."

"You mean break in?" she asked, raising an eyebrow.

I almost thought, Why not? The gang's already looting people's homes for their selfish reasons—why shouldn't we, to help the hospital? But thinking of them reminded me of the day when the guy with the truck shot that woman right in front of me, and my stomach turned. I don't want to follow their lead, not in anything.

"No," I said. "We don't have to. I know which houses are empty, from going out with Gav. We'll check the doors and only go in if they're unlocked."

So yesterday and this afternoon, we got Meredith watching one of her DVDs and then headed out. I make Tessa wait outside while I take a quick look around, to be sure each place really is empty. The first couple times I broke out in a sweat as I walked down the halls to the bedrooms. But I haven't come across anyone yet, well or sick, alive or dead. After a while, the memory of the dead woman and child in the summer house started to fade.

Which doesn't mean going in isn't awful sometimes. The summer houses were so polished and remote, I could pretend no one ever lived there. The places we're scavenging from now, they belonged to people I passed on the street or nodded to in the gro-cery store. People whose presence lingers in the photos propped on side tables and the notes left on kitchen counters, the toys scattered over living room floors and the posters hanging on bedroom walls. But none of them are coming back.

I've learned to keep my mind and eyes focused on the next drawer, the next cabinet, tuning out everything else as much as I can.

We haven't found a lot, mostly basic stuff like Tylenol and Tums, but anything's better than nothing. And we're grabbing any food we find, too. Gav might have enough stashed away for now, but who knows how long it'll be before we manage to take another delivery from the mainland. Tessa and I brought it all to the hospital, and I stuck the food in the kitchen there.

Gav came over last night to go over the self-defense training with Tessa and check that Meredith and I remembered what he'd taught us, and I saw him this morning for the usual rounds. But I didn't tell him what we're doing. It's not that I'm worried whether he'd approve. Of course he would. He'd get all excited and want to take over and make it part of the regular food run. And it wouldn't be mine anymore.

Maybe I should want to get more people involved. But for some reason it feels so important right now to have this one thing that belongs to me.

NOV 19

You might have noticed I haven't been talking about Dad very much, Leo. The fact is I hardly see him. Everyone who's left at the hospital looks up to him as the boss, and he's pretty much living there.

Which in a way is safer for everyone, because he doesn't risk bringing the virus here to Meredith or Tessa. He calls most nights just to check in, but he can never stay on the line for more than a minute or two. It's nowhere near the same as having him here. Sometimes I wake up in the middle of the night and wonder where he is, and he feels almost as far away as Mom or Drew.

I don't know how he keeps going. He smiles when we pass each other in the hospital, but the exhaustion is plain on his face. It must be quieter at the research center, so maybe he catches some naps over there. I hope so. At this rate, he'll make himself sick even without catching the virus. I can't lose him too. I just can't.

I finally got a chance to really talk to him this evening. He came into the hospital kitchen while I was putting away the food Tessa and I picked up in the afternoon, and started making himself a bowl of instant soup. At least now I know he's eating occasionally.

"Have you heard anything from the mainland?" I asked. "Is the radio picking up anything at all?"

He hesitated, and then he sighed. "Nothing productive's come of our attempts so far," he said. "But we'll keep trying, of course."

"I've been wanting to ask you," I said, "I took a look at the harbor the other day—it's deserted. And the boats..."

I could tell from the way Dad's jaw tightened that he already knew about them.

"I know you want to come to the hospital and help out here, and I think it's good for you," he said. "But I'd rather you didn't go anywhere else on your own, even in the car, all right? There's safety in numbers."

"Yeah," I said, which wasn't a promise, because I wasn't going to make one. I can't drag Tessa and Meredith with me everywhere. "So what happened to the boats?" I asked.

"The soldiers," he said as he tipped the kettle over the noodles, steam rushing up between us. "The ones who were stationed in the harbor. As far as we can tell, they became so afraid of catching the virus that they decided to disobey their orders and leave. But first they wanted to make sure no one here could follow them."

I swallowed. "So they destroyed all the boats," I said.

"Not all of them," Dad said. "You know some people keep smaller ones on their own property. If we wanted to send someone across the strait, we could. I just don't think it's worth risking the reception we're likely to get from the patrol boats. I suspect the military as a whole has taken a shoot-first stance toward anyone from the island."

What would they have done to Drew if they caught him? The image of his body washing up on the shore flashed through my mind, and I winced. Dad put his arm around me, and I leaned my head against his shoulder.

"Things have to get better, don't they?" I said. "This can't keep going on forever."

"Nothing's forever," Dad said, but the words weren't as comforting as I wanted them to be.

It's true, though. The epidemic has to end eventually. I need to focus on that—on the day in the future when the virus is gone, and all we've lived through will be just a story about something bad that happened a long time ago.

NOV 20

Gav made lunch for us today. He's a really good cook. Who'd have thought?

I hadn't planned it, but right after we finished the morning food run and waved good-bye to Warren, who's helping get the orphaned kids settled at the church, Gav said, "This probably sounds terrible, but I'm always hungry after we do this."

"You should come over to Tessa's and have lunch with us," I said.

"Yeah?" he said. My cheeks started to warm up. Hoping he wouldn't notice, I gave his shoulder a little shove.

"Unless you think our grub isn't good enough for you," I said.

"I guess I'll have to see," he said, arching one eyebrow.

The moment we walked into the kitchen he gravitated to the cupboards. In five seconds he was pulling out cans and poking through the spice rack while Tessa and Meredith and I just stared. He picked up a pot and then thought to check with Tessa. "You don't mind?" he said.

"Go ahead," she said, looking amused. Our idea of fancy cooking has been dumping a handful of frozen peas in with instant rice, so we weren't in any position to complain.

Compared to what we usually eat, the casserole Gav threw together was a miracle, even though he said he should have used

Parmesan cheese and fresh salmon instead of the canned. It's the first time I've enjoyed anything I was eating in ages. I let each bite roll around in my mouth before swallowing, ignoring my grumbling stomach, because at dinnertime we'll be back to basics again.

The moment would have been perfect, except that partway through the meal my hand bumped Meredith's glass. Her pre-boiled water spilled all over her lap and the floor, and the whole time we were mopping it up she kept saying sorry to *me*. After the twentieth time, I snapped.

"Meredith," I said, "it's not your fault. I knocked over the glass. Stop apologizing."

And then she did stop, because she started crying instead. I felt like I was about to win the worst-cousin-of-the-year award.

I wasn't really angry at her. But I'm so worried about her all the time, and of course that gets to me. Ever since I got back from the hospital, she's been all meek and cringing, apologizing for anything that's wrong, even if it's nothing to do with her.

Maybe she figures we'll be happier if she makes everything her fault. Like the documentary about wolves I saw a couple years ago that talked about the different rankings in the pack, with the omega way at the bottom. If the other wolves were pissed off about something, they'd take it out on the omega. But the omega didn't mind because it chose its role. It wanted to be the scapegoat so punishment could be dealt for whatever the pack was upset about and everyone could calm down. Maybe that's how Meredith's thinking too.

Or maybe she's so shell-shocked she's starting to believe everything really is her fault.

I don't know. I've tried to talk to her about it, and all she does is smile in this stiff sort of way and say she's fine, she's just happy she's still with me.

I wish Mom was here, so much. She would have known what to do. Better than me, anyway.

What I did do turned out not to be the greatest idea ever, but it seemed good at the time. "Let's take a little trip," I said. "You haven't gotten out of the house in ages."

"Can we go see the coyotes?" Meredith asked, still sniffling but sounding brighter.

I remembered the coyote I'd seen gnawing on the body outside Uncle Emmett's house. "I don't think they're feeling very friendly right now," I said. "We could go to the beach."

It was gray and windy outside and absolutely the wrong weather for beachcombing, but Meredith said, "Okay," gulped down the rest of her lunch, and ran to get her shoes and jacket. Tessa bowed out, saying she needed to do some work in the greenhouse. Dad's special nerve-medication plants might have been a failure, but she's still devoted to her own crops. Gav offered to come along.

"We'll take my car," he said. "I need to fill it up anyway." I gave him the keys to the station and showed him how to work the pumps a few days ago, since he's more likely to need the gas than me.

Once we got in the Ford, Meredith was quiet, and the silence felt too heavy.

"The casserole was really good," I said, to break it. "Did your mom teach you how to cook?"

Gav smiled, but it didn't reach his eyes. "You could say that," he said. "As soon as I was old enough to put together a sandwich, meals were basically a free-for-all. Everyone just made their own thing. After a while I got sick of sandwiches. There were cookbooks around. And I kind of liked that it bugged my mom if I made something better than what she'd thrown together for herself, and then ate it all."

"Oh," I said. I can't imagine being a kid and not knowing dinner at least will magically appear on the table sometime every evening.

He shrugged and said, "I didn't really mind, once I got used to it. You learn a lot when you know no one else is going to do things for you."

Watching him, I felt like he'd just handed me a piece of a puzzle I hadn't realized I was putting together. Suddenly I could see exactly how he'd become the guy I talked to in the park two months ago, who laughed at the idea of government aid and calmly went and emptied out a grocery store to provide his own kind of assistance.

I wanted to say something deep and sensitive to show I understood, but right then we drove past a row of stores, and instead I was shouting, "Wait, wait, stop!"

The gang's obviously worked over Main Street pretty well. Most of the store windows were broken, the sidewalk crunchy with glass. They'd gone into the garden shop, but I could see packets of seeds and bulbs on the shelves, and it occurred to me that I'd have to come by with Tessa sometime so she could grab anything she thought was useful.

But what had really caught my eye was Play Time.

I'm sure the gang assumed there'd be nothing useful in a toy store. Which is probably true, for them. The window with the swirling painting of two kids on a magic carpet ride was intact, if a little dingy looking. Beyond it, a huddle of stuffed animals peered out from one corner of the display, an army of action figures commanding the other.

It was better than the beach. It was, I thought, just what Meredith needed.

I tried the door and it opened. Whoever had come in last hadn't bothered to lock up. Maybe they'd assumed they'd be coming back the next day. I didn't want to think about the most probable reason they hadn't.

Gav had gotten Meredith out of the car. She walked up to the store hesitantly. "Can we really go in?" she asked.

"Yes," I said firmly. "Of course we can. You can pick out five things to take home. And we'll get some toys and games for the kids who are on their own now, too."

Gav looked up and down the street. "I'll take the car down to the station," he said. "Should only be a few minutes." But then he just stood there.

"We'll be fine," I said. "It's a toy store. Go on."

I pushed open the door and switched on the lights. It was like stepping through a portal into Narnia.

I used to love Play Time. When I was a kid, it felt like the hall of a fairy-tale palace, with the painted-stone floor, the mock-fur rug where volunteers would read from a book every afternoon in front of the gas fireplace, and the sweet cedar smell rising from the shelves lined with boxes and bins of treasures. I bought my minnow net there, and the big book of nature stories I read until the cover fell off, and those bird figurines with real feathers glued to their wooden bodies. But I hadn't gone in since before we moved back.

The shop seemed smaller now, more cozy cottage than palace hall, because, of course, I'm bigger. But there was still something magical about it. It was so untouched. A little piece of the life we used to have, hidden away in the middle of town.

Meredith just stood there staring, which wasn't what I wanted at all. I wanted excitement, dancing, laughter. So I picked up a bottle from the counter by the cash register and blew a stream of rainbow bubbles at her. She waved her hands at them and one of them popped on her cheek. Then she giggled.

"I want to try!" she said, and for a couple minutes, everything was spectacular.

I popped open a second bottle and we filled the store with bubbles, then ran through them from one end to the other, sending them whirling around us. A bunch of Disney Princess dresses were hanging on a rack near the back. I found Ariel's and tugged it over Meredith's sweater. She spun around in front of the mirror, grinning like I hadn't seen in months. We raced back to the rug and dove onto the beanbag chairs. While Meredith blew more bubbles into the air, I bent over the gas fireplace and tried to figure out how to turn it on.

When I heard the door open behind me, I assumed it was Gav back from the gas station. I didn't turn around until Meredith made a sort of startled squeaking sound, and then I froze.

Quentin was standing in the foyer.

He looked rough. His hair was bristly and uneven, as if he'd taken an electric shaver to it without a mirror, and his skin was sallow except for a broad, scabbed scrape on his cheek. Gang life doesn't seem to be treating him very well. But he still managed to sneer.

"Aren't you the one who was telling me off for stealing?" he said to Meredith. "What do you think you're doing now?"

Meredith's only answer was another squeak. She scrambled off the beanbag chair. I started toward her, but Quentin moved faster.

He lunged forward and grabbed her arm, wrenching it behind her back. She whimpered and went still.

Quentin was looking at me. "I hear you had the virus," he said. "They cured it."

I didn't have to wonder how he knew. All the guy with the shotgun would have had to say was he'd talked to some girl with light brown skin, which narrowed the options down to one.

I've felt uncomfortable and out of place before, but that's the first time I've outright wished I was the same color as just about everyone else on the island.

"I survived," I said. "They didn't cure it. I was lucky."

"Yeah right," he said. "The scientist's daughter just happens to get lucky?"

"My mom *died*," I said. "You really think if they knew how to cure the virus they wouldn't help everyone?"

He hesitated for a moment, still holding Meredith's arm. His grip had loosened enough that she didn't seem to be in any pain. But she was too far away—if I made a move he'd see me coming and hurt her before I got to him.

He wouldn't expect anything from a kid, though. If Meredith could get away from him, we could run for the door.

Making sure she was watching me, I rubbed my eyes, trying to be obvious without looking unnatural. She kept staring at me, her own eyes shiny with fear.

"So when's the government going to do more than fly by?"

Quentin asked, swaying his weight from foot to foot. "When are they going to get us out of here?"

"I don't know," I said. "They're waiting until the island is safe, and no one knows when that'll be."

"So they're really just leaving us here until we die, then," he said.

He glanced toward the window, scowling. I didn't know if I'd get another chance. I spread my pointer and middle fingers into a V and mimed poking them at my eyes.

That time Meredith got it. She looked from me to Quentin, who turned back toward me when she moved.

"They can't leave us here forever," I said, repeating the words that might as well have been my mantra the last few days. "We just don't know how long it's going to take." I held Meredith's gaze and nodded as subtly as I could. She bit her lip.

"They better fucking come," Quentin said, his voice rising. "I've got a buddy who's sick, and he's already—"

Meredith twisted around and jabbed her fingers into his eyes.

The rest was a blur. Quentin swore and let go of her to clutch at his face. I pointed to the door, already running. Meredith darted out ahead of me. I stopped for just a second to slam my foot into Quentin's shin as hard as I could, hoping that would slow him down if he came after us.

Out on the sidewalk, I realized I didn't know where we should go. Gav still wasn't back with the car. I grasped Meredith's hand and tugged her along in the direction of the gas station. Behind us, Quentin shoved open the toy shop door, muttering.

And then the rumble of an engine sounded from around the corner.

I think at first Gav only saw us, looking terrified. He stopped the car in the middle of the road and leaped out. Then he spotted Quentin.

They scrutinized each other, about twenty feet apart, Quentin favoring the leg I'd kicked, his eyes red and watering. Gav's jaw had tensed, his hands clenched at his sides. He took a step forward.

Quentin wavered, then turned and ran. If he'd had a tail, you could tell it would have been tucked between his legs.

My knees wobbled, and I sat down hard on the edge of the side-walk. My chest ached as if I'd just run a marathon, even though we'd hardly come half a block from the store. Meredith clutched at me. The taffeta of her princess dress rasped when I put my arm around her.

"Are you okay?" Gav said. "Both of you?" He moved toward us, and then stared after Quentin, his hands opening and closing like he didn't know what to do with them.

"Yeah," I said. "I am, anyway. How's your arm, Meredith?"

"It hurts a little," she said.

"Good thing you hurt him a lot, then," I told her. "You were amazing."

"Yeah?" she said, pulling back enough to meet my eyes.

"For sure," I said, and she smiled a little. I dragged in a breath. I didn't want our day out to end on such an awful note.

"Okay," I said. "We defeated the evil villain. Now you need to collect your reward. How about those five toys I said you could get?"

"I can still take them?" she said.

"Of course," I said. "And why don't you pick out the ones for the kids who've been all by themselves too? I know you can find the best ones."

"Okay," she said. I gave her a nudge toward the store, and she went. As soon as she was safely inside, I let my head drop into my hands. The breeze teased through my hair. Right then the chill felt kind of nice.

Gav sat down beside me. I spoke up before he could start.

"If you try to tell me this is all your fault for leaving us on our own for two seconds," I said, looking at him sideways, "I will kick you just as hard as I kicked Quentin."

He closed his mouth and cocked his head, as if considering his options.

"Where exactly did you kick him?" he asked.

"Shin," I said. "Like you showed me."

"Hmmm," he said. "Can I say that I wish I could have broken his shin into a thousand little pieces? And the rest of him too, actually?"

"Yeah," I said, and raised my head. "I guess that's acceptable."

At the same moment, we both cracked up. I don't know if we were releasing the tension or leftover panicky hysteria or what. But it felt good to laugh, even if there wasn't anything all that funny.

Then Gav leaned over, brushing his fingers across the side of my face, and kissed me.

It wasn't a long kiss. I hardly had time to react. He was somehow determined but gentle at the same time, the taste of the tea we'd been drinking at Tessa's still on his lips, his hand lingering against my cheek.

My heart started to thump in a totally different way. I didn't want him to stop.

But he did. His hand slid from my face to the back of my shoulders, and he hugged me tightly. I leaned my head against his neck. That close to him, I didn't feel the chill of the air at all.

"You're always threatening me with violence," he said, his breath warm against my ear. "What's that all about?"

"You're the one teaching me how to hit people," I pointed out.

"You're saying I'm a bad influence, then?" he asked. I could feel his grin.

"Oh, definitely," I said.

Meredith called my name from inside the store, and I shifted upright.

"Guess we'd better start loading the car," Gav said.

Meredith wanted to keep the princess dress, and she'd found a beading set and a fabric paint kit that she refused to let out of her sight. We picked out some stuffed animals and puzzles for the other kids, and I took a couple of games in case we get bored some evening at Tessa's and we've already watched all the DVDs ten times. In the end we filled the whole trunk.

After we'd stopped at the church, Gav drove us back to Tessa's. Meredith went running in right away to start on her beading.

Gav got out of the car with me. I hadn't been sure if what happened before had been some sort of momentary shock-related thing. It wasn't. He kissed me standing in front of the car, and I kissed him back. And I felt happy. Elated. Like I haven't in I don't know how long.

I can't help smiling even now, writing about it.

Is it weird that I feel kind of guilty about being happy, Leo? I mean, you have Tessa, and it was never like that with us, even if I wanted it to be. We haven't even been friends in so long. I needed this.

And now I'll have one less reason to be nervous when I finally see you again.

NOV 21

No food run today, so I spent the morning helping out at the hospital. The halls are starting to look less crowded. I'd like to assume that's because the people still out there in town are being smart and keeping themselves safe—not because there just aren't many of us left to get sick in the first place.

I was bringing breakfast around to the patients at what everyone's calling "Stage Two": low inhibitions and high social drive. It's not so bad. One of the nurses unlocks the door for me, and I wheel in the cart with whatever they're eating that morning, and the patients immediately gather around me, gabbing away and taking food if they're hungry. They're always excited to see me, like I'm the special entertainment at their party. And since they're keeping each other company, they don't cling too much when I need to leave. I just have to stop myself from thinking about what'll happen to them in the next few days.

Today I was a little spaced out. My mind was on yesterday, and Gav, and wondering what exactly is happening with us and if I was going to see him today and if I did would there be more kissing. I didn't even see Shauna in the room until someone tugged at my elbow. I turned around, and there she was.

Her nose and one side of her forehead, which she kept scratching, were red, and her lips were chapped, but somehow her hair still had that sleek wave to it, and she stood there in her hospital gown like she was wearing the newest fashion trend. Too much natural poise for any virus to knock her down. For a second, as I blinked, I felt as if we'd warped back to the school cafeteria two and a half months ago.

"Oh my god!" she said. "Kaelyn, what are you doing here? Are you volunteering or something? It's so cool to see you! You let your bangs grow out—they look kind of nice like that. How is everyone? I haven't seen anyone from school in forever!"

Before I got over my surprise, this elderly man drifted past us, running his hand over Shauna's hair like she was a pet. I remembered him from a couple days ago, when he'd spent half an hour telling me disjointed stories about his coast guard years.

"This young lady got better!" he said, pointing at me. "She's an inspiration! We're all going to be fine. Lovely to see you, lovely to see you."

Shauna gaped at me. "You were sick and now you're okay?" she said. "For real?"

Nell warned me not to talk about the virus once people get to this point, because you never know what kind of reaction they'll have. Most of them seem to forget they've got anything more than a cold, if you don't remind them. But I didn't see why I should lie when she'd asked me directly. Mostly I was wondering how the old guy had known. Must have overheard one of the hospital staff mentioning it.

"Yeah," I said, and then, trying to sound optimistic, "and other people have recovered too."

"What the hell!" she said. I'd forgotten how bright she can keep her voice even when she's completely pissed off. "*You* beat it? What's so special about you?"

I opened my mouth, but nothing came out. What could I say? That I wasn't special, just lucky? I didn't think that would make her happier.

Shauna kept going, her eyes narrowing. "You think you're so great because you lived in Toronto for five years," she said as I took a step back. "But you're a loser. You hardly talk to people. You spend all your time with your nose in your books or staring at squirrels in the park. Why should you get to be okay?"

The words hit me as if she'd pushed me. My skin went hot, and my jaw tightened with an anger I hadn't known I had in me. *Why shouldn't I?* I wanted to shout back.

The other patients in the room had noticed Shauna's agitation, and they clustered around us, murmuring to her in soothing voices, patting her back. I swallowed and reached for the door. She was sick, she couldn't help it. I should leave and let everyone settle down, and I'd come back and get the cart later.

"Yeah!" Shauna called after me. "Run away! Why should you be here? Mom, Dad, Abby—they should have made it!"

She was still yelling when I shut the door behind me. The nurse looked at me oddly, and all I could do was shake my head. I walked away, and kept walking all the way to the records room. It's quiet in there.

I crouched on the floor and wrapped my arms around my knees. A shiver ran through me. Part of me was rattled, hearing Shauna's voice echo in my head. Wondering if maybe she was right, if I did somehow steal a chance from someone else, from Shauna's parents or her sister, from all those doctors and nurses who've died. From Mom.

But part of me was still pissed off. And as I sat there, the pissed-off part ate away the rest.

What does it matter who I was before all this? What does it matter if Shauna was at the top of the social food chain and I was at the bottom? I survived. That is a fact. I am here and they are not, and I'm doing everything I can to make that count for something.

Which is a lot more than Shauna could ever say.

I stayed in the records room for about ten minutes, until I felt calm again. Then I went back and got the cart without even acknowledging her. When I came out, the nurse touched my arm and asked if I was okay.

"Yeah," I said. "I'm fine."

And you know what? I really am.

NOV 22

I was all jittery before I saw Gav today. Maybe I shouldn't be nervous—I mean, he's the one who kissed me—but I don't exactly have a lot of experience with guys. I don't want to assume we're a "couple" and come off all clingy. Maybe he's been with lots of girls; maybe a little kissing is no big deal to him.

But most of my jitters went away when I got out of the car at the hospital and he smiled at me from across the road. After we did the food run, it seemed totally natural to say, "Lunch at Tessa's again?"

Gav left his car at the hospital, and I drove. When I parked outside the house, I hesitated, knowing this was probably the last moment we'd be alone for a while.

"Hey," he said, turning toward me in the passenger seat. "Everything all right?"

I keep noticing new things when he's that close, like the few faint freckles under his tan, left over from the summer, or the way he only dimples on one side when he smiles. I like it, all of it.

"Everything's good," I said. Then it was like a gravitational pull took over. Without thinking I leaned toward him and he leaned toward me, and we were kissing again.

I felt like I'd been waiting for that all morning. This warm sort of tingling spread from my head to my toes, and my heart started beating so fast that after a couple of minutes I had to pull back and just breathe for a second. Gav traced his fingers down the side of my face and kissed my forehead.

We finally got out, because before much longer Tessa or Meredith was going to come to the window to check for me. Gav brought in one of the leftover bags of food from our rounds. I stood with him in the kitchen, and he taught me some of his cooking secrets while he worked. Maybe I can start making our meals without him a little more appetizing.

The warm tingly feeling stayed with me after he left. Tessa and I went out to scavenge some more, and even the sight of all those empty houses couldn't shake it. My good mood must have shown, because as we were driving back to her house, Tessa glanced over at me with the corner of her lips curled up, and said, "How long has this thing with Gav been happening?"

My face warmed. "Couple days," I said.

"He seems like a good guy," she said. "He cooks for you. And he cooks well. Definitely encourage that."

"Believe me, I will," I said, and we grinned at each other.

That's the first time I've felt like Tessa and I are really friends, not just acquaintances thrown together for convenience's sake. It was nice.

But the situation we're in, I guess it's impossible to keep feeling good forever. Before too long you have to face the bad parts again.

Nothing happened. I was just helping Meredith with her hair after dinner. The water's not any more safe for washing than for drinking—bacteria that gets in your eyes or nose can be more dangerous than anything you swallow—so cleaning up's gotten kind of awkward. Tessa's set a bucket of boiled water in the kitchen with a bar of soap that we use for our hands and faces. And every evening I've filled up the biggest pot, taken it into the bathroom for an all-over wash, and then filled it up again for Meredith.

We leave our hair for last, and then dunk it in. Mine's not too bad—it's shoulder length now, but if I use just a little shampoo, I'm done in a few minutes. Makes me glad I never gave in when Mom would comment about how pretty my hair would be if I let it grow out for once.

Meredith's isn't much longer, but hers is so much thicker, it's harder to work the shampoo in, and harder to rinse. So she works at the front parts while I work at the back, which makes the process go faster.

She'd just straightened up from the last rinse when she said, "Kaelyn, what was it like when you were sick?"

"The first part was like a bad cold," I said. "And having a bunch of mosquito bites at the same time. After that, I don't really remember. The virus stops you from thinking properly."

She sat still while I rubbed the towel over her head.

"Were you scared?" she said quietly.

I balked at answering, but what was the point in lying? "Yeah," I said. "I didn't know what would happen."

Suddenly I felt cold all over. Wondering why she was asking. "Are you feeling okay?" I said.

"I think so," she said. "Sometimes I get a little itch, but then it goes away. Does that mean I'm getting sick?"

I was so relieved, I hugged her until the dampness of the towel seeped through my pajama top. "Definitely not," I said. "Little itches that go away are normal. You don't need to worry, Mere. I'm not going to let that virus get anywhere near you."

She nodded, but her eyes still looked worried.

I'm doing everything I can to keep her safe, but I never feel like it's enough. Sometimes I wonder where the breaking point is. When she'll have gone through so much that, even after the epidemic is over, she won't ever be herself again.

Please, let us never have to find out.

NOV 23

I woke up this morning to the smell of smoke.

At first it didn't seem so strange, in that hazy time while I was still half asleep. Sometimes people burn leaves in the fall. There are those families who build campfires in their backyards and let their kids roast marshmallows now and then. But gradually I noticed that it smelled like wood, not leaves, and who would be roasting marshmallows at six in the morning when a killer virus is on the loose?

My mouth went dry, and I pushed myself out of bed. The ferrets were pressing their noses up to the bars of their cage, their backs hunched. The burning smell got stronger as I went into the hall.

From the front door, I could see smoke billowing up over the roofs south of us, darker than the cloud-filled sky. The tang filled my mouth. I went back inside and woke up Tessa so she could watch out for herself and Meredith. Then I drove to the hospital, hoping someone there would know what was going on. Everything's so damp, I didn't figure a fire could spread far, but I wouldn't have expected one to start in the first place.

I was almost there when the siren went off, the one they use to call the volunteer fire department. A short, choked sort of laugh jerked out of me before I could catch it. Because, really, who's left to answer?

In the hospital, Dad was on the phone at the reception desk. A nurse stood in a corner at the other side of the room, taking blood from a cluster of people. I sat down on one of the chairs and tried to relax, but my fingers kept curling into my palms.

As soon as Dad hung up, he came over. He didn't even ask why I was there.

"No one's sure what's happened yet," he said. "A group went out to take a look."

"Do you think the fire was set on purpose?" I asked, wondering if someone had lit it in the middle of a hallucination.

"Too early to say," he said. He put his arm around my shoulders and squeezed, but then he had to get back to work.

I figured since I was already there I might as well help out. I spent the next few hours with Mrs. Hansen, running sheets and gowns through the laundry, and then preparing pot after pot of Cream of Wheat for the patients' breakfasts. We were just ladling out the last few bowls when Gav walked into the kitchen, bringing the smell of smoke with him.

"It's out," he said. "Finally."

"I didn't know you'd gone to help," I said. Even though he was obviously safe, a little jolt of panic shot through me. I wanted to hug him, to feel for sure he was okay, but Mrs. Hansen was right there watching us.

She gave me a knowing smile and rolled the cart out of the kitchen. As soon as she was gone, I wrapped my arms around him. He leaned into me.

"I heard the siren, so I went out to see if there was anything I could do," he said. "A bunch of us showed up and tried to stop the fire. Only one guy had any training. I'm not sure if we actually helped or if it just ran out of fuel."

He turned his head away from me to cough, clearing the smoky rasp from his voice. Then he pressed his lips against my forehead. "At least no one was hurt," he added.

"It looked huge," I said.

"Six houses," he said. "All in a row. The hose wasn't doing anything to put out the fire, and we figured out why when we found a bucket that smelled like gasoline."

"Where would someone get a bucket of—" I started, and then stopped when I saw the obvious answer. My hands clenched, resting against the front of Gav's shirt. He nodded.

"After we found it, I went to check the station," he said. "The door was bashed up. They just helped themselves."

He didn't need to say who "they" were.

"But why would they want to burn down a bunch of houses?" I said.

"I don't know," Gav said. "Doesn't make any sense to me."

Maybe the gang thought it'd be fun to destroy a few buildings. These are people who'll shoot someone just for being sick, after all. But it seems to me like they're sick too—sick with fear, sick with selfishness. How can anyone do all the things they do without hating themselves for it?

NOV 26

The last couple days we've had fires in four different parts of town. All of them lit with gasoline. There hasn't been much anyone can do except make sure no one's inside the houses, and stop the flames from spreading farther.

For a little while I hoped all the smoke might get the attention of someone on the mainland, let them know we need more help. With no internet, no off-island phone service, and no luck using the radio, we might as well try smoke signals. But we haven't even gotten another helicopter.

Yesterday morning, Gav agreed to go with one of the adult volunteers down to the summer house the gang has claimed as their base of operations, to see if they'd be willing to talk.

"Why do *you* have to go?" I asked him while the other volunteer finished talking to Dad. "I think this hero complex of yours is getting out of control."

I was trying to sound teasing, but the truth is, I was scared. That guy in the truck would have shot me without blinking. I didn't exactly trust them to listen to reason.

"I've dealt with them more than anyone here," Gav pointed out.

"But we've locked the pumps," I said. "They can't have stolen that much gasoline in one go. When they run out, they'll have to stop anyway."

"And then they'll pull something else," he said.

Which is true. So I stood and watched him walk out to the car, my arms folded tight over my chest and a weight in my gut. I don't like how hard it was to see him go.

I only just got past two years of pining over you, Leo—the last thing I need is to get so wrapped up in another guy that I can't think straight. And Gav's not going to want some needy girl who'd wait by the window for him instead of having her own things to do.

So I boiled more water and brought lunches around, and tried not to look at the clock every two minutes. It was exactly one hour and fourteen minutes later that Gav got back. When I heard him coming through the doors, I stopped and let relief wash over me. Then I made myself take the cart back to the kitchen before I went to find out what they'd learned.

"We got held up a few houses down from their place," Gav told me while the other guy was filling in Dad and Nell. "A couple of them stepped out in front of the car—Lester from the ferry dock, and Vince's older sister, Andrea. She had a shotgun pointed at us. Neither of them would listen to anything we said. They just kept saying they were setting the fires 'for the good of the island.' 'We're cleaning the town up,' Lester goes. 'Bet the virus can't survive incineration!' I said people wouldn't either, and he just laughed. And then Andrea pointed her gun at us and told us we had ten seconds to leave."

So they're burning down their own town to try to take the virus with it.

I keep remembering how Quentin talked in the toy store. So angry, and desperate. I told him the government wasn't going to come with help until the island's safe and the virus is gone, and that we still didn't know a way to beat it. So now they're trying their own way.

And you know what? As long as they keep their bullets and their fires away from the people I care about, that's all right with me.

NOV 27

Today we decided to take a little break from worrying about viruses and gangs and the island falling apart. It's Mom's birthday, or it would have been, and Dad said we should make up for that lost Thanksgiving and honor her memory.

Tessa and I baked the last of the chicken breasts from her freezer, and we had a real salad with lettuce and tomatoes out of the greenhouse. Seeing Dad sitting there at her table felt so weird. It's the first meal he's eaten with us at Tessa's. But once we started eating and talking, everyone relaxed.

Dad talked about how he met Mom at university, and the day he worked up the nerve to ask her on a date, and I talked about how she taught me to ride my bike and kept cheering me on, even though she ended up more banged up than me by the end of the day. And then we got quiet, which seemed appropriate too. I wondered where Drew was right then, and whether he was thinking about Mom. Our words didn't feel like enough without him. The ache in my chest got bigger and hasn't gone away since.

After we cleaned up, Dad went off with Meredith so she could show him all the necklaces and bracelets she's made with her new beads, and Tessa and I flopped down on the couch. She glanced at the mantel over the fireplace, where a couple of photos of her with her parents—sitting on a log in a forest, squinting against the sun in front of a country landscape—are propped up. Suddenly I wanted to hug her, even though Tessa's about the least huggy person I've ever known. I miss Mom and Drew every hour, but I still have Dad. Tessa's been on her own so long.

"How do you do it?" I said.

"What?" she asked.

"You've stayed so calm and together, even though you don't have anyone," I said. "I wouldn't be able to stand it."

"I have people," she said. "I have you and Meredith."

"But you hardly knew me before the epidemic started," I said. "It's not the same."

She shrugged and said, "I know you now. I look at what I have and try not to think about what I don't. I don't know if I'd be any less worried about my mom and dad if they were here with me. I'd probably be more worried. At least, as far as we know, the virus never really spread on the mainland."

In comparison, I probably seem like an emotional wreck. I guess Tessa has her home and her greenhouse and the scavenging trips we go on, and she's narrowed down her life to those three pieces. Must be easier to stay sane that way. But I can't imagine leaving behind the work I do at the hospital or the food runs. Even when the things I see are hard to deal with, at least I know I'm helping. I don't think I'd be coping half as well without that.

I hadn't meant to mention this, ever, but it sort of fell out.

"Before," I said, tracing the pattern on the arm of the couch, "when school was still going, there was one day you came to class late and you wouldn't sit next to me."

She frowned. "Which class?" she said. "Where were you sitting?"

"It was biology," I said. "I sat at the front. Never mind. It doesn't matter."

"No," she said. "I know why. I always sit at the back. When we're doing review I like to start the homework from other classes, but most of the teachers get annoyed if they catch you. The front of the room doesn't work."

It was that simple. Sitting next to me just wouldn't have worked.

If I'd actually known Tessa back then, maybe I would have realized she hadn't meant to snub me. She doesn't waste time holding grudges or ranking people. She just wants to be able to do what she wants on her own terms.

Back then, her attitude looked like arrogance to me. But now I kind of admire it. Tessa shines, too, in her own thoughtful, steady way. She may not light up a room like Shauna does, but she wouldn't want to. Which I guess you saw a long time ago, Leo. And maybe I would have sooner if I hadn't been so busy resenting her for having you.

"Thank you," I said to her. "For letting us stay here. And everything."

For not realizing or at least overlooking the fact that a couple months ago I'd have happily stolen your boyfriend, was the part I didn't say.

I'd thought I didn't care anymore, now that Gav and I are, well, whatever we are, and now that Tessa and I are at least sort of friends. But I'm not sure I really let go until that moment. It felt like this thorn that had been digging into my side for months finally worked its way free and fell away.

I don't know what I'd have done without Tessa. She deserves you, Leo.

NOV 28

You know, for all the talk you hear about "Mother Nature" and the harmony of the natural world, the truth is, nature doesn't give a crap about anything or anyone.

Every scientist knows that. Nature doesn't have feelings or morals; it's just a bunch of random chances that sometimes work in the favor of this pack or that herd, and sometimes wipe one out. Some random chance gave this one virus the ability to infect our brains and spread itself by making its victims want other people's company. And as far as nature's concerned, whether we win or the virus does, it's all the same. There's nothing that stops and thinks about how much or how many are going to get hurt.

But every now and then I still want to have someone to grab and shake and shout at: "How could you?"

A question Nature's never going to answer.

I was at the hospital this afternoon. Tessa and I decided we shouldn't leave Meredith alone in the house for our scavenging trips, what with the gang lighting fires all over. I found a copy of *Never Cry Wolf* in the hospital library a little while back, and I've been reading chapters to the patients who are sick but not that sick yet, who get bored and depressed sitting around waiting for the virus to crawl deeper into their brains.

I was at my favorite part, where Farley Mowat chases after

a pack of wolves wearing nothing but his shoes, when I heard someone yelling. Which would have been normal in the hospital these days, except the voice was coming from the direction of the reception room, not upstairs, where they've moved the most sick patients. And it sounded familiar.

"I'll be back in a minute," I said, and went out to see what was happening.

The words got clearer as soon as I opened the door: "How long will the test take? When will you know?"

Gav was standing at the end of the hall, one hand splayed against the wall, the other clutching his mask. His face was flushed and his shoulders were shaking.

My heart didn't just sink. It plummeted.

"I need you to calm down," Nell was saying to him. "We're doing the best we can. Please put on your mask."

What does it matter? I thought. What good's the mask going to do if he's already sick?

He took a long breath and said, not quite shouting this time, "Are you going to do anything for him? Is there anything you *can* do?"

And I realized he was flushed with emotion, not fever. It wasn't him. Which meant there was only one person it could be.

"We're doing our best," Nell repeated.

"Great!" Gav said. "So I brought him here so you could just shut him in some room and leave him to die. Fuck that."

He wavered on his feet, looking like he wanted to say more but was too angry to find the words. When they didn't come, he spun around and stalked out through the reception room.

For a moment, I was paralyzed. Then my legs lurched forward and I ran after him, peeling off my protective gown as I went.

He'd already pushed past the front doors. I caught up with him on the steps outside. He didn't hesitate or glance back at the sound of my feet, so I said, "Gav, wait!"

It was like I'd hit him. He stopped and dropped down onto the steps amid the puddles left by the morning's rain, lowering his head into his hands. The coat he's been wearing is too big on him—used to be his dad's, he mentioned once—and suddenly he looked very small in it.

I sat down next to him and slid my arm around his back. It didn't seem right to talk first.

"I tried so hard to make sure he'd be okay," he said after a bit. His voice was ragged. I think he was trying not to cry.

"Warren?" I asked, even though I couldn't imagine who else he'd be this upset about.

"I convinced him he'd do the most help working with the kids in the church, because I knew they'd all been tested, so it was safe," he went on, without answering. "I made sure he wore his goddamn mask every minute of every goddamn day."

"Has he had the blood test yet?" I said.

"They're doing it now," Gav said. "But . . . I could tell. It hit him hard. He was fine the whole day, and then about an hour ago, all of a sudden he couldn't stop coughing. Or scratching his neck. I practically had to wrestle him into the car—he'd decided he was going to drive himself here, as if he even could. He was worried about *me*."

He shook his head as if that were the most ridiculous idea ever.

We sat there, not saying anything, for a few minutes. Everything inside of me felt like it'd been tied into tiny knots. Finally he raised his head and looked at me. The expression on his face made all the knots pull tighter, until I could hardly breathe. He looked beaten.

"What's the point, Kaelyn?" he said. "If nothing we do matters, if we're all just going to die anyway—what's the point of anything?"

I don't know. If even Gav can't see the point anymore . . . What if there isn't one?

But I couldn't say that. Not when he was looking at me that way. A thought started to uncurl in my head, so delicate I was afraid to touch it.

Maybe I don't need to be worried about the way I feel about him, Leo. This is different than it was with you. Maybe he needs *me*.

So I did the only thing I could think of. I kissed him. And he brushed his fingers into my hair and kissed me back, hard.

That was a good enough answer, for now. I hope I can find a better one. For both him and for me.

NOV 29

I went back to the records room last night. Wondering if there was something both Dad and I managed to miss. I pulled out the files for the six survivors, including me, and randomly grabbed another ten for comparison. As I was tugging out the last one, my eyes skimmed over the names behind it, and I saw your folder, and your mom's and dad's.

I hadn't seen your parents in my rounds. I'd hoped they'd managed to stay safe, but I didn't know. I could have asked Tessa if she'd talked to them; I could have gone by their house; I could have looked at the records earlier. Except I didn't really want to find out. As long as I didn't, it could still be good news. But yesterday, without really thinking, I set down the file I'd been holding and took out theirs.

I'm so sorry, Leo.

There's a reason I haven't seen them since I started volunteering. Your mom came in with the early symptoms a week after the quarantine was announced. Your dad followed her a few days later. They were both dead before I even got sick.

There's a folder for just about every person on the island in that room. Staring at them, I realized I could see how many of our neighbors the virus took, how many of our teachers didn't make

247

it, how many kids from school came to the hospital before Shauna and never left.

I don't know why, but the enormity of it hit me in that moment in a way it hadn't before. Five seconds later I was across the hall in the bathroom, crouched on the floor, trying to keep my dinner down. Even when my stomach finally stopped churning, the back of my mouth tasted like acid.

The quarry must be overflowing with bodies. So many people. People we spent most of our lives with. It has to stop.

When I could stand, I went back to the records room, shut the file drawer, and made myself get to work.

Organizing the information would be a lot easier on a computer. Drew could have made up a program like he did for those phone calls I was making...was that really less than two months ago?

If Drew were here.

But if the electricity goes, like almost everything else has, I'd lose all of it. So I started making charts on a pad of graph paper I found on the supply shelf, comparing numbers and dates and medications. How long it took each person to reach each stage. How much of which drugs at what time of day. Looking for any sort of pattern. The answer could be something so small, no one would see it unless they studied every little factor with incredible scrutiny.

There's so much data. So many factors. I filled six sheets of paper in three hours, and none of the information ended up looking remotely meaningful. Then Nell found me.

"What are you still doing here, Kaelyn?" she asked. "It's almost midnight."

I stared up at her, kind of dazed. My brain was swimming with medical notations it hardly understands.

When I didn't answer, her eyes went soft, but her voice got more firm.

"All right," she said. "Come on. I'm ordering you, as a doctor, to go home and get some rest."

As if sitting here in the same room as Meredith, knowing there'd be nothing I could do if she woke up and started sneezing right now, is going to make me feel any better.

I'm going back today. And tomorrow and the next day until I've accounted for every tiny detail. There has to be a connection. I'm not stopping until I find it.

NOV 30

It's rained at least part of every day since Mom's birthday. The cold driving rain that always comes at the end of the fall. Not pleasant, but we're taking a car everywhere we go anyway, so I haven't had much chance to be bothered by the weather.

The good thing is, rain and fire don't mix well, and Quentin's friends obviously know that. As far as we can tell, they haven't tried to light up any more houses. Maybe they're just saving the gasoline they stole for when they can do the most damage. Or maybe they'll finally get a clue and realize burning down a few buildings here and there isn't going to solve our problems. Unless they do us a favor and burn themselves up too.

Since the fires had stopped as long as it was raining, I figured it was safe to leave Meredith on her own for a little while—as safe as it ever is. So Tessa and I set off for a quick scavenging trip this afternoon.

We went through a bunch of houses not far from Main Street, but half of them looked like the gang had already gotten to them. They've mostly focused on food and electronics, though, so at least we sometimes found pills and creams in the medicine cabinets.

When we came to the third place with a vacant TV stand, Tessa shook her head.

"I don't know why they think a bunch of televisions and DVD players are going to keep them alive," she said.

"Maybe they're planning on taking everything over to the mainland and trying to sell it," I said. "When they figure out how to do that without getting shot."

Then I remembered seeing the garden shop the other day, so we swung by there. Tessa looked at the shelves for a few minutes, picking up packets and cartons and then putting them back, frowning.

"I used to come here almost every week," she said. "The woman who owns this place would special-order things for me. She loves this store."

"Chances are those guys will come back eventually and grab anything you don't take," I pointed out. "Or burn the place down."

Chances also are the owner's already dead.

"You're right," Tessa said. "And I can always bring back what I haven't used and pay for what I did when she opens up again."

She took all the seeds and bulbs and as many bags of fertilizer as she could fit in the car, and a bunch of pots and planting trays. After she closed the trunk, she paused for a moment under the awning.

"You okay?" I asked.

"Yeah," she said, and laughed lightly. "I was just thinking—Leo used to come here with me, help load the car. I'd be talking the whole time about all my plans, and he'd nod and grin so you couldn't tell he didn't have any idea what I was going on about most of the time. He wasn't into gardening or farming or any of that. But he would be, right then, because of me. That's the way he was."

She lowered her eyes and turned her head away. I hadn't realized before how much she misses you. An uncomfortable mix of my own missing, and guilt—for the times I thought she couldn't have cared about you enough—swelled in my chest.

"He's a great guy," I said.

"Yeah," she said. "The best." And slid into the car. That was it, subject closed.

"Is Gav all right?" she asked on the way to the hospital. "He hasn't come by in a while."

"He's okay," I said. "He's just—his best friend got sick. He's been spending most of his time keeping him company."

Even though it hurts talking about Warren, knowing how worried Gav is about him, and even though I had an extra twinge of guilt realizing how hard it must be for Tessa to see us together when her boyfriend's hundreds of miles away, I still got that warm, tingly feeling thinking about him. I floated in it, wondering how I could possibly be so happy about something when so much else is going wrong, the whole way back to Tessa's house.

She parked the car in the driveway. Everything looked normal. Then the upstairs window jerked open and Meredith's voice brought me back to earth.

"Kaelyn!" she called down. She gasped a couple times, that breathless gulping sound people make when they've been crying and are trying to calm down. "Be careful!" she said. "I think they all went away, but I don't know."

My heart stopped.

"Who?" I said. "What happened?" But she'd started sobbing and couldn't answer.

Tessa walked to the door and yanked it open. The knob fell off in her hand. Inside, the floor was caked with muddy footprints, and I could see that all of the cabinet doors in the kitchen had been flung open. Tessa hurried in that direction. I dashed up the stairs.

The door to the master bedroom was closed and locked. I knocked on it.

"Meredith," I said, "you can come out. Whoever it was, they're gone now. Are you okay?"

She sniffled, and the lock clicked. The second she opened the door, I knelt down and pulled her into my arms. She buried her face in my shoulder.

"It was that guy, the angry one who came into the toy store," she said. "And a bunch of other people too, but I didn't know them. He grabbed me and told me to show them where we kept the stuff you and Tessa have been taking from the houses. I said that you gave it to the hospital, and he got really mad. But then they started going through the kitchen, and he wasn't paying attention, and I got away from him and ran up here. That was good, right?"

"Really good," I said. I was so angry, my voice shook. If I'd had a gun, and Quentin had stepped in front of me right then, I think I could have blasted him away without hesitating.

I eased Meredith back and looked her over. Her wrists were already starting to bruise, a purplish pattern of fingers against the dark brown of her skin. I hugged her again and kissed the top of her head.

Then a thin wail split the air, so pained it made the hairs on my arms rise.

My first thought was that I'd been wrong, someone was still here, and they were hurting Tessa. "Stay here," I told Meredith. "Keep the door locked until I come back." She nodded solemnly, and I crept to the stairs, peering over the banister.

I hoped I'd have more of a chance if I took our enemy by surprise, but I didn't see anyone, just the ransacked kitchen and, as I edged into the hall, the back door swinging open in the wind.

When I reached it, Tessa was standing on the patio just outside, her pale hands clasped in front of her. The rain was soaking her clothes and hair.

She must have been the one who'd made that sound, but she was totally silent then. Just staring at the greenhouse. Seeing it, I jerked to a halt behind her.

They'd smashed the entire front wall, and part of the south side too. Wet glass glinted on the patio stones. Boot tracks crisscrossed the garden areas, leaves and stems trampled in their wake. There were dips and pits in the dirt where plants—I guess the ones that were clearly edible—had been uprooted and taken, and others stood at half-mast, their upper parts torn off.

The rain started to trickle down my neck, under the collar of my jacket. I shivered, but I didn't want to move until Tessa did. I was waiting for her to spring into action, to start picking up the pieces and fitting them back together into the best shape she could make; to tell me that while what happened was really awful, it could have been worse. It can always be worse.

Instead, she turned around and looked at me, her eyelashes dark and wet.

"They knew when we'd be out," she said. "They were watching us."

"Meredith said they were looking for the food we've been taking from the houses," I said. "I guess they must have seen us. . . ."

I stopped. Because I knew how they'd happened to see us. They'd seen us because they'd known I'd survived the virus, and

Quentin had been convinced I knew something about the cure, and so they'd been watching *me*. Possibly ever since that first guy aimed his shotgun at me. How else could Quentin have known where I'd be the day we went to the toy shop?

And since that day he must have been waiting to take his revenge for the way I embarrassed him. The gang didn't need the little bit of food we'd been gathering on our own. They had tons.

Tessa had heard the story of the toy shop from Meredith. She'd obviously drawn the same conclusions I had, just faster.

"It was because of you," she said. Simply, stating a fact. Then she brushed past me and walked inside. As I hurried after her, her bedroom door thumped shut. She hasn't come out since.

If she hadn't invited me into her house, this never would have happened.

I don't know what to do. How can I make up to her something so enormous I can't imagine where to begin?

DEC 1

First snowstorm of the winter. Not even really snow—sleet. Gray, slushy rain pattering against the windows since early this morning.

Meredith and I were watching *The Little Mermaid* after dinner for the eighth time when the lights and the TV flickered and died.

I don't know whether the outage is temporary or permanent. Hopefully temporary. No electricity means no fridge, no oven, no microwave. Maybe no heat too.

Gav called a little while after the power went. I could tell he was at the hospital because of the jumble of voices in the background.

"The entire hospital went black while I was hanging with Warren," he said. "They only just got the generator going. I heard the whole town's gone out. Are you okay?"

I'd had to grope through the dark for the phone. Meredith was still curled up on the couch, breathing shakily. I crouched down by the wall and closed my eyes. "Yeah," I said. "Tessa's looking for the candles her parents kept for emergencies. It's kind of spooky, but we'll live."

"I'll come over," he said. "Just got to say bye to Warren."

I wanted to see him. Wanted it so badly, my stomach ached that he wasn't already here. I've hung out with him and Warren at the hospital a bit, but I feel uncomfortable intruding on their friendship, so I haven't seen him much the last few days. But as I opened my mouth, the window beside me rattled with the wind and the sleet, and I could see in my mind the long slippery roads through the pitch black between him and me. The image of the shattered glass from the greenhouse rose up behind my eyelids, shifting into the Ford's smashed windshield, and before I even knew I was going to, I heard myself saying, "No. Stay there."

"They don't need me," Gav said. "They'll be doing lights-out for the patients in a half hour anyway. I'll just—"

"Gav," I said, trying to sound firm, even though the ache in my stomach had turned into a heavy lump. "Don't. I don't want you to come. We'll be fine."

There was a pause, and a sharp intake of breath, and he said, "Okay. Sure. Fine," like it wasn't fine at all. "I'll see you later, then," he added, and suddenly I was saying, "Bye," even though I'd meant to explain.

"Kaelyn?" Meredith said, as the dial tone droned into my ear. By the time I made it back to her on the couch, Tessa had come in with the candles, and we went to our rooms.

Meredith finally dozed off a few minutes ago. The ferrets are perched on the upper platform of the cage, heads bobbing as they follow the flickering of the candlelight. I probably shouldn't be wasting it on writing here. The box Tessa found only had a few left.

Besides, it feels kind of fitting right now, to be adrift in the dark.

DEC 3

So I'm here in Uncle Emmett's living room again, where we sat a million years ago while Dad talked about a virus that had killed one person, that *might* be a risk. It feels so strange to be back.

I took a nap on the couch this afternoon, and when I woke up and heard someone moving in the kitchen, for a second I thought it was Mom.

"You don't need to go to so much trouble, Grace," Uncle Emmett used to say, and Mom would answer, "I want to know you're having a decent meal at least once in a while," and then he'd mutter something to himself and plop down in the armchair to watch TV. It used to drive me crazy how he'd complain about her making dinner, but never offer to help.

I'd give my right arm to have them here, griping at each other again.

We moved in yesterday morning—Meredith, Tessa, the ferrets, and I—because the electricity seems to be gone for good, and unlike Tessa's house and mine, Uncle Emmett's has a generator. Dad helped me fix the front door, and between our car and Tessa's, we were able to move everything important in one trip. The gang took the computer and the TV when they came through, but those would have been luxuries we'd hesitate to use anyway. We don't want to risk overloading the generator. We have the stove for boiling water and cooking, and we've got light if we have to use it. Which is all we really need these days.

I'm not sure what everyone else in town is doing. The hospital's fine, of course—it's got the biggest generator on the island. And some other houses have private generators, so people can get by. Dad said there are a few empty places like that near the hospital for anyone who needs shelter. The church has one too, so the kids should be okay.

Meredith and I are sharing her old bedroom. It's a little cramped, but I brought the binoculars, and I've started watching the mainland from her window whenever I have a free moment, even though all I've seen so far are faint lights through the fog rising off the strait. Since we're the hosts now, I figured I should offer Tessa the master bedroom.

I don't know what she's feeling—but then, I've always had trouble telling. She went out to the backyard before we left her house, and came back in with nothing. I guess there wasn't much she could salvage. There's a stiffness in the way she moves, the way she talks now, that I don't remember from before. Like she was broken and the parts didn't fit together quite as well when she got put back together.

So I've been doing all the cooking, such as it is, and I let her decide when she feels like talking to me. Small offerings. If I could think of something better, I'd do it.

I didn't hear from Gav all yesterday. This morning as I was putting away the breakfast dishes, there was a light knock on the door. When I opened it, he was standing on the front step with his shoulders slightly hunched and his hair rumpled, looking just as wary as he did the first day he came to my house. For a second it felt as if nothing that'd happened since then was real.

"Hey," he said, and I said "Hey" back, and then I reached toward him instinctively. He caught my hand and stepped inside, interlacing his fingers with mine. He held my gaze as if he was searching for something. After a moment he leaned in to kiss me. And I was pretty sure that it had been real after all.

I slid my other arm around his waist, and he eased back slightly. "I'm sorry I didn't come sooner," he said. "I went by Tessa's yesterday afternoon, and you were gone. I wasn't sure where to look."

"It's okay," I said. It didn't seem worth mentioning our awkward conversation on the phone the night the power went out. "I figured if you didn't find us before then, I'd see you at the hospital when I went in today. How's Warren?"

Gav shrugged, but his jaw tensed. "As comfortable as they can make him," he said. "They give him a little aspirin for the fever, and tea and mint candies to help his throat, but I guess that's about all they can do anymore."

"It's not their fault," I said. I suspect Dad would swim across the strait during a snowstorm if he thought they'd give him the medications we need when he got to the other side.

"I know," Gav said. "And it's not like any of the specialized drugs made a difference before. Maybe the real cure's been mint all along." He tried to smile, but his mouth wavered.

"I think it's been hard for him," he added. "His dad took his little sister to stay with their grandparents in Dartmouth and didn't make it back before the quarantine. And his mom's afraid to go in the hospital. He's had to make do with mostly just me for company."

"You think he'd like me to come by again?" I said. "I'm happy to visit more—I just wasn't sure how he'd feel, since he doesn't know me that well."

"I think he'd like that a lot," Gav said, and really smiled. "I was going to head over there after I'd seen you—why don't you come too?"

So I did.

They have Warren in one of the smaller rooms that used to be an exam room when the hospital was operating normally. An elderly woman was lying on the exam table, having a sneezing fit as we walked in, and a boy who was maybe ten sat against the wall and kept pausing his handheld video game to scratch the top of his left foot. Warren was sprawled on a folded blanket on the floor, his back propped up against a pillow, a book open on his knees.

"Kaelyn!" he said when he saw me, and raised his eyebrows at Gav. "Got tired of coming on your own, eh?"

Even with the mask covering his face, I could tell Gav was grimacing at him.

"I keep telling him to stay home," Warren added, to me. "If you want to catch that thing, this is the place to do it. But like always, he ignores me."

"I always listen to you when you say things worth listening *to*," Gav retorted, and Warren grinned at him for a moment before he started to cough. He picked up a mug beside him and sipped his tea until the cough subsided.

I had to grope for something to say that had nothing to do with the virus, or the hospital, or anything else depressing. Finally I settled on, "What're you reading?"

"This political thriller someone left here," he said. "Not really my genre, but there aren't many alternatives."

"There's a library on the second floor," I said. "It's small—really just a closet—but they try to have a little of everything. What do you want?"

His eyes lit up. "Where would I start?" he said.

He kept up the same cheerful tone as he suggested authors and topics: "Politics is fine, as long as it's nonfiction—but not biographies, political biographies are even worse than this." That sort of thing. Like it was no big deal he was there, like he'd just caught a bug that would clear up with some rest. But the truth is, he's been sick nearly five full days, which means chances are he won't be himself by tomorrow, and I could tell he knew that just as well as I did. His hand shook whenever he picked up the mug of tea, and his eyes flickered away from us when he laughed. And any time he mentioned the hospital, or alluded to being sick, his smile got bigger.

Gav and I weren't the only ones wearing masks. I watched Warren hold up his with jokes and banter, and a sharp little pain dug into my chest.

He's scared, like anyone would be. I don't know how much of the cheerful act is to boost his own spirits, and how much is for Gav's benefit, but it's not really important. Because either way, there was nothing I could do except stand there and notice, and go upstairs to grab him a new book.

And then I come back here and write all this down, like I would have recorded the habits of coyotes and my observations of seagulls before.

Useless. So incredibly, completely useless.

DEC 5

I found it! Oh my god, Leo, I really did! The answer was there the whole time. I just never looked back far enough.

I probably would never have seen the connection if it wasn't for Howard—that survivor who takes the bodies out of the hospital.

I think he's been living there since the electrical service went out. I went into the hospital kitchen this morning to boil some water, since we were getting low again, and he was there mixing up a glass of powdered milk to pour on his shredded wheat.

I'd never seen him without his gurney. He's taller than I realized, I guess because he has to bend over to push it. And even though his hair's mostly gray, up close you can see he's not that old. Younger than Dad—in his thirties, maybe.

I said hi, and he said hello, and it was a little awkward because I don't know anything about him other than what he does for the hospital, which isn't exactly a great conversation starter. I filled up a pot and put it on the stove, and he picked up his bowl and headed out into the cafeteria. That was when I noticed the way he walked.

"You okay?" I said. "You're limping."

"Oh," he said. "That's nothing new. 'Bout a year ago, I was working with the boats, managed to drop an anchor on my foot."

I winced and said, "Ow!"

"Yeah, it smashed my toes up good," he said. "Couple of them didn't heal straight, that's why the funny walk. Had a hell of a fever afterward, too."

"A fever?" I said, and memories from our summer trip to the island last year rushed into my head. The two days right before we went back to Toronto, when I was stuck in the hospital here, feeling like I was on fire.

I'd been by the water when it happened, just like Howard. Cut my heel on a mussel shell as I was climbing onto the rocks after a swim. I'd never thought the two might be connected. Dad had said it was probably something I'd eaten.

I turned off the stove and ran out into the hall without another word. Howard must think I'm insane.

But the truth's there in the hospital records. Five of us who survived the virus, we were in the hospital between April and October of last year with a bad fever. I'm sure the other guy must have had it too—maybe it just didn't get bad enough that he needed treatment.

Having that fever protected us. Kept us alive. Which means if we can figure out how, there's got to be a way we can keep other people alive too.

Dad must have missed the connection for the same reason I did. Too focused on the virus itself, not bothering to check back beyond the start of the epidemic.

I have to talk to him. I looked all morning, but I couldn't find him. Nell said he might have gone to the research center, but the doors were locked when I checked there. I'll go back after Meredith's had lunch. The sooner he knows, the sooner we can do something.

Finally. I can't believe I found it!

DEC 6

I had to wait until this morning to write this. Last night all I wanted to do was scream. I don't think I could have held the pen without snapping it in two.

That connection, the fever, it doesn't mean anything.

No, that's not true. It means plenty. It just isn't going to help us in any way at all.

Dad didn't get back to the hospital until the evening. I was so excited I didn't even ask him where he'd been. I dragged him into the records room and pulled out the files. I couldn't talk fast enough, as if I had to explain everything as quickly as possible or he might stop listening. I had this idea that maybe, if he knew soon enough, we could save Warren. I could already see Gav's face lighting up when I told him.

After a minute, Dad put his hand on my shoulder. "Kae," he said. *"Kae."*

He must have said my name three or four times before I really heard him and forced myself to stop.

"I know," he said. "I saw it as soon as we had our first recovery."

I stared at him. I felt like I'd run smack into a wall. Like a bird that soared toward what looked like open air and crashed into a pane of glass.

"So why haven't you done anything?" I asked. "All the people who caught that fever beat the virus! Isn't there some way we can use that?"

I knew if there had been a way, Dad would already be on it. But I'd been so sure, so relieved. I couldn't let the idea go without a fight.

"At first we weren't certain there was a connection," Dad said. "Our second survivor said he didn't get sick at all last year. And by the time the third patient recovered, I'd already looked through the files. The fever isn't a sure indicator, Kaelyn. Not even close. If it was, I wouldn't have been so worried about you. But there are other people who came down with the fever last year, who caught this virus and died. From the information we have, I'd say the previous infection raises chances of survival to about forty percent."

"Forty percent is a lot better than the zero everyone else seems to have," I said. "Do you even know what caused the fever?"

"Yes," he said. "No one had identified it at the time, but the doctors kept samples, and we analyzed them again after the epidemic started. It was a virus. A virus that was an earlier form of the one we're facing now."

Right away, I understood. "That's why having the fever before made a difference," I said. "We were already a little bit immune." Then the rest of what he'd said sank in.

"If you have samples of the old virus, of the one from last summer, you could give it to people who haven't been sick yet, right?" I said. "Maybe it wouldn't help people who've already got the new virus, but anyone who hasn't, like Meredith and Gav and Tessa —they'd have a better chance."

"I wish we could, Kae," Dad said. "Maybe if we'd known in the very beginning. But with the hospital in its current state, we don't have the resources available to make sure people survive even the less potent form of the virus. Without proper medication, the fever might be fatal on its own. At the very least, it would weaken a recipient's body and make them more susceptible to the mutated form, despite the partial immunity. You and Howard and the others had a year or more to recover before your immune system had to fend off the new virus. I talked the idea over with the doctors and the Public Health Agency staff, and no matter how we look at it, the risk just doesn't balance out."

"So it's useless," I said, my shoulders sagging.

He shook his head. "It did help us in the early stages," he said. "If we hadn't been aware of the illness last year, and didn't have the samples to compare, we wouldn't have been able to isolate the new virus as soon. Or to start the blood tests and work on the vaccine."

Blood tests that just confirmed what people already knew. A vaccine that, if it worked, had never returned to the island. But that wasn't what stuck out to me.

"What do you mean, you were 'aware of' it?" I said. "Did you already know I wasn't the only one who'd had the fever—that it wasn't just food poisoning?"

"Nell asked for my professional opinion after I brought you in last year," Dad admitted. "She was concerned because the patients in the previous cases hadn't been responding quite the way she expected. I told her to monitor the situation carefully. All of the patients had recovered, but it was obvious we could be dealing with something unfamiliar, and we had no way of knowing how the disease might evolve."

I jerked away from him. "You were worried whatever caused the fever might turn into something worse," I said. "You kept asking me if I was feeling okay—you weren't sure it was totally gone. You knew something like this could happen before it even started!"

He looked at me like I'd pulled a knife on him. "It was a condition we'd never seen before," he said. "Any responsible scientist would have been concerned. But we couldn't predict the future. We did everything we could with what we knew, Kaelyn."

"No you didn't," I said. "You could have told the hospital to call in Public Health back then, and maybe they'd have found a way to deal with the virus before it got this bad. You could have said we had to stay in Toronto last spring instead of letting us move back. And then none of this would have happened, Mom and Drew would be okay, everything would have been okay!"

I was yelling by the end, and then my voice broke and I almost burst into tears. Dad said something, but I didn't want to hear it. I just left. Marched out to the car, slammed the door, and leaned my head against the steering wheel. And then the tears leaked out.

I know I wasn't being totally fair. Of course the hospital wouldn't have called in the national health agency over a dozen people with a fever. No one could have known how the disease would change. And if we'd stayed in Toronto, it wouldn't have made any difference to the virus. Rachel's dad would still have gotten sick, and Rachel, and everyone after, exactly the same, except Dad wouldn't have been here to help, and everything would have been even worse for the island.

But it would have made a difference to us. Mom would still be alive, and Drew would still be with us, and we wouldn't be living like this. I'd be able to walk across the hall right now and hear Drew's fingers clattering away on his keyboard, see Mom standing in the bathroom putting her hair up for the day. I wouldn't have to wake up every morning and remember that they're not here anymore, and feel the pain hit me all over again.

I'm not sure I can forgive him for that. Right now, I don't even want to.

DEC 7

Do you know three months ago I honestly believed that all I had to do was change how I acted, and everything in my life would be okay? That asking myself, "What would the Kaelyn I want to be do?" would solve all my problems. Remembering it now I want to laugh.

What would the new me do? I've pissed off the only friend I have left and she might not ever totally forgive me, and I don't know if my boyfriend is really my boyfriend because we aren't in a position to do normal boyfriend-girlfriend things like go on dates and have conversations that aren't about disease and starvation, and Mom is dead and Drew's missing and most of the other people on the island are dead too, and we still don't know how to cure this horrible unstoppable virus so it's going to keep killing more, and the mainland has just about abandoned us, and there's a gang going around shooting people and setting fire to houses and stealing stuff, and as of today only one of the pumps in the gas station has any fuel left, so soon we won't even be able to use our cars for protection.

On days like this, the me I am wants to curl up in the corner with my arms around my head. There's no part of me that isn't scared. There is no me that knows what to do. I'm already doing my best, and that's all I've got.

DEC 8

Gav showed up at lunchtime today with a box of macaroni, a jar of pasta sauce, and a black eye.

"What happened?" I asked as I let him in.

He headed straight into the kitchen, threw the food on the counter, and grabbed a pot. "My fault," he said. "They told me Warren started hallucinating last night. But I said I was going to see him anyway. He didn't know who I was. And whoever he thought I was, he really didn't like."

"I'm sorry," I said, which seemed totally inadequate. Gav smiled at me a little painfully before he started poking through the cupboards. I pointed him to the spice jars.

"Thanks," he said, and kissed me so quickly I hardly had time to feel it. Then he busied himself sloshing water into the pot and jerking around the knobs on the stove. Every movement said he didn't want to talk. So I left him to his cooking.

By the time the pasta was ready, he seemed calmer. He still didn't say very much, though. The four of us plowed through the meal with less than ten words between us. When we finished, Tessa said she'd take care of the dishes, and recruited Meredith as her dryer. Gav looked around and said, out of nowhere, "You can see the mainland from here, can't you?"

We went up to Meredith's room, and I handed him the

binoculars. "I've managed to spend at least a few minutes watching every day since we moved in here," I said, trying to sound hopeful. "Hard to see much, but lights go on at night, so there must be people around."

"Patrol boats are still staked out," he said.

"Yeah," I said. "I think they've moved closer to the mainland than they were before—because of the weather probably. But all week I haven't seen them budge."

For a while he just looked. Then he lowered the binoculars and set them on the window seat.

"The first time we talked," he said, "you told me the government was going to look after us. You still think they'll come through?"

"They have to do something eventually," I said. "Eventually someone's going to ask why they haven't heard from us in ages, and try to see what's happened."

"Eventually," he said. "That could be a really long time."

"I know," I said.

I stepped closer to him, hooking my hand around his elbow and gazing over the strait. Through the fog, the buildings across the water seemed to melt into the gray of the sky.

"What would you be doing if everything was normal?" I asked. "If there was no quarantine, no virus."

He paused. "Doing just enough work to scrape by in class," he said. "Picking up odd jobs in the evenings to make sure I had enough money to get out of here the second I earned that diploma. Trying to convince Warren he should come with me." He stopped, the silence more heartbreaking than anything he could have said. After a moment, he slid his arm around my waist. "Probably hoping a certain girl would come too," he added.

I smiled, but my throat had gone tight. "You think you'd have noticed me if I wasn't the girl with the inside scoop on the epidemic?"

"Sure," he said automatically. "Can't imagine missing you." He turned, pulling me closer, and leaned in to kiss me.

He said the words so easily, as if there couldn't be any doubt, but I don't know. I don't know if I would have opened up to *him* if I hadn't seen how he acted when the town was falling apart. I want to believe that we'd have ended up together no matter what, that our feelings go beyond the awful circumstances that've thrown us together, but it's not like either of us can say for sure.

But maybe that doesn't matter. Because when he was kissing me, and I was kissing him back, I didn't care. And for a few minutes I wasn't terrified of how long "eventually" might take.

DEC 10

Last night we had to go on a little trip.

Meredith woke me up after midnight, with a yelp like she'd been bitten. Nightmares. It took me a whole minute to wake her up, and then she was sobbing so hard it was another five before I figured out what she was babbling about.

She forgot one of her stuffed animals at Tessa's house when we moved. A fluffy cat she named Purr that Aunt Lillian gave to her when she was three. She couldn't stand the thought that she'd left Purr alone in the dark, that "those guys" might come back and hurt him.

"He's fine," I told her. "No one will come back—they took everything they wanted."

"He doesn't know that," she said, shaking her head. "He's really scared."

I said we'd go get him in the morning, but she wouldn't calm down, just kept insisting he needed her to come, with tears still trickling down her face. I started to get choked up too. She's lost so much already, and there I was arguing with her over something so small. Something that was one of the few things I could actually give her.

"Okay," I said. "I'll go get him. It'll just take a few minutes."

"He doesn't know you," she said. "And I don't want you to go by yourself. It's so dark."

By then, we'd woken up Tessa too. When she peeked in to see what was going on, there was more babbling and more tears, and somehow all three of us ended up piling into the car to rescue a toy cat. It seemed like the easiest solution at the time. None of us was really thinking straight.

The town was eerie in the middle of the night, with only the headlights guiding us. They didn't catch any color, just turned everything ghostly gray. And the world beyond them was pure black.

Meredith couldn't stand to be alone in the backseat, so I thought to hell with road safety, and let her sit on my lap. She curled up with her arms around me and her head tucked under my chin. As I watched Tessa drive through the darkness, it felt good to have someone to hold on to.

With the electricity cut off, we couldn't turn on the lights at Tessa's, but there was a flashlight in the car we've used when scavenging. We followed the thin beam to the guest bedroom. Purr was lying half hidden under the nightstand. Meredith snatched him up and squished him in her arms.

Good, I thought. Now we can go back to sleep. I wasn't totally sure it wasn't a dream.

We were almost at the front door when a figure swayed into our light.

I flinched back, and Meredith shrieked, and Tessa just went still. The figure stepped closer, and Quentin's face shifted into the flashlight's beam, thin and yellowed. A sour odor rolled off him

—the smell of someone who hasn't washed in a long time. He was holding something in his right hand that glinted. A carving knife.

"What are you *doing*?" I said. The light shivered. My hand was trembling.

Quentin squinted at us, then sneezed three times against the back of his hand.

"Oh," he said, his voice scratchy. "It's just you."

"You're sick," I said, nudging Meredith behind me.

"Why are you in my house?" Tessa demanded.

"They would have shot me," he said. "I wanted to talk to Kaelyn. No one was here, so I thought I'd wait. That was . . . That was a while ago." He looked at me accusingly and added, "Took you long enough."

We hadn't left any food in the house. I wondered what he'd been eating. *If* he'd been eating. Had he brought bottled water with him, or had he been drinking it from the tap, unboiled? He stepped to the side, wavering, as it occurred to me that he might be sick from more than just the virus. Maybe not even the virus at all.

"You should go to the hospital," I said.

Quentin shook his head. "No way," he said, and coughed. "Too many sick people. Who knows what I'd get?"

"You've already got something," I said. "At least they'd try to help you."

"You'll help me," he said. "Your dad knows stuff. He made you better. You can tell me what to do."

"I don't know anything!" I said. "I told you that before. I can't do anything for you."

"You have to!" he said. "I'm sick!"

He staggered toward us, reaching for me with the hand that

held the knife. In the same instant, Tessa's arm shot forward. Sparks crackled and burst between us, and Quentin cried out. He collapsed on the floor, limbs twitching, the knife spinning from his fingers. Tessa stared down at him, then at the thing she was holding, which looked like an electric shaver.

"What is that?" I asked when I found my voice. "What did you do to him?"

"Stun gun," she answered. "Or maybe it's a Taser. I'm not sure. I found it in one of the summer houses when I was going on my own. Thought it would be useful to have it on me, just in case."

She looked at Quentin again. He was trying to get up, not very successfully.

"I expected that to feel more satisfying than it did," she said. "Let's get going."

She stepped around him and headed for the door. Meredith bolted after her. Quentin was saying something, so slurred I couldn't make out the words. He pulled himself onto his hands and knees, his arms wobbling with the effort. Watching him, my stomach twisted. No matter what he'd done, how many screwed up decisions he'd made, he was still that kid I'd gone to school with since kindergarten.

"We're going to leave him here?" I said.

Tessa turned back toward me, expressionless. "Why not?" she said.

"He's *sick*," I said, but I couldn't blame her if she didn't care about his health. So I added, "If we leave him, he won't stay here. When he gets sick enough he'll go out and try to find other people, pass the virus on. If we get him to the hospital, they'll make sure he stays there."

"Don't want hospital," Quentin muttered.

"No one asked you," I said. I held Tessa's gaze for a moment. Her lips pressed flat, and then she nodded.

I put Meredith in the car first, and brought an extra mask to put on Quentin. Then we dragged him over to the backseat. Thankfully, he'd recovered enough from the shocking to stay on his feet, but he was too sick to put up much of a fight. He tried to push past us when I opened the door, and Tessa held up the stun gun.

"Get in or I zap you again," she said.

She handed it off to me when we were ready to go, since we'd taken her car and she had to drive. I kept it trained on him the whole way to the hospital. Quentin mumbled something about his rights and illegal weapons, but mostly he just slumped there, shivering and coughing. He started to protest again when we parked in front of the hospital, but one of the volunteers spotted us through the windows and came out to help.

And then we went home and fell back into our beds.

I felt like I must have dreamed it when I woke up this morning. But I was still wearing my shoes, and Meredith had Purr tucked tightly under her arm in her bed. And when I went downstairs to make breakfast, the stun gun was lying on the dining room table. Because that's what our life is now.

DEC 12

Oh fuck fuck fuck.

Meredith's hot and she's crying because the inside of her elbow won't stop itching.

She cried louder when I went to put on my coat, so I'm still here and Tessa's gone to tell Dad.

If there is a God I would punch him in the face ten times harder than I ever kicked Quentin.

When is the virus ever going to be satisfied? When does this stop?

Why can't it just leave us alone?

DEC 14

Meredith keeps apologizing to me. She coughed so hard that she threw up the tea she'd been drinking and said sorry over and over the whole time I was wiping it up. She said sorry when *I* started to cough because my throat was dry from reading the third book in a row to her. She says sorry when I need to bring her a new box of tissues, and sorry when I check her temperature and even with the Tylenol it's still four degrees higher than it should be, and sorry when she can't stop sobbing because she wants her mom and dad.

Every time she says it, I feel the horrible weight of all the things I'm not doing—I can't do. And I wish she wouldn't say it. And then I feel even worse for being bothered by this when she's the one

I feel like I'm condemning her if I write "dying."

She might not, right? There's that one guy who recovered even though he never had last year's fever. Meredith could be the second one. It's possible.

Not a single particle of me believes it'll happen. But it's possible.

Gav came back from the hospital with Tessa and Dad yesterday. He was here again this morning. He takes over reading to Meredith and making her tea when there's too much for me to do at once.

He wrapped his arms around me in the kitchen, and my eyes prickled, but I didn't cry. Crying seems like condemning her too.

He hasn't said anything, which means Warren isn't any better. Which means Warren could very well be dead. I don't have the strength to ask him.

This is what we do. We make tea and read books and watch people die.

DEC 15

Most people think the scariest thing is knowing that you're going to die. It's not. It's knowing you might have to watch every single person you've ever loved—or even liked—waste away while you just stand there.

It has to end sometime, I keep telling myself. And that's true. And some point, there'll be no one left.

And then it won't matter that I survived, because anyone who might have cared will be dead.

DEC 17

I could only manage to spend an hour with Meredith this morning before I lost it. She's in Stage Two now. Throwing her arms around me, grabbing my hands, chattering about how much fun we'll have, asking why we can't invite Tessa and Gav in to play too. Even though I know it's not absolutely safe, I've been taking off my mask when I'm in there with her, because she hates seeing me with my face covered.

I was doing a pretty good job of distracting her, I think. I let out Mowat and Fossey and had them run around with her for a while, and then we made a huge necklace out of the last of her beads, which she draped around and around my neck until the strands hung at the right length.

I've still got it on. The beads click whenever I shift my weight.

Then Meredith looked out the window, and her face suddenly went solemn. "Why doesn't Mommy come back, Kaelyn?" she asked. "Doesn't she know I miss her so much? She always told me she loved me. If she loves me, why isn't she here?"

"I'm sure she'd be here if she could," I said, and swallowed. For a second I was afraid if I tried to say anything else, all that would come out was a wail.

"I'm going to get you a snack," I managed, and got out of there. Dad put a lock on the outside of the door this morning, just like he did for Mom, and for me too, presumably. I could hear him fiddling with the tap in the kitchen downstairs—he found some filters that might at least make the water taste better, even if we still have to boil it.

I took a couple of deep breaths as I pulled off the protective gown I wear when I'm with Meredith, and looped it over the doorknob. After I'd bought myself a little more time washing my hands super-thoroughly, I decided I'd better get that snack ready before she got too restless.

Gav looked up from the living room couch as I came down the stairs. "Kaelyn," he said, "what are these for?"

He was holding a pile of rumpled papers. It took me a moment to recognize them. All those charts I'd written up and pored over in the records room. I'd shoved them into the coffee table drawer.

When I sat down next to Gav on the couch, he scooted over so our legs touched.

"I was comparing the medical charts of the people who got better and some who didn't," I said. "I wanted to figure out what made the difference."

"And you didn't find anything?" he said.

"No, I did, actually," I said. "It just wasn't anything the doctors can use."

I explained about the fever, and how it was caused by almost the same virus. "When you get sick, your body makes antibodies, right?" I said. "To fight off the disease. So I already had extra antibodies that could attack the mutated virus, at least a little bit. More than most people have."

"That's why everyone who gets better is safer than the rest of us,"

Gav said, nodding. "Because you've got the right antibodies to fight the virus off if you're exposed again. You told me about that when you insisted on being the one who drove people to the hospital."

"Yeah," I said. "Except the immunity only works as long as the virus stays the same. If it mutates again, like the flu always does . . ."

We sat for a minute contemplating that awful thought. Then Gav looked at the papers and said, "It's too bad they can't take some of the antibodies out of you and give them to someone else who needs them."

I opened my mouth, and nothing came out. My pulse was suddenly racing. I read this story, years and years ago, in a kids' book about animal contributions to science, that I hadn't remembered until he said those words. About these doctors who put some sort of virus in a horse so that its body would produce antibodies. And then they'd used those antibodies to cure people who caught the virus.

If they could do a procedure like that with a horse, I thought, why *couldn't* they do it with me?

As soon as it crossed my mind, I knew it was pointless. If I could come up with the idea, someone at the hospital would have given it a shot ages ago. Did that mean the procedure hadn't worked? They'd already stopped trying by the time I recovered? Why?

"I have to talk to my dad," I said.

Gav followed me into the kitchen. Dad was bent over the sink, peering at the fixture he'd screwed into the faucet. He'd just turned on the tap, and a stream of water that was maybe a little less brown was gushing out. Unfortunately, a bunch of tiny streams were also trickling from the space where the fixture was attached.

He frowned and turned off the water. "Your mother was always better at this sort of thing than me," he said.

"Here," Gav said. "I think I see the problem."

Dad stepped to the side to let him adjust the fixture. "Dad," I said, as he dried his hands on a dish towel, "Gav made me think of something."

I repeated our conversation about antibodies, and the story I knew about the horse. "You tried it, didn't you?" I said, and when he nodded, I asked, "What happened?"

His face fell. "There has been some success with that sort of procedure in other cases involving unfamiliar viruses," he said. "When our first recovered patient was well enough that we felt we could safely draw blood, we attempted to give some patients in the early stages a boost with a serum. It slowed down the disease's progression, but that was all."

"If you were trying to use one sample for a bunch of patients, you couldn't have given each of them very much," I said. "Did you ever try giving them a larger dose?"

"We used a reasonable amount, Kaelyn," Dad said, sounding like he was pleading with me. "And after contributing that one sample, our survivor started to feel weak and had to be readmitted to the hospital the next day. There are only six of you—maybe seven now. Not to mention—"

"Okay," I said, before he could come up with even more arguments, "I realize you can't do it for all the patients. But maybe you could get enough for one person. I'm blood type O negative; I can donate to anyone. We talked about it in school last year. So use me. I'll give you as much blood as you can safely take, for Meredith."

I held out my arm. He looked at it, and then took my hand in both of his.

"We can't," he said. "This isn't as simple as a regular blood transfusion, Kae. Meredith is already very sick. If we inject her with a large amount of what is effectively a foreign substance, she's at a far higher risk of allergic reaction. It will almost certainly raise her fever even higher. There's a possibility her body will reject the foreign cells outright. Even if it doesn't, the most likely outcome is she'll only suffer more. And we don't know how giving the blood will affect you."

I pulled my hand away from his. "So it's not that we can't," I said. "It's that you're scared to." I was so angry at him for saying no, for shutting down yet another idea, that my whole body went rigid.

"It's not about being scared," he said.

But you know what? It is. I never looked at it that way before, but Dad's scared of a lot of things. He was scared of Drew kissing boys. He was scared of Meredith getting eaten by coyotes. He was scared of us leaving the house before he even knew the virus was dangerous. He's scared of me going anywhere in town on my own now, even though I've done it more than once, and the only times I've ever gotten into trouble were when there were other people with me.

The problem is, that doesn't mean he's wrong. This is his field. He's supposed to know the best way to deal with a virus.

"Kaelyn!" Meredith called from upstairs, breaking the silence between us. "Kaelyn, where are you? Uncle Gordon?" She managed to sound petulant and panicked at the same time.

My stomach flipped. Because imagining making her even more sick didn't just scare me, it petrified me.

So I said, "I know" and "I'm sorry" to Dad. And then Gav turned on the kitchen tap and let out a little cheer.

I still can't help Meredith, but we have slightly cleaner water. Hurray.

DEC 18

Today I told Gav not to come back.

I'd just had lunch with Meredith in her room, and was coming down with the dishes, and he was rummaging in the basement to see if Uncle Emmett had anything stashed away that might be useful. I was stepping into the kitchen when he sneezed so loud you could have heard it in the backyard.

I stiffened. The plates tipped in my hands, and Meredith's plastic cup bounced on the floor. The basement stairs creaked.

"It's okay," Gav said, poking his head through the doorway. "It was just the dust. I'm fine."

He spread out his arms, as if that proved anything. But he didn't sneeze again, and he didn't cough, and he didn't look like he was fighting the urge to, either. And the basement really is dusty. His shirt was already streaked with grayish smudges.

I picked up the cup and set the dishes on the counter. I didn't even realize I was crying until everything started to go blurry.

Gav reached for me, and I said, "Stop!"

I turned toward him and took a step back at the same time, crossing my arms in front of me.

"Kaelyn," he said, moving forward.

"I said stop!" I yelled, and that time he did. He looked at me, confused.

"I was just upstairs with Meredith," I said. "I've been touching her dishes. I haven't even washed my hands yet."

And suddenly I was remembering all the times Gav has sat by me, touched me, since Meredith caught it, and I felt like throwing up. I'd been so careless. What did the protective gown and the hand-washing matter when the virus could be creeping up from my feet or through my hair? We haven't been able to wash properly in weeks. I've been re-wearing clothes that seem clean, because every time we run a load of laundry I'm afraid the generator will short out. And I was too wrapped up in this miserable situation to consider how dangerous that could be for anyone else. I was just glad to have him here. How could I have been so selfish?

I should never have let him in the house after Meredith got sick.

"You should go," I said.

"Kaelyn," he said calmly, like his life wasn't on the line, "I've been talking to sick people on the route, going in and out of the hospital, for *months*. If I was going to catch the virus, I would have already."

"You don't know that," I said. "Meredith was fine for months, and now she has it. You've been okay because you've been careful. You can't just stop and think you'll be fine. It's not safe in here. I'm not safe."

"So I've decided to take that risk," he said.

"I don't want you to," I said, my voice shaking. "I want you to go. Now."

He opened his mouth to argue some more, but something in my expression must have convinced him I wasn't changing my mind.

"Okay," he said. "I'll go. But I'm going to come back tomorrow."

"I'm not going to let you in," I said.

"Then I'll talk to you through the door until you do," he said. "That's how we started, isn't it?"

Watching him walk to the hall and put on his boots hurt, right through the center of my chest. Because he meant it. He would keep coming back. As if I'm . . . as if *anyone* is worth taking that kind of chance for.

"Gav," I started.

"I'm going, I'm going," he said, holding up his hands. "I'll see you tomorrow."

"No," I said. "When Meredith's . . . When this is finished. Not until then. And not here. Okay?"

He didn't answer me. Just gave me one last look and then went out the door.

It was the right thing to do. I knew that then. I shouldn't feel so awful now.

I hesitated for a few seconds after he left, and then locked the door. When I turned around, Tessa was watching me from the living room doorway.

"I'm not leaving," she said, in the same tone she'd used when she was threatening to zap Quentin.

I hadn't thought that far. I don't know if I would have. We've been with Tessa so long—hell, she practically gave her house to us—I can't imagine telling her to get out. Where would she go?

"I know," I said. "Of course."

Does that make me a bad friend, for wanting to protect Gav more than I'm willing to protect Tessa? Or a good one, for letting her decide for herself?

DEC 19

I told Nell I wanted to go home, so she brought me here. But this isn't home. This is a cot in a room where Meredith should be but isn't. Home is gone. There's nothing left.

She was screaming. Ten o'clock at night. I had to take her to the hospital. She tore up the Little Mermaid dress with her hands and scratched my arm, but I didn't want to call, I wanted to take care of her myself. I told Tessa not to worry, I could do it. I carried Meredith out to the car and strapped her into the backseat, and she squirmed and cried, but she didn't remember how to release the belt. So we made it there. She started screaming again when she saw the hospital, and she bit my hand trying to make me let go of her, but I got her in and I found Dad, and he gave her a shot. Just like he must have for me, and for Mom.

She has her own room. Everyone's dead now. No more need to cram bodies into every available space. She got one little bed in what was supposed to be a storage room on the second floor.

I don't usually go up there where the Stage Three patients are. The yelling's louder.

When the shot wears off, that'll be Meredith yelling too. There are only enough drugs to keep the patients calm when bringing them in. They strapped her arms and legs down to make sure she won't hurt herself, or anyone else, when the hallucinations take over.

Dad said he'd walk me to the car. I let him. I should have said I'd be fine. But it wouldn't have mattered. It wouldn't have mattered that I wanted my dad there with me for just a few more minutes if I hadn't seen something moving in the darkness from the corner of my eye. If I hadn't turned, trying to figure out what it was.

"What?" Dad said, and I said, "I thought I saw someone over there," and I even pointed, because I didn't think, I didn't think at all.

Then there was a scraping sound off around the side of the building, and Dad started jogging over to see, and I followed along, because I didn't know what was happening, and then he was running and shouting, "Stop! Stop right there!"

I should have run too. I don't know why I didn't run. I saw the woman with the gasoline can, and she spun toward Dad, and I froze. All those moves Gav taught me, and I had nothing. So there was no one close enough to stop her when Dad reached for her and she raised the can and slammed it into his head.

I screamed. Dad swayed and fell. The woman dropped the can and took off. And then, then my legs started working again.

People were rushing out of the hospital. They must have heard me. I screamed so loud, my throat's still sore. I was kneeling on the concrete walk next to Dad. Everything smelled like gasoline. The blood was seeping out through his hair so fast. I pressed my hand against it, but I couldn't stop it. I wanted to think I felt a breath, but his eyes kept staring, just staring, and he wouldn't blink.

Nell says they were trying to set the hospital on fire. There were two men with the woman. A few of the volunteers checked around the building after they saw Dad, and chased the guys off before they could do it.

Nell says they must have thought they'd get rid of the virus if they burned down the place where just about everyone who's had it ended up.

She says Dad is a hero because he stopped them.

She said, "I'm so sorry, hon."

I'm the one who should be apologizing. I'm the one with Dad's blood on my hands.

I don't know where they took him. Somewhere in the middle of everything, Nell pulled me away from him and hugged me, and then he was gone.

Everyone's gone. It's only me.

DEC 20

It's cold up here on the cliff. There's frost speckling the rocks, and the wind coming off the water numbed my nose in all of about five seconds. I wanted to breathe the ocean air one last time, but now I can't smell anything.

I wore my fingerless gloves so I could write, but my fingers are already aching, so I don't know how long this entry is going to be. I just felt like I should give some sort of explanation before I do this. To show I really have thought it through.

When I've read about people jumping off a bridge or a rooftop, it always sounds like some melodramatic fit, flinging oneself off into nothingness. But it isn't really like that. Looking at the edge of the cliff, I can picture stepping into that empty space on the other side without hesitating, without flinching. Like it's a perfectly reasonable thing to do. Like taking that step doesn't mean anything more than starting down a staircase.

You can't even say I'm out of my mind. Young gorillas will let themselves waste away when they've lost both their parents. They stop eating and playing, and eventually they get sick and die. What I'm doing here is a completely natural response.

This way is just more efficient.

I'm not one of those people who shine, whose light is going to be missed the minute I'm gone. I never have been. Dad looked after the hospital, and Gav organized food for the whole town, and Tessa is going to create better crops for the entire world. What the hell have I done?

The only thing I'm good at is watching. Birds on the beach, coyotes in the forest, all those people dying.

But I tried. I tried to go out and help, and look where it got us. I put ideas into Quentin's head, I led him back to Tessa and Meredith. I arranged for Gav's group to start bringing sick people to the hospital, and now his best friend's dead. I didn't take enough precautions and caught the virus and made Drew feel he had to run off in some crazy plan that's probably gotten him killed. Maybe I even brought it home to Mom. It had to be someone.

And then I just watched—as Mom died, as Meredith got sicker. I stood by and let some woman bash Dad's head in.

There's nothing left. I can't do anything but hurt. I want it to stop.

Gav will be all right. It'll be better for him—one less person he'll feel he has to risk his life for. And Tessa takes care of herself just fine. I feel a little guilty about Meredith, but she won't even know I'm gone. If I stayed, it'd only go one of two ways. I'd ignore everything Dad said and convince Nell to try the antibodies treatment one more time, and Meredith's last days would be agony. Or I'd sit and watch her fade, never knowing if there was something I could have done that I missed.

So I'm putting things right. I should never have been one of the ones who survived. Maybe there is some kind of higher power that will see this, that will let me pass my luck on to Meredith. She deserves it.

Trading my life for hers—seems fair, doesn't it?

Damn it's cold. I can hardly feel the pen.

My heart's already pounding. My body knows what it's going to do. It's just four steps from here to the edge. I'll put the journal down, and it'll be over in less than a minute. I won't look down. I won't even cry.

Here I go.

I'm still here, Leo. I came back.

I feel like I should thank someone, like I've been given a gift, even though the decision was mine the whole time.

I should thank the cormorants.

I went right up to the edge. And then I couldn't help looking down. All that choppy red-brown rock dropping away into the waves. All those clumps of sticks and seaweed nestled on the tiny ledges. Hard to believe anything can perch there, let alone raise a family. The wind was tearing at my hair, wrestling with my coat, ripping twigs and bits of sea grass from the nests.

And I thought, how long must it have taken? How many failed attempts before the first cormorant figured out just the right way to arrange those sticks so the wind didn't blow them away? How many eggs slipped out and cracked open on the rocks, or tumbled down into the surf?

They could have gone somewhere else, somewhere that looked easier. But the easier places have predators hungry for bird meat and eggs, other birds competing for space and food, all sorts of dangers. So really not easy at all.

If they were going to survive, they had to make life work here. But they didn't just know how. They made mistakes. They must have.

They made nests that fell apart. They lost eggs. And slowly, trial after trial, they figured out one piece of the solution, and then another.

It's impossible not to see it, once you look. If they hadn't kept trying, even when they were screwing up more than they were succeeding, there wouldn't be any cormorants. If they'd given up, they'd have all died out. It didn't matter how long it took them to find the right way. The trying was what was important.

All of that went through my head as I looked down at the nests and the long, long fall. My heart was in my throat. And I realized, that's what I'm really throwing away if I jump. The chance to keep trying. It doesn't matter if I don't shine like Shauna. Shauna's dead. It doesn't matter if I'm not as confident as you, Leo, or as strong as Tessa. We're on a cliff, all of us, and surviving isn't about who's the best or the brightest. It's about holding on as long as we can, and trying, and failing, and trying again until we've inched a little closer to getting through this.

If I go back, maybe I'll screw up again. But maybe I'll help, if only a little bit. If I walk off the edge of the cliff, that's the end of everything. I'll be standing by, letting the virus and the gang and hopelessness win, for the rest of eternity. I can't imagine anything worse than that. No matter how much the trying hurts.

Maybe I'm not good at much other than watching, but sometimes when you look, you see things you wouldn't have otherwise. Important things. Like what's really scary here, and what the person I am can do about it.

I want to laugh, and cry, and hug someone, but I've got to look after Meredith first.

Dad knew viruses, but he didn't know everything. And sometimes he let himself be too scared. Meredith will die if we do nothing. That's a fact.

So if I can give her even the smallest chance of surviving, the risks don't mean a thing.

DEC 21

Yesterday feels like a million years ago already. Like I walked a long way after coming down from the cliff, even though I went straight to the hospital.

When I saw the front doors, for a few seconds I couldn't move. I could only think about coming down those steps with Dad the night before, and the pain tore through me from belly to throat like a gutting knife. My eyes welled up and my stomach lurched.

But Meredith needed me. I still knew that. Thinking about her got me through the doors.

I wandered the halls until I found Nell in one of the rooms. As soon as she'd finished checking on the patients, I pulled her aside and told her about the antibody transfusion.

"I remember that," she said. "We tried the procedure using a blood serum with five of the patients, but it wasn't successful in the end."

"Do you know how to prepare the serum?" I asked, and she nodded.

"I want to try doing the transfusion one more time," I said. "With Meredith. I want you to take as much blood as you can from me and give it to her, all of it."

"Kaelyn," she said, "I know you want to help, and I know how awful you must be feeling right now, but I don't think—"

"What could it hurt?" I interrupted. "Just once. Just try it. That's all I'm asking. I need to know we did everything we could."

She looked at me sadly for a few seconds, and then she sighed. "All right," she said. "Give me ten minutes to get the equipment I need, and I'll meet you in the reception room."

So I had my blood taken lying across the reception room chairs. Two times Nell said it was enough, but I didn't feel that bad, so I insisted we keep going. The third time, my head swam when I raised it.

"Okay," I said.

"Good," she answered. "I was putting my foot down now anyway."

She had me drink a couple of juice boxes and eat some stale cookies, and told me to rest in the reception room for a little longer. "If you feel at all out of sorts in the next day or two," she said, "come straight back here. Don't hesitate."

Then she hurried off to prepare for the procedure.

I know she's only doing the transfusion because she figures Meredith's dying anyway. But the why doesn't matter. I'm just glad she agreed.

The sun was almost down when I left. I heard Gav's footsteps before I made him out, weaving through the cars blocking the road around the hospital. I hesitated on the stairs. He stopped when he saw me. His eyes looked dark in the dim light.

"Kaelyn," he said, sounding worried and relieved at the same time, "I've been looking for you all afternoon."

He moved like he was going to run right to me, but then he seemed to check himself. I thought back to the last time we'd talked. How I'd told him to stay away from me. Right then that seemed almost as ridiculous as what I'd been going to do on the cliff.

I held out my hand. And then he ran.

He threw his arms around me, kissed me hard, and pulled me even closer so my head rested against his shoulder and his jaw against my ear.

"Where were you?" he said. "I went by the house, and I looked all through the hospital, and I drove around town, and I was about to do it all over again."

"I just went for a walk," I said. "I needed to think."

But stopping there felt like lying. Leaving out so much, it went from omission to dishonesty. What was it Mom accused me of, all that time ago? Pushing her away, shutting her out. Because I'd wanted to keep everything I was going through to myself.

A lump rose in my throat, remembering. I made myself swallow it. "It's been hard," I said quietly. "I'm really scared."

"Me too," he said, and gave a ragged sort of laugh. "I'm scared all the time. But a little less scared now that I know you're okay."

He pulled back, just slightly. "They told me about your dad," he said. "What happened to him. I'm going to go and tell those idiots with their guns and their gasoline how stupid they're being, and if they don't like—"

"Gav," I said, breaking the string of his words. I curled my fingers into his coat. All the desperation that had left me when I walked away from the cliff started to well up inside me again. I had to stop it.

"Don't," I said. "I know you want to be the hero. And if that's what you need to do for the town, all right. But I don't want you doing it for me."

"It's not about being a hero," he said. "They killed him. They hurt you more than I can even think. I can't just leave that alone."

"Yeah, you can," I said, shifting away so I could look him in the eyes. "You know what would hurt me more? If you risked yourself because you thought it would help me, and something happened to you. The most important thing to *me* is that you're okay too. You get that, don't you? But if I'm trying to protect you, and you're trying to protect me, it's all going to cancel itself out. And neither of us will be okay."

"So what do you want us to do?" he asked, his voice tight. "Just not be together?"

I dragged in a breath. "No," I said. "Of course not. But maybe... You remember the other day, you said you thought you'd have noticed me even if the epidemic hadn't happened? Can't we just act like this *is* a world where our lives aren't in constant danger and horrible things aren't happening every minute, and be normal together? Stop worrying about who needs to protect who?"

"Normal," he said. "You mean like, chocolate and flowers, and school dances and curfews and arguing about whether we hang out with your friends or mine?"

"Well, maybe not totally normal," I said. "Normal-ish."

His shoulders rose and fell, and then his lips curved with a faint smile. "All right," he said. "I could give that a try. I already know what I'd be doing right now in a normal-ish world."

He tugged me close and kissed me, and right then I wasn't so scared anymore. Right then I felt like maybe everything could work out after all.

I understand better what Drew meant, back in September, when he said there wasn't any point in locking ourselves away from the world just to stay safe. It's the rest of the world that makes it worth being alive. But I don't ever want Gav to feel like I did, pushed to the edge, blaming himself because he couldn't save everyone. Because he couldn't save me. If I need to be saved, I'll do it myself. I think I can handle that.

DEC 22

Yesterday when Gav came by for lunch, I started feeling faint, and I slipped on the stairs and nearly fell, so I asked him to drive me to the hospital. Nell tutted at me and had me lie down in the reception room with a constant supply of juice and soup. By the evening I was feeling better again, but she made me spend the night.

Other than a few hospital staff and volunteers, no one came through the whole time. In the morning, I said to Nell, "It's not so busy anymore."

"No," she said, squeezing my shoulder. "We didn't have to admit any new patients yesterday. The numbers have been going down, but it's the first time that's happened since the outbreak started."

I know it isn't a huge breakthrough. There are a lot fewer people left to get sick. But the town's not empty. Those who've survived this long must be taking all the precautions, and the precautions must be keeping them safe. And if the virus can't claim any new victims, it'll start to fade away.

I went up to see Meredith before I left. She's still lost in a delirium, but for moments now and then she settled into a sort of calm. I think that's at least a little better.

When I got back to the house, Tessa was filling flowerpots with soil by the living room window. "I think there might be enough sun here to get something growing," she said, and I could have hugged her. Instead I settled for making us a pot of tea. We sat in the dining room for a while, sipping from our mugs and not saying anything. Then a couple of squirrels started chattering outside the window, some dispute over who was the true owner of a stash of acorns probably, and we looked at each other at the same moment and smiled.

There was something perfect about it. This one peaceful moment, understanding each other without speaking.

Tessa said once that she got by because she focused on the people she had with her, not the ones who were gone. The ache of missing Mom and Drew hasn't gone away, and now there's a sharper pain for Dad on top of it. But I've got people. People who care, who I care about. Maybe they're not who I'd have picked to be with if I'd been given the choice four months ago. But that doesn't mean they're not exactly who I need.

DEC 23

Another day, and Meredith's still with us. Her fever broke around noon, and for a few minutes her mind seemed clear. She held my hand and said my name and beamed at me when I kissed her cheek.

Nell says it's too early to tell if her improvement will continue. "Try not to get your hopes up, hon," she said when I was leaving. But that seems like terrible advice. Why would it be better to expect the worst than to hope? Expecting the worst almost sent me off a cliff.

I don't expect the best, either. But I'm hoping for Meredith as hard as I can.

That's probably why I still do this too. Sit by the window in her bedroom and watch the mainland. The water in the strait is rougher in the winter. I think the patrol boats have moved again.

I've started keeping a record of everything I see over there, which means mostly just notes like "three lights on at the south end of the shore at nine o'clock." I have to wonder if

Something's moving out of the mainland harbor. It looks almost like the ferry. Hold on.

*   *   *

It is the ferry! The patrol boats are letting it go by. I can't see who's driving it, even with the binoculars, but that's definitely our ferry, cruising toward us across the strait. And not just that.

I can see *you*, Leo. Standing on the deck like you're ready to jump in and swim if the boat doesn't move fast enough.

Someone's coming for us. I don't know what that means, but it has to be good. Maybe they're bringing us more medicine, or parts to fix the phones and electricity. Maybe they've got the vaccine. Maybe Drew's there.

And you're coming home.

I've got to go tell Tessa. I can't stop grinning. In a little while, you'll see it. I'll finally be able to talk to you face-to-face, like I promised you I would. And then we'll be one step closer to recovering the world we had before.

ACKNOWLEDGMENTS

I could not have written this novel without the help of four excellent books on viruses and disease—*Virus X* by Frank Ryan, *Deadly Companions* by Dorothy H. Crawford, *How Pathogenic Viruses Work* by Lauren Sompayrac, and *The Hot Zone* by Richard Preston—which helped shape my conception of my fictional epidemic and the response that would follow. I am also indebted to Jacqueline Houtman for sharing her expertise in medical microbiology during the early drafts. Any mistakes in the science are mine, not theirs.

Many thanks to Cyn Balog, Amanda Coppedge, Saundra Mitchell, and Robin Prehn for their invaluable feedback on the manuscript; to my agent, Josh Adams, for finding the novel the home it needed and for his unfaltering enthusiasm and expertise; to my editor, Catherine Onder, for loving the story I wrote while having the wisdom to see all the ways it could be made stronger; and to the entire team at Hyperion, for skillfully transforming it from words on a screen into an actual book and for helping it reach the hands of readers.

Much love to Chris and my family and friends both online and off, for your unwavering support and faith in me. I wouldn't be here without you.